A REFUGEE
in its
OWN NATION

A REFUGEE
in its
OWN NATION

Surinder Sardana

PARTRIDGE

A Penguin Random House Company

To order additional copies of this book, contact
Partridge India
000 800 10062 62
orders.india@partridgepublishing.com

www.partridgepublishing.com/india

2nd May 1947

It was a very hot and sultry day and Bhagmal was lying on a cot under a Neem tree as he was feeling very tired and depressed. The depression had been caused by an information brought to him by Allaudeen, his old friend and classmate in the school who was working in the office of Deputy Commissioner, he had informed that it has been finally decided that the India will be bifurcated and a new nation of Pakistan will be carved out of India, as demanded by Ilama Iqbal and Pakistan will be Muslim majority nation and where Hindus will be second class citizens.

The information was very disturbing as Bhagmal had a family comprising of his charming and beautiful wife, aged about 25, mother of two sons and two daughters. Sulakshni his wife had born these children in the last seven years of their married life. Sulakshni was married to Bhagmal because of her own liking and fondness for him, since he was close friend of Labh Chand brother of Sulakshni and Bhagmal was a regular visitor to her family house. Her father was a school teacher and mother was seamester of repute in her locality.

Apart from the immediate family of Bhagmal through his marriage, he had a father Purshottam, mother Rampyari, sister Rajjo and sister Bhucho both younger to Bhagmal. Her two elder brothers Brij Bhan and Lekh Raj were working in government offices in Pasrur a nearby town, Lekh Raj in irrigation department and Brij Bhan in land revenue department. Both the brothers had built small houses for themselves and living with their wives, both did not have any child at the present time though both were married a very long time. Brij Bhan's wife gave birth to two children but both died at birth Lekh Raj was medically found impotent.

Bhagmal was not sure as to what course of action need to be taken and followed finally he decided to ask his father and mother whom he did not appreciate much but always trusted their wisdom whenever he found himself in a turmoil if any kind.

In the afternoon he took his wife to the room of his parents, his father Purshttam and mother Rampyari were rather surprised as in the past he had never came to their room with his wife. His father was quick and eagerly asked him if everything was in order and both of them are well Bhagmal in the presence of his mother told them about the information which he had received and his concerns over the information. There was a subdued silence for some time before his father spoke that he has a friend in a place which will be part of India and not Pakistan and someone will have to go and meet his friend at a village near Rohtak a district town and he will be able to provide the detailed address, but the question is as to who will go there as it will take about 24 hours to reach there and the whole process will take about five days since Brij Bhan and Lekh Raj are not very wise and government servants and will have to seek leave and necessary permission to leave their headquarters which may take a long time and will involve a lengthy and cumbersome procedure. It was finally decided that Bhagmal will have to travel and meet Bhanna Ram, a landlord near Rohtak who may extend necessary help in the resettlement. Keeping the decision in view a telegram was sent to Bhanna Ram informing that Bhagmal is coming to him and he should confirm his availability by wire. Bhagmal was asked to visit the Imperial Bank and get the account opening form duly certified by the branch agent so that he could open an account in the bank at Rohtak. Rampyari agreed to make two ser Pinnies (a sweet made at home) and to take five yards of muslin for the wife of Bhanna Ram.

Next day the Bhanna Ram's telegram came late in night confirming his availability to receive Bhagmal at Rohtak railway station. Bhanna Ram was informed that Bhagmal will reach Rohtak by Punjab mail on 4th of May and will need about Rs. 500 and will need lot of help. Bhanna Ram sent another telegram confirm that he will be receiving Bhagmal at Rohtak station at the train arrival time and shall be driven to nearby village Dobh by a fast mule cart driven by Bhanna Ram.

Bhanna Ram received Bhagmal at Rohtak Railway station at 4 AM in the midnight, served him some tea in a kasora (an earthen pot) and some eatables and Bhagmal was asked to sit on the mule driven cart with his luggage consisting of two bags and water pitcher known as Surahi (an earthen pot having a pot belly and a long round neck).

Bhanna Ram enquired about the welfare of his friend Purshottam, the father of Bhagmal and about the other members of the family including his mother, brother and sister and their kids. By 4:45 they had reached at Dobh village nearly 4 miles away from Rohtak. The night was not warm in the early hours when the dawn was spreading its wings and various birds had started chirping in their different voices.

Bhagmal was well received by the family of Bhanna Ram including his wife who was not ugly but in no way could be called any presentable her name was Todomai as he was told. Bhagmal touched the feet of Todomai who put her dirty hand on his head. She told Bhagmal to go and get fresh so that she could give him some hot milk and something to eat as he might have been hungry, then Bhagmal should take some rest and then Bhanna Ram will sit with him and find out from him the real situation so that whatever needs to be done should be done in a proper manner.

Bhagmal went to the open field after defecating, took a bath at the well by drawing fresh water changed clothes, putting on a tehemat (A loose 2.5 meter by 1.5 meter cloth which is wrapped around the waist and knotted and baudi (A vest made of coarse cotton cloth having three, four pockets)

When Bhagmal after getting fresh came back to the main room, Todomai brought him hot milk in a peetal teen Pava glass (Brass made tumbler which can hold about 750 ml liquid) and mathari (A fried pancake made of fine floor with salt and condiments, mostly and usually made at home) after enjoying breakfast Bhagmal lied down upon a bed made up on a cot under a pepal tree (Peepal is a tree which always gives out oxygen only at day and night and usually have a very long life upto 300 years and have very deep roots. It was lunch time, by the time Bhagmal came out of his slumber. In his slumber Bhagmal had a dream in which he was sleeping with his wife Sulakshni and she was stark nude and he was playing with her breasts and was weeping for his helplessness and given predicament. The dream lingered on even after he was fully awake and in the company of Todomai and Bhanna Ram.

The lunch was served to him and Bhanna Ram when his two sons had came back from school. Both the boys named Mool Chand and Phool Chand had came back from school. Mool Chand was student of 7th class and Phool Chand was in 5th class. Boys' three elder sisters were married long back and were living at their homes at nearby different places.

After the lunch was over and Todomai and the boys were gone to different room. Bhanna Ram asked Bhagmal to accompany him to the fields so they could talk in peace without being disturbed once in the field both of them sat at a Takhtah (A wooden cot) under a Banyan tree. Bhanna Ram asked Bhagmal as to what was the problem and how best he could help and be of use, as he was deeply indebted to his father Purshottam, who had bestowed upon him lot many favours in his bad times.

Bahgmal told him about the confidential information he had received from his classmate and friend Allaudeen who was working in the office of Deputy Commissioner, Bhanna Ram listened very intently and asked Bhagmal as to what kind of help he should extend so that he could be at ease and feel somewhat sure about the very unknown future.

Bhagmal told him that he will need rupees five hundred to open a bank account at Imperial Bank Branch at Rohtak as he has brought a duly signed recommendation letter from the branch manager of the bank branch at Jhang. Further that he will have to rent out a house at District Headquarter at Rohtak so he could establish himself there and send his children to school and he will be happy to buy around eight Killas of agriculture land preferably irrigated with good soil. That he will need to rent out a shop in the main bazaar (Main Market)so that he could establish his books and stationery shop there.

The plan is that he will transfer a good amount of money from his present bank account, so that as and when he shift and migrate to this part of India his own nation now being partitioned simply to keep Nehru, Gandhi and Jinnha happy, without any thought of population, its feelings suffering and uprooting which will cause them most irr-reparable loss of physical and mental well being. The partition will cause social up vheal and destruction which may take decades to settle before a new social order is established. Suddenly Bhagmal stopped talking as he heard the name of Bhanna Ram being called very softly and slowly. A man was standing at some distance, whom Bhagmal did not know and he was calling the name of Bhanna Ram. Bhagmal drew the attention of Bhanna Ram towards the man standing there, Bhanna Ram recognized the man Ladha Ram his distant cousin and partner in his business. Bhagmal was duly introduced to Ladha Ram and was told that Ladha Ram has a very good knowledge of district town Rohtak and he knew many people there.

Then Mool Chand came running and asked his father that the mother was asking them to came home and take their food. Bhanna Ram invited Ladha Ram to come along and have some food, but Ladha Ram said he had his food and had called on Bhanna Ram to discuss something urgent about some problem in their business. Bhanna Ram asked Bhagmal to go home with Mool Chand and have his food and he will be back soon after sorting out the matter with Ladha Ram.

Bhagmal and Mool Chand walked towards the house, Mool Chand was curious to know about the place and people of the place from where Bhagmal had come. Bhagmal told him about the place and people of his area and answered curious and pointed questions of Mool Chand

and soon they were at the house. Todomai welcomed them and enquired about Bhanna Ram and was told that he had some business matter to discuss with Ladha Ram. They both were told to wash their feet and mouth so that food may be served to them.

Today Todomai was looking good and presentable, she was wearing a salwar (Loose Tunic with string to tie the waist) Kameez (A shirt) of pink colour and her cleavage could be seen from a distance and she was in happy and cheerful mood. She laid the food in a Thali (Big Saucer Plate) in which there were three Katories (Bowels) the vegetable was matter – paneer (Peas - Cheese) Bhurtha (Meshed and fried egg plant with onions) and Alloo Raita (Meshed curd with chunk of boiled potato) A Gadavi full of Lassi (A round tumbler with curd milk in it) with two glasses) she asked them to start eating, because she was not sure as to when Bhanna Ram will come back, by the time they started eating, Bhanna Ram came washed his feet and mouth and sat squat there on the floor, food was also served to him. After the main food course they were served with cold Phirni (Thick boiled and sweetened, sweetend milk allowed to cool over night) in ice box. Ice brought from the town for the purpose. After the food was over I was asked to have after noon siesta and in the evening I might be shown the agriculture land in the nearby village and Bhanna Ram went out of the home. Mool Chand and Phool Chand were put to sleep by Todomai and after that she took her food.

I went to the adjacent room and lay down on the cot then I spotted my bag and cursed myself for my foolishness as I had not handed over the gifts I had brought with me. I immediately got up and went to the next room and saw Todomai changing her cloths I kept on standing and was caught and with a guilt rpropusly apologised. Todomai came forward and kissed me on my lips I lost my balance and fell down, now Todomai was perplexed while I got up she went out of the room loudly saying very sorry.

After half an hour Bhanna Ram came in told Todomai to prepare some tea, I also got up and said that I shall also have some tea.

The tea was brought in and Todomai was looking much shaken up and she could not look straight at me. After having the tea I and Bhanna Ram went out Todomai was told that we may be back at about dinner time.

The village where the land had to be seen was about 3 Kos (A Kos is nearly 2 and half mile). Bhanna Ram brought out his mule cart saddled the mule attached and I was told to sit on the cart, a bundle of sugarcane and fodder for the mule was put on the cart.

It took us nearly forty five minutes to reach the house of Mulkh Raj at Itana Paana, Lahli. Mulkh Raj welcomed us by a Namaskar (folded hands) and made us sit comfortably on a wooden cot and loudly called for some water after few minutes a young man of 25 years very tall and well built came out with a jug and three glasses kept them at the cot and touched the feet of Bhanna Ram and saluted me in affable manner, then he filled all the three glasses from the jug and handed it over to us. The water was not cold and had a jaggery in it and was awfully very sweet. Bhanna Ram told to Mulkhraj that I was a close friend's son and was looking for some piece of land the good one I was told that as of moment he had nothing on the offer but assured that within next two days he will get back to me with an offer. After spending about another fifteen minutes of small gossip we took leave of Mulkh Raj. We started back on our mule cart to our place. Bhanna Ram felt very sorry that he could not help much. I assured him not to worry, somenothing, good will sure come up soon.

We were back at Bhanna Ram's house by 6:30 PM. Lamps were on but there were no street lamps it had became dark and gloomy. The village was not quite but there was no noise except the sudden barks of the dogs and braying of mules.

Most of the household women were busy cooking evening meals to be served at dinner time.

I was sitting in the varanda with Mool Chand and Phool Chand who were trying to be friend me and know more about my place, my family, my train journey, they were planning to came with me to Rohtak as and when I boarded the train for my home and family. Bhanna Ram came and sat there and told the boys to go and complete their school home work and help their mother. Bhanna Ram asked me If I have been to Delhi even once and I said no never he said that he had been to Delhi about 10 years back for two days and he had seen big bazaars and buildings, he did not go to Delhi by train but had gone by a mule cart with some goods to be delivered at a rich man's house in Fatehpuri the journey on one side taken more than 18 hours and then the back journey took less than 16 hours because they had a very less load in all it took 4 days and he had earned twelve e rupees and free food in the bargain, I was impressed fascinated by the episode and said that I will like to visit Delhi but not by a mule cart but only by train and shall be happy to bear his expenses if he accompanied me to Delhi. But I did not know anybody in Delhi nor Bhanna Ram had any one known in Delhi, while we were planning, talking and budgeting the Delhi visit, Todomai was standing there and over hearing us, she made a big laugh and said to Bhanna Ram that he was so forgetful that he did not remember that his Saala

(Brother in law on looser side – wife's brother) her mother's sister's son Bodh Ram was running a tea vend at main Delhi railway station. I and Bodh Ram knew Bhanna Ram quite well as he had spent about 10 days with them a long time back. So the biggest hurdle was over come and they decided to visit Delhi after two days but they will came back within two days even if they had to walk or crawl, it was a condition laid upon them by Todomai.

Next day being the Sunday they did not want go to Rohtak as the bank will be closed for a weekly off. It was planned that Bhanna Ram will borrow a bicycle from Ladha Ram and they shall go to Rohtak on bicycle as both of them knew cycling and both of them went their way. Bhagmal came to his allotted room which was 15 feet by 12 feet with a high roof made up of wooden cross beams. He sat on the cot and suddenly remembered that he has not prayered for about two days since he took the train journey, he felt very uneasy and guilty and sat down on the ground after spreading a mat he did not have a Diyya or Aggarbati or Dhoop (Small earthen lamp in which oil is put and a cotton stick is lighted, Aggarbati and Dhoop are incense sticks. He sat in squat like position, folded his hands and invoked the God and recited the path (a well designed prayer to the God). He was now saying slowly in a very low voice.

Oh, my God
Very - very sorry
I did not sit
In your presence for last
Three days
Please do not punish me
I sincerely offer my apologies
Oh, God accept my apology

And forgive me for my lapses
Oh, God, you are my savior
You are my only hope
I solely depend on you
And without your kindness
I cannot be there
Oh, God, have mercy
Oh, God, have mercy

He sat praying there for about half an hour and after that he drunk a glass full of water and went to bed and fell into deep sleep. In his sleep he saw his father and mother both seemed in deep worry as if something was disturbing them, saw all his children sleeping peacefully and then suddenly he saw his wife Sulakshni tired di-shelved and sobbing in her bed, in his dream he called softly the name of Sulakshni. She did not seem to hear him as she did not respond in any manner, he extended his hand towards her. She took his hand in her hand and put it at her chest and started sobbing loudly, he was perturbed and asked her as to what was bothering her, but she did not give any reply but continued sobbing, he bent forwarded and embraced her, she went limp but did not withdrew he started stroking her breasts tenderly. She did not protest or stop him. Suddenly he woke up as he was bursting at the bladder, he went out in he street and relieved himself came back took some water and went back to sleep and dozed off.

He suddenly woke up after hearing a loud noise, he looked at his pocket watch lying near his pillow it was 3 O' Clock in the morning he could gather from hushed voices in the next room that Bhanna Ram was leaving for his field to irrigate the land as it was his day of turn for getting water from the canal and he will be in his field for about two hours.

Bhagmal again went to sleep, he had slept for less than half an hour when he felt that someone was touching him, he turned his side but the touch was not powerful he used his right hand towards the cough as he thought maybe he has put the pillow on his side instead of keeping in below his head, as he was not used to keeping the pillow under his head. The touch became very persisting and very close, he had to get up and see as to what was the cause of touch he got up, it was pitch dark he adjusted his eye sight and searched and tumbled for his torch he found the torch and he put the torch on and in the beam of light he found Todomai lying stark naked in his bed, he was non-plussed and could not fathom out as to what is happening and he decided to get out of the room without asking any questions and making any noise, but in the mean while Todomai got up went up to the door and bolted it and came back and slapped him on his face and pulled him down to her breast and put her left breast to his mouth, he was very badly shaken and had lost all his senses, he was not sure as to what could be done to get rid of his predicament without making noise and let anybody to know about the situation in the mean while Todomai took his number in her hand by pulling down his Tehmat (Loose Cloth tied at the waist) and started masturbating his number very fast and vigorously, it seduced him very strongly and he started caressing her breasts and then took her one breast in his mouth and sucked it and bit it. Now Todomai was on high and he took her hand and guided his two middle fingers to her vagina in pushed his fingers in to her vagina and make a rotating motion. She started moaning in a minute and let him take her to the bed. He took her to the bed and let her lie on her back and then he mounted her penetrating, pushing, she gave out a cry of joy and he came out, they both remained tied in each other's arms for few moments and then he got out of the bed tied his Tehmat and went out, Todomai also got up put on her clothes and went out quietly feeling very satisfied and enthralled, because she had what she was yearning for a long time, as Bhanna Ram was not able to satisfy her after he had gotten physically sick with an undetermined disease, though he slept with her almost every week, but he was unable to satisfy her desires and Todomai thought that this was a chance of her life, as she was sure in her mind that Bhagmal will not relate this incident to anyone including his wife. Todomai always thought that she was a good judge of man and she was certain that though in the beginning Bhagmal was perplexed, unwilling and surprised but gradually he has availed the opportunity provided to him and finally he enjoyed it and did provide lot of enjoyment to Todomai.

Bhagmal came out of the house and started walking furiously towards the village well and then decided to go to the canal and meet Bhanna Ram and tell him the whole truth about as to whatever had happened to him, he was so immersed in his thought and it was not even dawn, he stumbled and fell down into a side ditch, he came out of the ditch and sat on the nearby stone. He was feeling lost and gloomy and felt very sad and shaken by whatever had happened half an hour ago and suddenly started weeping and tears started flowing from his eyes, he was trying to fathom as to how and why it happened and what was his fault or could he help and prevent it from happening, he did not and could not find any answer, even his sub conscious was not throwing any light or signal or answer. He sat there very silent and motionless but fully awake but in great mental pain.

Someone came near him and said Ram – Ram (God's name) he was completely shaken but numbly said Ram – Ram, the man asked him if everything was alright and he was fine, he slowly replied I am very fine and thank you.

Bhagmal kept sitting there just starting at the sky without thought in his mind, he was feeling completely drained out and felt that he has no strength move a flock of sheirking crows brought him out of his sudden stupper, he got up and started wandering on the road and he did not know where did the road will lead him to but he kept walking slowly without any sense of his environment.

The dawn had come and there was a low light and glow there, birds had started chirping, the cacphoney of dog bark, people everywhere, almost everyman had a having stick of Neem (Margosa) in his mouth, on which he was chewing with a rhythm to make it into a brush to clean his teeth, some were defecating in the nearby fields around the bushes for a cover, all these people ultimately reached the village well and pond to have a bath. Bhagmal was as yet not ready to wash himself, so he lingered on with his wandering.

He saw an old man bringing out a pocket watch and enquired from him as to what was the time like and was told that the time was Ten minutes past five in the morning, he asked the old man, if anyone in the village had a Radio and was told that he has never seen a radio and will not know if anyone has a radio and asked him to tell him as to what was a radio and what did it do, Bhagmal explained him as to what was radio and what did it do, the old man was astonished and asked him as to how did he know about the radio and where from he is and how come he in this village and whose guest he was.

Bhagmal told him that he is from a distant place known as Jhang and he was a guest of Bhanna Ram. The old man

Loku Ram knew Bhanna Ram and had been to Jhang, when he was a Naik (Corporal) in the Indian Army. Loku Ram asked Bhagmal to accompany him to his house and have some breakfast. Bhagmal thanked him for his offer and told him that he has as yet not had his bath. Loku Ram told him that he also has as yet not had his bath, Loku Ram told him to go and have his bath and come to his house for which was at the fag end of the road and have his breakfast as and when he was ready to eat it.

Bhagmal hurried back to his staying place, took his clothes and said in the air in the direction of the inner room that he was going out for a bath and will return little late as he was going to have his breakfast with Bhanna Ram came out and asked him where did he go that early, Bhagmal told him that his sleep was disturbed, so he had gone out and was just wandering about the village then he left for his bath and to keep his appointment with Loku Ram. After taking bath and a small prayer to the God, in which he complained to the God about the injustice met to him inspite of the God being in heaven and observing everything in his whole kingdom. He asked for God's forgiveness and guidance so as that he may be in peace with him. On his way to the house of Loku Ram, he was thinking only of Todomai and her fury and his madness which compelled him to succumb to his lust and lustful demands of Todomai, he was as yet not able to find out any good reason or justification for whatever had happened and how will now face Todomai and how will, she face him.

When he reached the fag end of the road he saw a big pucca house (well built house) an old lady was sitting at a cot outside the main door of the house. Bhagmal went near the house and said Ram – Ram (God's name) in the direction of the old lady and the old lady also said Ram – Ram and looked at him very enquiringly, he asked for Loku Ram and was in turn asked if he was Bhagmal the guest of Bhanna Ram and he said yes. She asked him to sit on the opposite wooden cot and she will go in and send Loku Ram out to meet him, she went in and Loku Ram came out and put his right hand over his head and said that it was good that I have come as he was feeling hungry without breakfast. Loku Ram called for his wife Bhartari.

Bhartari came slowly with two big bowls in her both hands and put them before both of them. She brought out two spoons from her pocket and asked us to enjoy our breakfast. The breakfast was Baajere Ka Daliya (A porridge made of Pods of Millet), she appeared again with two glass of curd milk. The daliya was cooked deliciously and the curd milk was very refreshing and I enjoyed my breakfast and sat there for some time chatting with Loku Ram who was asking leading questions about my business and my parents and family, after some time I asked leave of him, he told me in the end that one of his half brother Jhaver was at Pasrur a nearby town near Jhang and he was working in the Post Office and I can call on Jhaver for any help.

Bhagmal left the place of Loku Ram to return to the place of Bhanna Ram. He was in two minds whether to go to Bhanna Ram and Todomai, and he was mentally not prepared to face them. He wandered in the village and its fields to while away his time but unknowingly started walking towards his staying place in about ten minutes he was outside the house. Bhanna Ram was coming out of house and he told him that he was going to nearby village to buy some good seeds for wheat, and he had been told that this seed gives very good yield and asked Bhagmal to accompany him, if he felt like coming with him. Bhagmal took about a minute to say no, because he did not felt like walking in the scorching sun. Bhanna Ram said it was fine with and told him to go and lie in the shade and have a chat with Todomai and boys.

Bhagmal sat on the cot lying outside the house under the Neem Tree (Margosa) he was silent, his eyes half closed and in deep thought, he was thinking about the past three days since he left Jhang and the train of events, his dreams of sad faces of his parents and weeping of his wife Sulakshni and his liaison with Todomai. He was thinking that most of the men were fool and they moulded by the God to remain foolish. So that God may chaste ties them, punish them, so that they strive to improve their behavior and ultimately start acting wisely so that they may be deemed and given a permanent adobe in the God's heaven. He fervently prayed and hoped that the God will guide to the path of redemption and on of these days he will ultimately settle in the abode of God.

His train of thought was suddenly and rudely broken when Phool Chand loudly shook him and gave him a glass of water and asked for Mool Chand. Phool Chand louldly called out the name of Mool Chand and he came running Bhagmal went inside his allotted room and found out the time from his pocket watch, it was Nine 'O clock, he put the watch in his pocket. He felt like having some time, he told Mool Chand to go to his mother if she could cook some tea for him, Mool Chand and Phool Chand both went inside to their mother to find about the tea, they both came out and told him that the mother was taking bath and she will cook the tea in short while on hearing that Todomai was taking bath Bhagmal started visualizing her supple body and full breasts. In the mean while Phool Chand asked him to tell him about his four child and his house, Bhagmal told Phool Chand about his child and house Mool Chand wanted to know if in his town, there were kites, he told him that his both sons flew lot of kites and he will make them a kite if they can get him some big size of paper, they said they will find out some paper and went inside the house, after some time they both came out with a very old calendar for him to make a kite, he asked for some gum, the boys had no gum, so they were asked to bring some flour, they brought some flour, from which Bhagmal made a paste, he told them to bring two big twigs and knife, they brought twigs and knife. Bhagmal straightened the twigs with knife and made out a kite, and ask them to put the same under the sun shine so as to dry, and mean while the boys should find some long length of thread. Boys brought a real of thick thread. The kite was made up and was ready to fly, Bhagmal helped the boys fly the kite and the boys were not only happy but were enthralled by the joy and new experience. They kept playing with the kite and were much engrossed in the new fond joy.

Todomai came out and called for Bhagmal in a low voice. She had brought the steaming hot tea and some homemade salted pancakes. She was wearing a see through transparent shirt and was not wearing under shirt, which she used to put on. She looked straight at Bhagmal and their eyes met he tried to evade her direct look as he could see and feel lust in her eyes. She whispered slowly that he should be ready and happy to have her again at night. Bhagmal was filled with a gleeful joy, a distant fear and strong guilt and sincerely wished to escape the situation, but could not make up his mind, as how to avoid and escape the opportunity coming his way. He felt strong sympathy and pain for Todomai and was ashamed at her lust predicament and helplessness.

He took the salted pancakes and munched them without feeling its taste and gulped the hot tea and than started sipping it slowly. His mind was busy, confused and moving very fast in different directions and he could not come up with any tangible solution. The moment the tea was over, he got up and came out of the house and started walking slowly towards the canal. He was thinking furusionly as regard to his position, he thought that he should leave the village once Bhanna Ram is back and catch a train back to his place, it was a corroding thought but he knew that in given circumstances he will not be able to do like this because he may not be able to convince Bhanna Ram with his reasons and will not be able to convince and satisfy his father as he has not taken even a single step towards his mission for which he had come to this place. So the thought was found to be futile and not worth much pondering. The other thought was to sneak out of the house in the night and wander in the village or may be he can go to the place of Loku Ram and spend the night there but for this he will have to make a reasonable storey which he could tell Loku Ram, since Loku Ram never asked of him to sleep at his house and any such action will tarnish the image of Bhanna Ram and his wife. This thought was also abandoned as impractical then he thought that he will stay awake the whole night and sit in prayer before the God, as he wil light a lamp before the God and ask for his forgiveness and seek his guidance to meet the situation. He was not very sure as to whether prayer will help him in anyway and he shall be able to resist the lust full overtures of Todomai or he will be able to stop and restrain himself from falling prey to his own lust and shall let go the God given opportunity waste and cause pain to the lusty and sex starved and hungry Todomai. He knew it for sure that whatever was happening was not any good and he also knew that he has no way out of it as he could resist everything but temptations and it was a very – very big temptation, how so ever bad it might have been.

He was unable to make his mind as what course he should follow, he kept on walking and reached at the corner of the road at an intersection where the village road met to the town road, he saw a barber shop a wooden cot was lying there and three-four people were sitting there possibly waiting their turn with the barber. He went there and sat on the wooden cot to wait for his turn with the barber, few minutes later the barber came out and asked him if he was in need of a shave or hair cut. He had not shaved since he had left his place so he told the barber that he will like to have a shave, he was made to sit at a raised wooden plank before smudgy mirror and the barber started putting shaving soap on his face, and then the barber sharpened the razor and started shaving after doing once the barber repeated the process and finally his face was washed with smattering of cold water and a dirty cloth was used to wipe his face. The shave was done and over, the barber was paid a takka (32nd part of Indian Rupee)

While Bhagmal was having shave he had been intently looking at his gloomy face and worry lines on his forehead when he came out he again started walking along the road saying Ram – Ram to passer-bys but his mind was in a big muddle. Suddenly he had a day dream and a vision of his wife Sulakshni she was looking tired, depressed, forlon and lost brooding God knew what, but he heared that she was saying to him that he should not worry too much abvout his liaison with Todomai and she understood his position and knew that he had no options but to do whatever was asked, Sulakshni assured him that she will never take up the issue and he should shun his guilt and enjoy himself as long as he was capable and ready to satisfy her in the bed as usual and she will not complain at all. Now he felt light and his mind was clear and he became cheerful and started back to home.

When he reached the house, Bhanna Ram had came back with the seeds and was having his tea. Tea was also brought for him. Todomai was no more wearing the transparent shirt.

It was five in the evening and dinner was three hours away. Bhanna Ram asked him to come along with him for a walk and while walking they will firm up the plan for visiting Rohtak to open bank account and renting out a shop and the house, they will also plan their proposed visit to Delhi. Bhanna Ram paid him rupees two hundred and told him that he will give him more money on Wednesday. They came out of house and walked towards the main road. Cattles were coming back to home, peasent women with some kind of fodder over their head were also walking back to the village. Some bullock cart with green fodder and dry wood twigs were headed towards the village. Dogs were following the carts and there was noise of bell chimes, braying of the cattle's and barking of the dogs and different but loud voices of human being were making a likeable cacophony.

Bhagmal was immersed in his thought which had no particular direction and rhythm so was Bhanna Ram thinking and puffing on his Beeri (A hand rolled cigarette made from particular type of Tendu leaf which grew wild and was collected and transported to beeri rolling stations)

They stopped at the house of one Kishu and Bhanna Ram asked him to lend us his bicycle, Kishu brought his bicycle and handed over it to Bhanna Ram. Now both of them took the handle of the bicycle at both ends and walked it was decided that they will leave at about Nine in the morning after breakfast and Todomai will cook then their lunch and pack it and they shall carry it with them along with some Lassi (Curd Milk) and once in town they, the first thing they shall do is have some tea at a famous shop which sold good masala tea cup for a Takka (Thirty Second part of a Rupee) which was big money by their standards. After they will go to the Imperial bank and open their bank account and once it is open they will scout for shop and the house supposed to be taken on rent, as Bhanna Ram knew few people in the town, he will seek their help in the matter. Whenever they get a chance they shall sit under the shade of some dense tree and enjoy their lunch and Lassi and be there for about an hour so, and then they will take some more tea and cycle back to their village. Both were satisfied by their plan and walked back to the house.

On reaching the house they were told to get fresh and sit for dinner, both of them washed their feet and mouth and sat for dinner. The dinner consisted of Dall Fry (Fried Cooked lintle) Papad (A thin rolled and Sun dried pancake made of lintel floor) Papad is fried on fire or fried in oil) and some Aachaar (Pickle usually made at home)

The food was brought out in big Thalli (Platter) by both the boys, water was served in glasses both of them had their food in complete silence, as it is taught in India and is mostly and commonly practiced. After the food they both were given some jiggery and flanel seeds as a desert and digestive aid. They were told that the milk will be served to them before they go to bed.

At that time people of small places did not have radios as there was no electricity in the villages and hence fans or lights could not be only oil lamps mostly without chimney were used, the school going boys they were hardly in any good number, who went to the schools and girls were not sent to the school, whatever little was taught to them at house only, the girls were mainly trained in cooking, embroidery and sewing and tailoring, quilt making, pillow making, spinning, weaving were also taught to some of the girls and women most of the women learnt knitting and would knit woolen sweater etc. sewing machines were unheard of most of the stitching was done by needle by hand only most of the torn clothes whether gents or ladies were hand patched and patches could display the competence of patch maker, only white thread was used, coloured thread was hardly available and nobody bothered about it.

At nine in the night Bhanna Ram retired to his bed after having his milk. Bhagmal also had his milk but did not go to sleep, instead he spread his Tehmat on the ground and sat on it in lotus position, crossed leg and folded hands. He went in to meditation invoking the name of God very humbly and kind of reciting some Vedic mantra (Vedic Hymens). It was almost half an hour when he in his meditation started visualizing the form of God in the form of Lord Shiva, the destroyer, he mentally postrated before the image of his God and started speaking fast loudly in un intelligible slaybu. He asked the God as to why did it happen to him that he could not resist his lust and went along with the flow of lust of Todomai, the God smiled and said well you wanted it and he said he never stops any human being from doing anything they were willing to do inspite of the best kind of intelligence and wisdom ordained to them by him, he was told that he could have prevented whatever had happened, since he was enjoying himself in the act. So he did not stop it and prevent himself from doing whatever he was doing and enjoying, as his past karmic debts have not been exhausted and he shall continue to suffer for his all doing in his all and many lives.

Bhagmal had got his answer to his predicament he bowed before God and thanked the God for enlightment. Now he was feeling at peace and ease his turmoil totally gone, he was ready to sleep, he tied his Tehmat and lay on the cot and went into deep slumber. He was woken up by his urge to go for a pee, he went out, relived himself and had some water.

When he came back to his bed he realized that someone was lying in his bed it was Todomai without a fragment of cloth on her, he lay alongside her and started playing with her supple and well shaped breasts, Todomai pushed his mouth to her left breast and inserted the nipple in his mouth, he started sucking it vigorously, after few moments she shifted his mouth to her right breast and he sucked it. She took his number in her hands and tenderly started playing it and then she took one his hand to her vagina and put his middle finger into her vagina, he did not need any encouragement and started pushing it inside in deep and rotate it with some force. She embraced him tightly and begged him to fuck her, he mounted her from the top and used whatever force he could command after few stoke she came out her vagina was flowing wet, she was biting him and begged him to push more, he did try but hardly could do it and brust ejaculated and went limp on top her.

After some times she pushed him to the side, took out a piece of cloth cleaned herself and him, kissed his forehead and touched his feet and went out without a word. When she was at the door she thanked him and came back and asked for forgiveness and exclaimed that at least her long waiting physical thirst has been quenched and promised to remain chaste rest of her whole life and then left.

Bhagmal felt restless and sat in prayer, he closed his eyes and tried to concentrate upon the image of the God but felt tired and felt like dozing off. He went out relieved himself, had a glassful of water and went to sleep in his sleep he saw his father in deep worry and discomfort, his mother Rampyayari was sitting by his bed and was trying to console him asking him and not to worry as she was sure that Bhagmal was quite well and safe and once his work was completed will come back and it was only the third day since he went away.

When Bhagmal woke up it was clear dawn, he got out of his bed went out to freshen himself, he took his towel and other clothes, went to an open field to defaced, went to the well had a bath, washed his cloths and came back, Bhanna Ram was waiting for him, both had their breakfast and in the mean time Todomai, packed their lunch and lassi. It was eight thirty by now, they both started for the town.

Bhanna Ram was paddeling the cycle and Bhagmal was seated on the carrier, the food pack was hanging on the handle. After some time Bhanna Ram stopped the cycle got down from it, handed over the cycle handle to Bhagmal and he lighted a beeri and started puffing on it, once the puffing was done with, they were both ready to move ahead now Bhagmal was paddeling and Bhanna Ram was astride on the cycle carrier.

By twenty minute past nine they were in the town and in five minutes they reached at the planed and appointed tea shop, they went in, ordered two cups of masala tea and waited anticipating the savoury taste of the masala tea. The tea was brought to them in glass tumblers, they started sipping the tea from glass tumbler. They enjoyed and appreciated the tea taste and promised themselves that they will have more tea once they were ready to go back after ending their designated work.

Exactly at ten by their watch they entered the bank, the clerk at the counter asked them about their purpose of visiting the bank, Bhagmal explained that he wanted to open a new bank account, he was asked to meet the Head Clerk

Mouddin, they were asked to sit on chairs lying there and a form was brought out, it was an account opening form, Bhagmal was asked his name, his father's name and address, the head clerk filled in the details and asked him to sign at crossed spaces and then he was asked to get it signed from someone who knew him and had a bank account with them, Bhagmal signed at three crossed spaces and told the head clerk that he did not know anyone, who had an account with them, but he himself has a account at their Jhang branch and he had brought a recommendation letter from the Agent of Jhang Branch. On hearing Bhagmal, Mouddin asked him to meet the agent Mr. Brut in the chamber.

Bhagmal took the filled up form from the head clerk and went to the chamber of Mr. Brut. Mr. Brut was a strong looking man, with big moustaches and was puffing on his unlit cigar. He was asked to sit down and explain his business, he put the duly filled account opening form and the recommendation letter he had brought with him, Mr. Brut glanced it seriously and asked Bhagmal as to what brought him here in Rohtak from Jhang because it could not be education or business and not even agriculture as the land around Jhang was better than around Rohtak. Since Rohtak was a town of ruffians, no one will like to settle here or live here unless he was in the service of Government or Police or Railway.

Bhagmal felt uneasy and uncomfortable and he told him as to what brought him at Rohtak and why he was trying to open the account at Rohtak. Mr. Brut went into deep thought, because he also had heard some unconfirmed reports in this regard at the Service Officers Club but not bothered himself much, as he being Anglo Indian thought that being a member of the privileged class as long as the

British were in control, he and his family's life and rights were safe even if the partition of India did take place.

Suddenly Mr. Brut came out of his deep thought, had one more look at the recommendation letter before him and then opened an Index – book and matched the signatures on the letter with the signature in the Index Book, on finding that the signatures matched well. He took the account opening form, signed it and called for the Cashier, when the cashier appeared, he told Bhagmal to give rupee one hundred to cashier. Mr. Brut called for the Peon Imtiaz and asked him to bring water. The water was brought and given to Bhagmal and he had a half of it, meanwhile the cashier came back with the receipt, Mr. Brut made few entries in the form and called for the Head Clerk handed over the form to the head cashier and asked him to prepare a pass book and issue a cheque book, as fast as possible.

Bhagmal was asked to come back in half an hour and collect his pass book and cheque book, Bhagmal came out and met Bhanna Ram and told him that the bank account had been opened and he has to collect pass book and cheque book after half an hour or, so they both came out of the bank and Bhanna Ram lighted a Beeri and started puffing on it, Bhanna Ram was of the opinion that going to Railway Road to look for a shop to be rented out was not possible in the short time, so it was decided that they both will while away the time near the bank, they came out and sat around a tea shop, which was beneath a mighty Peepal tree, many wooden planks had been laid on the bricks and few peoples were sitting there some just lazing around, the others had a page of Hindi newspaper. When Bhagmal saw the newspaper, he went near the man who was holding the paper, he glared over and on seeing the date on the side he found that it was an old paper of November of the last year, he found that Rohtak got only few English News papers each costing four annas (one fourth of a rupee) and the only Hindi newspaper was a fortnightly, which did not carry any worthwhile news.

People sitting around was not prone to chatting and everyone was looking in the other direction instead of engaging with his neighbourer Bhanna Ram asked of a man sitting beside him as to how was the situation of canal water supply in his are, the man said that he had come from Jhajjar, Jhajjar is a place whose ruler the Nawab of Jhajjar Principality, Nawab Jhajjruddin, had revolted against the British by joining the force of Emperor Bhadur Shah Jafar, proclaimed the first Emperor of Hindustan during the first Indian war of independence in 1857 which was brutally crushed by the British and declared it as mutiny and more than 5000 Indians were hanged to death and there was hardly any canal in the area and the agriculture mainly depended on the mercies of the God and his whims of making rain, whether scanty or plentiful and this year so far he has not been merciful and he was in the town to meet his Lawyer in regards to a land dispute he was having with his father and brothers as both of them have refused to give his rightful share, because they did not like and approve of his wife, because she will not observe Purdah (Covering of face on seeing a man who may be senior in age or relationship.

On hearing the version of the Jhajjar man Bhagmal went back in his mind as to refresh that he also had somewhat similar situation, but his father and brothers were not involved in any manner, rather it were other relative or neighbor who had shown great resentment for the reason that Sulakshni was not observing a stretch purdah and had to be reminded every time she appeared without purdah, but she mostly complied though with a smirk.

It was more than half an hour when Bhagmal re-entered the bank and went to the head clerk and asked for his pass book and cheque book and was told that he should collect it from the Agent. He went back to Agent Mr. Brut, who was little busy and asked him to sitdown and later asked him to write down on paper his residential address in Jhang and the address of place where he was staying in Rohtak, so that he may contact him if needed, and then Mr. Brut handed over the pass book and cheque book to him and advised him to keep them safe.

It was Tweleve in the afternoon of Seventh May 1947 when he and Bhanna Ram started scouting for a shop at Railway Road, Rohtak. Bhanna Ram knew one Lala Ghassi Ram, a kirana merchant, and he took him to his shop, he was well received by Lala Ghassi Ram, after the pleasantries, the water was served and Bhagmal was introduced to Lala Ghassi Ram and he was also apprised of their purpose of their visit to him, on hearing their purpose Ghassi Ram called on Ghasita and gave him a key and instructed him to take them to his other shop lying vacant, so they could have a peek of it Ghasita, took both of them to the other shop a short distance away, the door was opened and Bhanna Ram and Bhagmal entered the shop and saw it acutely, then they both came out surveyed the neighborhood and then Ghasita was asked to close and lock the shop, and they all moved back to the shop of Lala Ghassi Ram, when they were back in the presence of Ghassi Ram some Red Sharbat (A sweet red drink) was served to them, it was real tasty so they both had a repeat serving of the Sharbat.

That Bhagmal asked Lala Ghassi Ram as to what will be the monthly rent for the shop if he took it on rent, Lala Ghassi Ram told him that since he is known of Bhanna Ram and Bhanna Ram has brought him so the rent will be rupees three and eight anna's per month, this point Bhanna Ram intervened and said, Lalaji, please agree to rent it at Rupee three per month and he will stand surety for the regular and timely payment of the rent and the rent will start from 01st July, 1947. Finally everything was agreed upon by everyone and the deal was done, at those times the word of man was the most powerful and most trusted system of all arrangements, as all the people carried out honestly even in dire circumstances, Lala Ghassi Ram asked Bhanna Ram to take Bhagmal to the temple, place a tekka and repeat the deal before the God, so that the deal had the approval of the God. Bhagmal along with Bhanna Ram and Ghassi Ram went to the temple and bowed before the God and repealed the details of the deal made and prayed for its approval and success.

Now it was thirty minute past one they both along with their bicycle started looking for some shade, so that they could eat their lunch. They found a shaded places beneath a mamonth peepal tree, they sat on the ground under the shady tree, spotted some water nearby, it was a rack of four pitcher filled with water, there tumblers, they used the tumblers to bring water out of the pitcher, washed their hands and mouth and sat for their lunch, they started their lunch along with lassi, when they felt satisfied, they took the balance food to nearby cow and dog and offered the food to the dog and cow, and washed their hands.

Now the time was twenty minutes past two clock in the afternoon, they decided to be dawn there on the shade, they dozed off. In his day dream Bhagmal, he saw his father Purshottam who was sitting by the side of his mother Ram Pyayari and they were engaged in discussing something very serious, as was evident from their hush tones and gestures, he tried to fathom out as to what his parents were discussing and then, suddenly he saw his elder brother Brij Bhan and his wife Amrit cloisted together and sitting ideally and saliently by his parents. The scene in the dozed off situation made him worried and he longed to be near his parents and with his wife and children.

Exactly at three 'O Clock they got up took their bicycle and started moving to the tea shop, once at the tea shop, they both had tea and came out. Bhagmal went back to the shop and brought Burfi (A sweet meat made of milk and sugar) for the kids. He somehow decided to not to look for the house on rent for now and told about it to Bhanna Ram, nw they had done their work and moved back towards the village, Bhanna Ram astride the carrier and Bhagmal paddeling the bicycle in a furry and haste. At four in the evening they were home, Bhagmal handed over the Burfi to Todomai, telling her to give it to the kids and to have some of it herself.

After some times Bhanna Ram asked him, if he will accompany him to a near by village, so that he could have a look at the possible land of piece he may like to buy. Bhagmal agreed upon and they both went to the village Bhali. The land was owned by one Pandit Bhikka Ram, on the look of it, it seemed to be shallow land not having much of irrigation, on prodding the owner it was found that, indeed it was a shallow land, but the price asked for it was exorbitant. Bhagmal told the Pandit Jee that he will get back to him with his answer in about a fortnight. After that they walked back to Dobh, enchanting Ram – Ram on the way back to home.

By eight in the night they were back at home, the dinner was announced and they both washed their feet, hand and face and settled for the food.

The food was brought today it was cummies fried Rice and Kadhi (Kadhi is made through Curd milk in which ground gram flour (Besan) is added, some oil is also added and it is boiled till its somewhat thick and then it is fried with fenugreek seeds, coriander seeds and some Astofiedia is added to it and if one has curry leaves, these leaves are put in it.

Mool Chand, Phool Chand also sat with them and had their meals, after the food a mango was peeled and sliced and served as a dessert.

The food over both men went out Bhanna ram lighted a Beeri and puffed it, Bhagmal was given a Green Cardamom to chew, they were out on the road for about one hour, both came back and lied upon their bed.

Bhagmal was not feeling like sleeping he got up spread his Tehmat on the ground and sat on it in Lotus position and closed his eyes trying to meditate and visualize the God, Today he was very lucky he could visualize the God in a brilliant form very soon he bowed before the God and asked for his blessings and foregiveness, for this wrong acts and thanked the God for his benevolence and requested the God to shower mercy on his parents, his family and his brother and their wives. Somehow he felt that the God was not paying attention to his requests he repeated his requests once again and started weeping and he realized, that the God has disappeared, now he was in great distress he called for his mother and she appeared and asked him as to what was bothering him, he told her that the God just disappeared from his vision, without granting him his wishes. His mother assured him that God will consider his requests and if the requests were good, honest and worth and beneficial to all concerned the requests shall be granted, otherwise the request will not be considered at all. Ram Piyari his mother told him that Azam Khan the Naib Tehsildar (A Junior Land Revenue Officer) had came to meet his father this evening and had told him that the partition of India was a certainty as Mahatama Gandhi to keep Pandit Jee in good humour has succumbed to the pressure brought on him by both the Congreess led by Jawahar Lal and Muslim League by Mohamad Ali Jinha has finally agreed upon the partition of the Great Indian Nation and the formal announcement is likely to be made by the Secretary of State to the Government of India on 31st May 1947. It will be followed by issue of notification in which the exact date of partition and its modalities will be announced and Extra – ordinary Gazette Notification will be widely circulated.

That his father Purshottam was very much worried and was making a plan for future including that whether he should trust and rely on the assurance of complete safety to all Hindus who choose to stay in Pakistan and all Muslims who stay in New India. On this issue he is in double mind and is completely confused and is unable to make up his mind in the matter and he is waiting your return back to the house after completing your assigned work.

The news passed by his mother was very disturbing and did not make him feel like sleeping, so he got up. tied the Tehmat around his waist and went out of the house, the roads were pitch dark and silent except for stray bark and a whiff of dry cough, he kept walking aimlessly for about an hour and then came back had a glass of water, he had already relieved himself and went to sleep. Since he had to go to Delhi, he was woken up at 2 'O clock in the mid night and was told to get fresh and ready in a jiffy. So they could hitch hike on mule cart carrying milk for the train, which was bound for Delhi, the train departed Rohtak Railway Station at four fifteen in the morning.

He was ready by three, was given some hot milk and few biscuits and a pack which had lunch in it which consisted of Prantha (fried pan cake of salt and condiments) and Aachhar (Pickle) they came out to the main road and waited for the milk mule cart when the cart came, they got astride it and squated on the wooden plank in about half an hour they had reached the Railway Station, they got down and Bhanna Ram went to the ticket window and brought two tickets for Delhi. Bhanna Ram lighted a Beeri and vigoursly puffed on it, they reached the plate form and boarded the train and sat on wood plank berth in the compartment and slowly before the departure of the train, the compartment went more than full with men and milk cans.

The train departed at the scheduled time after about seven minutes, it stopped more people and milk cans boarded it, it again sounded a buzzer and started chugging "after about ten minutes it stopped few more people and milk cans boarded it, after hooting the horn, it again chugged out, the speed of the train increased and after about fifteen minutes it reached Sampla, where it stopped as it had to collect coal and water, it. After coal and water it chugged out of the station and stopped at few stations and then at Shakur Basti most of the passengers and milk cans deboarded the train, Shakur Basti is a part of Delhi. The train reached Main Delhi Railway Station on plate form No. 12 at six thirty in the morning.

Bodh Ram the sala (A relative) of Bhanna Ram had a tea shop at plate form No. 9, they both alighted the foot over bridge and landed at plate form No. 9. There was only one tea shop, so both of them went to the Bodh Ram, was busy cooking tea, as some train was soon expected to arrive at his plate form, when he saw his Jeeja Bhanna Ram, he waved happily and asked to wait for fifteen minutes. I was introduced to Bodh Ram, he touched my feet, we both were asked to come inside the tea stall and sit down on some small iron stool lying there. We were served tea in Kullahars (Glasses made of earth dried and brunt) and Mathi's (flour made pan cake with salt and well fried) we took tea etc.

After half an hour Bodh Ram apologised for his in-attention and asked Bhanna Ram about his wife Todomai and his kids Mool Chand and Phool Chand said that he will soon find a replacement to look after his Tea Stall and then he will spend time with them. He was told by Bhanna Ram that they had came to Delhi to see around and visit some book shops. At eleven in the morning Bodh Ram's friend came and relieved him, we the three came out of Railway Station and started walking towards the Red Fort via fountain, we saw the fountain, but it was not working, then we were shown Gurudawara Sheesh Ganj where the ninth Guru of Sikhs, Shri Guru Teg Bahadur along with his disciples was beheaded by the order of Moghul Emperor Aurengzeb for refusing to convert to Islaam, with great efforts a Gurudawara was built at the particular site of beheading, the entire work was done through donations and karsewa (free voluntary labour). After praying at the Gurudawara Sahib they saw and prayed at Gouri Tample (Devoted to Gouri the wife and companion forever of Lord Shiva the Hindu God). When they reached the Lal Quilla, the Red Fort and the palace of the Mughal Emperors, which was built by Emperor Shah Jhan, who later built a Mausoleum in love and memory of his beloved wife Mumtaz Mahal and was named Taj Mahal, a supposed to be very beautiful building, built very skillfully with white stone called Sangmurmur, brought from a long distant place known as Makrana in Rajputana by an army of Elephants. It said that about hundred thousand craftsmen worked for about fourteen years to create the beautiful monument which is known as the Eighth wonder of the world. All the crafts man had to pay a very heavy price as everyone lost its right hand fingers, so that the building may not be repeated at a future date.

Now they were at the outer door of Red Fort, they were denied entry as some Army General was inspecting the Garrison in the Red Fort. They were dismayed and started moving towards Jama masjid just across the road from the Red Fort. Bhagmal did not find the Jama Masjid at Delhi as great as was the Shahi Masjid at Lahore.

Delhi being a very old city which is supposed to have been built as Inderprasth by the legendry Pandavs of Mahabharat, the first land plough of the area was done by Balrama the elder brother of Lord Krishna the all powerfull Hindu God, who was friend, guide and mentor of Pandav brothers.

Delhi had been built and destroyed many times by various invaders including Nadir Shah, who had taken the Moghul Thorne known as Takhte Touse wholly made of Solid Gold in the form of dancing Peacock with inlaid diamonds including the world's costieliest and heaviest diamond Kohinoor which has been cut in two parts and the larger part has been inlaid in the British Crown Kohinoor is said to be not very lucky for its bearer. The Peacock Trone and Kohinoor are still in the possession of the British Empire. Delhi was made capital of India in 1911 and a very large Caronation Darbar (Crowning Ceremony) was held at place now known as Kings way camp, the Civil Lines and University of Delhi and the Legislative Assembly and other buildings and the Town Hall were constructed, all these activities helped the business grow very fast, Chandni Chowk spread out in all directions and the business prospered.

By now it was afternoon, Bodh Ram told that he will buy them some lunch, when we told him that we had brought our lunch with us, he said that it did not matter and he will get us some Pranthaa's (stuffed flour pan cake deep fried on hot steel plate on fire in lot of pure butter). We were taken to Gali Pranthey wali (Fired Pan Cake Cooking street) to the shop of Bablu Halwai. We ate pranthas with pickle and chatni, and then had sweetened curd milk, it was a quite fill but the price paid for its was really exhorbritant. It was rupee three in all. Then Bodh Ram took us to another shop of Pandit Bhola Ram three leaf Donga's (curved plate bowels made out of leaf of Dhaak Tree) were brought to us it had a good looking pudding, we savoured it and yearned for more, but did not ask for the same again as the price was stately rupee one for each bowel, the pudding was made of wet and grounded paste of (Mung ki Dal) lentil with Khoya (boiled and shortened milk and then allowed to cool into a lump in air) Then the paste is mixed with khoya and fried and boiled in clarified pure butter and lot of dry fruits and sugar and Attars (extract of flowers) added to it.

We all were full to our throat and felt like sleepry. I asked Bodh Ram if we could go to Connaught Place, he said fine with him but must decide whether we want to walk about two miles or go by Tonga (Horse driven carriage) Which charges four anna's per pessanger (one fourth of a rupee) we decided to walk, so that we may also digest our food. In half an hour we reached New Delhi Railway Station and a short distance was the Connaught Place on the way we met a woman bagger with four kids, we gave our lunch to her and walked into Connaught Place, we reached Madras Hotel and then went to Hanuman Mandir (Temple of God Hanuman) I prayed there and put a paisa (One sixteenth part of a Indian rupee) before the God Hanuman and asked for few bows, after that we went outside Rivoli Cinema, Regal Cinema and then we went to Jantar Mantar (A structure based on Astronomical positions of the sun at all hours to find out the position of other stars in relation to the sun). Jantar – Mantar was built by one of Sawai Raja Maan Singh of Jaipur (The princely king of Jaipur state in Rajputana) he had also a similar in Jaipur which was bigger in size and scope than the Delhi Jantar-Manar. After seeing the Jantar – Mantar, I felt very sad and very much concerned about my future and the future of the family, my friends, my town and the future of new devided India, at that moment and that situation in Delhi the capital of India and which was bound to remain the capital of new India, being created to satisfy the greed and political authorities of two powerful politicians who could fool the people on various ground, Mohammad Ali Jinnah on the basis of pure Islamic nation made of total Islamic population Gandhi and Nehru on the promise and premise of independent India, free from the alien rule of the British Empire, people on the entire sub continent were carried over by the hopeful promises, about which they were not sure and were quite apprehensive, but dare not protest feeling that it will be anti national to have any such sentiments. People of India as whole were ready to suffer any indignities just to fulfill the wishes of their leaders. The voices of dissent were cowed down harrunaged and chased away and finally silenced by might of political force through the police. Somehow on the occasion I was not feeling very happy about my sightseeing of Delhi and so I asked Bodh Ram that if there was any train leaving for Rohtak by the evening, he said there was a train at fifty minutes after five in the evening and if we hired a Tonga we could get that train for sure I looked at Bhanna Ram, he said he will be happy to be in his bed than to be on railway platform at Bodh Ram's tea stall. We fetched a Tonga and asked the coach man to take us to Delhi Railway station fast, he already had three passengers and with the three us, he harked the horse and put the horse on tight leash, the horse understand his master and trolled very fast at fifteen past five we were at the station, Bodh Ram hurried away to buy us the rail tickets and soon were at his tea stall sipping tea and Bhanna Ram puffing on his beeri. Since the train left from the same platform we took our tea at ease, and then said our good byes and thanked Bodh Ram, Bodh Ram gave two rupees to his Jeeja (Brother-in-law on the gainer side) for his wife and touched the feet of Bhanna Ram. He paid one rupee to me and also touched my feet. I protested but he brushed me aside.

We boarded the train, and the train departed at its appointed time, it stopped at few stations some people deboarded it some got in, when it reached Shakurbasti many milkman got in, Shakurbasti is an ordnance depot of Indian Army, where Army tants are fabricated, it also has freight train repair shop, and a big loco shed, it is an important military Railway Station on Ferozpur – Delhi track. When train reached Bhadurgarh, it became atmost empty. At eight thirty we reached Rohtak railway station, we got down went to a tap had some water which was very hot which made us yearn for tea, Bhanna Ram lighted a beeri and puffed on it, we were making our selves ready for a long walk of about four miles. We left the station and started walking briskly towards the village. When we reached at Bhiwani road, we saw a bullock cart, we harked the cart man and asked him as to where was he headed to, he replied oh to Bhali, without stopping he told us, we asked him can we hopp on he said, he will not mind, if we sat on the cart, we requested him to stop he pulled to strings and the cart almost stopped, we jumped up and sat on the cart, thanking the God, that it was our good luck that we got this God sent cart.

When we were seated on the cart the cartman looked at Bhanna Ram and said Jai Ram Ji ki (A gesture of acknowledgement of someone) and asked was he not the big land lord of Dobh. Bhanna Ram said yes he was indeed the land lord of Dobh and said Ram Ram. I was introduced as a guest on a visit who has came from Jhang on hearing this the cart man looked at me and asked me, if it was true that Jhang will not be part of New India and will be part of Pakistan and many people from the Pakistan part of India will be forced to migrate to new India, I was stunned by his question and acknowledged, I was a big fool to think that I was one of the only few who had this kind of knowledge, before I could answer his query, I asked him as to how he knew all this, he laughed and said only the fools did not knew it. Then suddenly a beam of light baffled the bull driving the cart and cart man. A man with a turban on his head and wearing police dress was throwing the torch light. The bullock cart was stopped, he hopped astride the cart and told the cart man that he wanted to go to Lalhi, the cartman said he was going only up to Bhali, he said good at least the major part of the foot walk can be avoided. After the usual introductions between all sitting there, the police man addressed me and asked me as to what was the news in Pakistan, and will the Pakistan be reality and not one of more new game of treachery of the British, the Congress and Muslim League, I said as far as I have the knowledge and understanding of the situation, it is going to be true very soon, on hearing me the policeman sighed very heavily and said that it was going to be very bad luck as the new

Kaptan (Captain) will not be a Gora (A British) but a brown Indian with all dirty habits and inhuman nature, as he know this in his fifteen years in the police force, he said once he completed twenty years of service which was necessary for getting pension, he will resign and plough his meager land instead of obeying the Kala Angrez(Black British).

Then the man with the turban, who was a police man, said his village Lahli had only one family of a Lock smith which was Muslim family but very poor and had no land in the village except the house in which they lived, the house was very big and its court yard had two good mango trees and the mangoes when ripe were very – very sweet and the lock smith was very kind to him and always gave him a bunch of mangoes twice in the season, but the ruffians of the village always stole many of the mangoes and the old couple cursed them for their thievery. Now once the Pakistan is created, the lock smith and his family shall have to migrate to Pakistan, but I don't think they will ever migrate as the lock smith family had always lived among and with Hindus of the village and had always participated to every Hindu festival and ritual, and the family never cooked or ate mutton or fish or even egg, of course they could hardly offered to eat mutton or fish and he planned to ask them if they were planning to migrate to Pakistan, they should sell their house to him and he will pay a handsome price for the house and rupees twenty extra for the two mango trees.

While they were busy in talking and listening the cart man told Bhanna Ram that we have reached Dobh, so we got down from the cart, Bhanna Ram paid one Anna to the cart man (One anna is sixteenth part of one rupee) which the cart man accepted only after lot of persuasion.

When we reached home, it was pitch dark the dog barked came near the main door, scented Bhanna Ram twice over and then ran back to the entrance door and started barking and thumping the door with its paw, Todomai suddenly got up and heard the commotion and sound lighted torch and asked in a loud voice as to who was there, than Bhanna Ram coughed and said it was Bhanna Ram, this was repeated once again and Todomai opened the door probably the cough and its repeat was the shared secret and a code.

When Todomai saw me and Bhanna Ram, she asked if everything was fine, because we were supposed to come the next day night, Bhanna Ram assured Todomai, that everything was fine, and they had came back as they had nothing to do in Delhi, then she asked was the behavior of Bodh Ram was any good and idd he treat them well and showed them around and hosted them well, I and Bhanna Ram said in unison voice, that Bodh Ram was real good host and he had spent more than eight rupees in treating us to delicious Pranthas and Halwa plus a Tonga ride, and he also brought us the return tickets, hearing this Todomai it is good that Bodh Raj treat them well.

She said she will cook some food for us, Bhanna Ram asked of her, if she had enough milk, she said she had plently she was told to bring them milk with some thing worth eating, she went to the kitchen and in about ten minutes, she was back with two glasses of milk and four grilled pappads and a water tumbler and gulped large quantity of water straight from the tumbler and passed on the tumbler of Bhanna Ram, who also gulped water, we took milk and pappads and then said Ram Ram and parted so as to go to our bed.

Once in my room, I changed and spread my Tehmat on the ground and sat over it trying to meditate and to have a vision of the God. After about good ten minutes I closed my eyes shut and started thinking about the day's events and was quite stunned to note that so many people knew about the bifurcation or partition of India, and everyone was having different and his own strictly private view of the situation, the question of the cart man was very disturbing and the thoughts of the police man were not very comforting, I was more perplexed in the process and could not think in any appropriate and proper direction, the situation seemed so fluid that I was unable to keep any count of the waves and furries being created by the proposed but certain partition of the great Indian nation the jewel of the British Empire, its most vast, powerful and resonceful land mass with vast fields good culture produce, its varied climates, land mass with large and powerful rivers, vast majority of English speaking people, who were more than useful and helpful in administering the nation, its brave and strong army, which fought for it in both the world wars with gallantry and died for it and that too at the lowest salary and perks. India had a very rich cultural heritage and it had many enlighted people, some of them having made scientific discoveries like Dr. JC Bose and Nobal Lurate Dr. Ravindra Nath Tagore, it also had great warriors like Tipu Sultan, Rani Jhansi, Tantya Tope, Nana Phadnawees, who gave a very long fight to the British in 1857.

India also had vast mineral resources like iron ore, magnese, liganite, lime which were the back bone of steel industry in England apart from huge quantity of good quality of cotton which helped the Manchester's Textile Industry live.

More over Indians were poor, obedient and good slaves and most loyal to the English in general and to the British Crown in particular. The British Empire could not and will not find better subjects anywhere in its empire, barring few exceptions like Subhash Chander Bose the founder of INA, the revolutionary Chander Shekhar Azad, Bhagat Singh, Sukh Dev, Ashfaqullah, Madan Lal Dhinghra, Veer Savarkar.

It had great Indian Religious leaders like Arbindo, Swami Viveka Nand, who had a large following in the USA and Swami Daya Nand Saraswati and Mahatma Hans Raj of Arya Samaj movement.

The British could never forget a pioneer Indian Industrialist the great Jamshett Ji Tata, who pioneered steal making in India, starting with salt and opium, the Tata's has made India as their country of domicile, after coming from Persia.

There were too many Indians who were great in many respects and they could not be forgotten though they could not be ever officially respected or regonised as most of them wanted the British to leave India because these people thought that the British had already looted and skimmed too much and are trying to kill its culture and its independent identity and the British are favouring only the British minded sycophants to grow and Indian ness was being crushed under the guise of reforms and developments. Bhagmal's train of thought stopped and he could visualize the form of Lord Shiva the destroyer, he saw the god in a trance and in dance form, which was very fearsome, he closed his eyes to avoid the furry of God, the eyes closed the God disappeared and there appeared the Hanuman (The Monkey God) the vision showed Hanuman flying over the sea with a great speed as if it bring more Sanjeevani (the life giving herb, found at very high altitude in the mountain of Himalaya) for the survival of dying and defeating India, to be partitioned ion two countries on the basis of religions identities and in the process killing the original and true religion and all this was happening to whet the political appetite for more power to add more subjects and to add to the suffering of masses who will be uprooted from their homes, hearths and souls to fend for themselves in hostile lands and hostile and unfriendly terrains. So that the politicians could make themselves as savior of mankind and attain everlasting glory, fame and a false immortality. The vision of Hanuman disappeared as Bhagmal dozed off.

It was six in the morning when Bhagmal woke up, he went out to freshen himself up, came to the house and took his clothes, went to the village well and had a bath and then he came back to the house, and was informed by Mool Chand that the breakfast was ready and he should eat it. He went to the main room and sat on the floor, breakfast was served to him alone as Bhanna Ram had his breakfast earlier and had sat for prayer.

After Bhanna Ram came out of the prayer, he told Bhanna Ram that if he agreed than he will leave for Jhang by today's train Punjab Mail and he will be obliged if Bhanna Ram made proper arrangements for his travel to the Rohtak Railway Station. Bhanna Ram asked him as to what was the hurry and he has yet not seen the agriculture land, he planned to buy, at this Bhagmal said something was bothering him strongly, which he could not exactly pinpoint but at the sometime he would to be near his parents, his wife and kids. Todomai who was sitting nearby was also listening to their talk, she said in very jocular way oh, yes. You must be missing your wife the most and she could understand it well, Bhagmal said of course he missed his wife very much, but what was bothering him to be at his house at the earliest was not very clear to him, but he was very sure that there was definitely something amiss. Somewhere, which was very perturbing him.

Bhanna Ram told him that he will take his mule cart and will ensure that he catches the train, and they shall leave for Rohtak at Seven Thirty, though the train left only at Ten O'Clock in the night and they shall have their dinner and tea at the Railway Station.

Since they had to take their dinner with them. Todomai assured Bhagmal that she will prepare lot of food for the journey so that he will not have to eat any dirty food on the way to home.

Bhagmal was wandering as to what was making him chirpy, fidgety, but in the corner of his mind and heart he had a deep feeling of premonitions of something really bad happening at his house. To acquire some kind of peace of mind he came out of the house and walked down towards the village well, where he was sure to find some cool shaded area, where he could lie on the ground and have a sound nap to put his mind at peace and rest. When he reached the village well it was almost deserted and not many human souls were to be seen there, he went near the well, had some refreshing water dabbed his face with fresh water, wet his head and hair, then started towards the shaded area under the mamonth Peepal tree, he lay flat on the ground and went into a deep slumber he slept for about an hour, he did not dream anything, he got up, felt at ease and peace within his mind. He walked back to his house as he was feeling hungry and was longing to eat something. Since the schools were closed for summer holidays, he found Mool Chand and Phool Chand in their court yard, playing Gulli Danda (Gulli is about six inches in length and about two inches in dia, tapered down at both the ends and the Danda is straight wooden rod two ft in length, the Danda is used to strike at the tapered end of the Gulli to dispatch the Gulli to a distance, the distance depending upon the face used while striking the Gulli). It is one of the most widely played games by the boys in the land of five rivers known as Punjab. But Alas Punjab will not have five rivers anymore once the partition took place, Pakistan getting two rivers and the new India having three rivers. These rivers were the back bone of agriculture in the existing undivided Punjab and these rivers had made the irrigation canals net work, which was dotted with Dak Bungalows around the canal net work, where the visiting Government official could spend their nights while on duty and also enjoy in secluded Dak Bungalows. Near here the village Lahali also had a Dak Bungalow, and it was a common knowledge that the Sahib (A common Term used to Identify the Deputy Commissioner) used to have orgy parties here in the Dak Bungalow with many society women who had the access to the Sahib.

After some times the lunch was announced as Bhanna Ram had come back home. Bhagmal washed his feet and mouth, went in and sat down for the Lunch, after few minutes Bhanna Ram joined him, the Lunch was served, it consisted of fried root potato, Aloo Raita (potato) Chatni (Ground paste made up of mint leaves and onion, lot of dried mango powder and other condiments and salt added to it.

I enjoyed the food and had two servings of root potato and three servings of Pudina Chattney. Kharbooja (Musk Melon) was served as desert, it was very sweet and I had plenty of it, having done with the food, I got up went out washed my hands gargled and went out to relieve myself. I came back went to my room, spread my Tehmat on the floor and laid down and dozed off. It was four O'clock in the evening when I was woken up and was handed over

a telegram which read "COME BACK VERY SOON"
PURSHOTTAM

The telegram was sent express double the price and it made me doubly panicky Bhanna Ram, consoled me and said that whatever was happened everything was good and fine at the other end and I should not worry at all because I could not help in any manner and anyway I was already going back to home and shall be there with my family the next day two hours before noon. I re-read the telegram and prayed in silence to the God to have mercy upon me and my family at home please God by merciful. Bhanna Ram asked Todomai to cook some tea, after about fifteen minutes Todomai brought two Tumblers of tea, Bhagmal and Bhanna Ram splurged their tea in silence and then Bhanna Ram and Bhagmal went out of the house and at some distance from the house Bhanna Ram lighted his beeri and made few quick and deep puffs, exhaled lot of black smoked, coughed for a moment and asked Bhagmal, whether he has any inkling for the reason of telegram or as to what might have gone wrong and Purshottam, the father of Bhagmal had to send the telegram. Bhagmal with a big sigh and remorse said that he does not have an iota of inkling as to whatever had happened at his place to result in an urgent telegram and said that he had prayed to the God to have mercy on him and his family and hopefully things at house will not be as bad as he was imagining and he can't help in any case and shall come to know of the facts, as and when he reaches home and hopefully he will reach home tomorrow fore noon. They both walked along the road in silence they budged about two mile and they turned back came back to the village and into the house.

Once they were home Bhanna Ram asked Bhagmal to pack up his things and called for Todomai and said to her to keep the dinner ready and packed in an hour and told her to cook some tea for both of them.

At seven sharp Todomai came out and brought two tumblers of hot tea, she also carried the packet which had dinner for both of them and the extra food for the journey. She looked for Bhagmal and when she located him, she told him not to worry on the way as everything will be fine at his house. Bhagmal was quite touched by her gesture.

After taking tea Bhanna Ram went out and was back in fifteen minutes along with the mule cart and told Bhagmal to keep his luggage on the mule cart, Todomai, Mool Chand and Phool Chand also came there Mool Chand and Phool Chand touched Bhagmal feet in good bye, he paid rupees two each to both of them and then Bhagmal said farewell to Todomai and thanked her for the good food she had given to him and also the other comforts provided to him on leaving Bhagmal referring to comforts, she blushed and folded her both hands in good bye.

Bhanna Ram and Bhagmal both came out, Bhanna Ram sat on the left side of the mule cart, held the horse strings, Bhanna Ram sat on the right side, the luggage lying tied in the middle of the cart. Bhanna Ram pulled strings and harked the mule to move. The mule started moving slowly towards the road once on the road, the mule got into rythematic stroll they both were keeping a studied silence, both busy in their own thoughts, which were only known to them. At fifteen past eight on the 08th May 1947 they reached at Rohtak railway station. Bhagmal got down of the mule cart, removed his bag and the food pack, Bhanna Ram un-harnessed the mule tide and it to a pole, put the cart by its side and came back, took the food pack and they both moved towards the ticket window, Bhagmal went to the ticket window asked for a Third Class ticket for Jhang and paid rupee nine as fare.

The train Punjab Mail from Bombay was expected to arrive at its right scheduled time Nine forty five PM. They both went into the railway station, selected a vacant bench on the platform which was almost deserted. They sat on the bench, both in turn went to the nearby water tap, washed hands and opened the food pack, brought out their dinner portion and ate it in silence. After having food, they went to tap, drank water from the tap and ordered tea at the nearby tea stall, the tea was brought to them in Kulahar (tumbler made of dried and brunt earth). Bhanna Ram paid the price of tea, both took tea, Bhanna Ram lighted his beeri and puffed on it, while sipping his tea.

After forty minutes past nine the train was announced, and they both stood up, Bhagmal holding his bag on a string on his left shoulder moved ahead in the direction of engine, when the train chugged into the plate form, Bhanna Ram folded his hands in farewell and asked for forgiveness, if he lacked in attention or hospitality and also begged pardons on behalf of his wife Todomai, if the food was not good or tasty and asked Bhagmal to pay his best regards to his parents and also send a telegram to him on his arrival at home and to confirm that everything was good and fine at home. Bhagmal boarded the train and made himself comfortable in half empty compartment the train locomotive sounded three hoots and chugged out of the platform Bhanna Ram waving his hand in farewell.

Bhagmal was looking out of train window, the train picked up speed after the outer signal and there was pitch darkness all around and even in his third class compartment only one blub in the corner was throwing a flickering lights, the over head fans were not even stirring, the hot air coming from the window was giving the most welcome relief. The train stopped at Jind and then moved, Bhagmal slumped down on his seat and kept dozing off till he heard the shrill voice of someone selling hot tea, he woke up with a starts and found out the train was stopping at Jakhal to have coal and water, he again dozed off.

And was woke up by flies, noise and the urge to relieve himself the train had reached Bhatinda and it was five in the morning, he checked his bag, it was lying intact, he found out from a passenger that the train will stop here for half an hour, change its locomotive and staff and shall leave for Firozpur at six In the morning, he got up from his seat, collected his bag and deboarded the train went to a water tap, washed his face found out a tea stall, had a cup of tea and a Rus (Dried slice of bread) he went to the book shop looking for a newspaper, but did not get one, came back boarded the train into a compartment, sat at a vacant seat near a window soon train left out and finally reached Jhang at about eleven in the morning, he came out of the railway station breathed deep into the familiar air and hired a Tonga to his Mochhi Mohalla locality. He was outside his house by eleven thirty. He felt eleated, depressed, worried and over whelmed by the events of last week. He knocked at the door, his son Kaka opened the door looked at his father touched his feet and wept, his weeping brought his father Purshattom out, who embraced him and gave a loud cry and started weeping, Bhaagmal was more perplexed and non plussed as he did not know as to why everybody was weeping on seeing him, he touched the feet of his father looked at him and ask sternly why was he crying, his father took him inside where his mother Ram Payari was lying dishelved, tears rolling her ears wetting the bed, he touched the feet of his mother and lay besides her, put his one arm around his neck and strongly hugged her and wept openly in very loud voice.

Ram Paryari came out of her long upon and embraced Bhaagmal saying slowly in a very low voice, hey Bhaagu Oy Bhaagu how unlucky you are, you have been looted in day light and your mother could not provide you any security and protection, Oh how sad it is and how unlucky we all are, and what about your old father, pretending to be brave and your chaste wife Sulakashni had been defiled, defied, deshelved and we could not do anything nor did we do anything, how cowardly we are, and we are not entilled to live and rather should die of shame, but oh, God will not allow us to die nor the God came to protect us or came to save Sulakashni from utter devastation and the God also failed badly in preventing this to happen, nor did he kill or punish the preparotor of atrocities, the God has become merciless and no more cares for the poor like us.

Kaka came forwarded with a glass of water and Nikko also brought another glass of water. I took the glass of water form Nikkoo and gulped it over, go and asked my mother Ram Payari in stern voice to stop crying and to get up and cook food for me and the family, on hearing my stern voice, she got up and went to the bathroom had a bath and lighted a lamp and offered prayers to the Gods and went to the kitchen prepared some tea, offered tea to her husband and his son and then went about corking the food, since no body had eaten anything for the last 48 hours.

My other son Didu and daughter Chhotti, came and embraced me and asked me to why did I go out for such a long while I kept my quiet trying to understand the situation.

Lost in my thoughts, I told myself that I shall have to be brave hearted and have to withstand the unwarranted on slaught. I got up, took out my clothes from my trunk and went to the bathroom to fresh me up so as to fathom the course of action to be followed in the given situation.

When I had my bath, I came out lighted the lamp and prayed to the God who simply did not help and prevent the devastation and defilement of my wife and said to the God, that he must justify his unjustified apathy and his derilication of his assigned and prorogated duty to help his devotees, as Sulakashni my wife was her great devotee, who always observed a fast on Ekadeshi(eleventh day of fort night) and Poornimashi (End of lunar month when the Moon was full and the brightest) for the last twenty years.

My father called me loudly and said that the food was ready and waiting for me I said I shall have my food after some times after he has eaten and the kidds and mother had eaten.

I went to my room, it was almost dark and hot and humid, I went near my wife touched her forehead and said in a low and loving voice Hey Sulakashni, get up, drop and forget whatever did happen how so ever bad it might have been, but she has to get up and give me the courage, so that I may live and she dies as Sadhawa (Married woman with a living husband).

Sulakashni threw her coverlet, stood up she was without a shred of cloth on her body and she was bruised at her body at many places. I could visualize the devastation and the agony she must have faced; she did not weep nor cover herself, came towards me and touched my feet, and went to the bath room outside the room. I brought out the First Aid Box and knocked at the bath room door she opened up without protest. I cleaned her bruises and removed the dried blood from body and then put on a medicinal lotion at the open bruises and came out telling her to have a bath and in the mean while I shall fetch her some clothes, She did not say a word, I came out she closed the bath room door, after I had brought her clothes consisting of salwaar, Kameez and dupatta (Slawar Kameez is a loose tunic and a long shirt and Dupatta is a stole). I knocked at the door, she was done with her bath, and opened the door slightly I handed over her clothes to her. Then she came out of the bathroom went to her room lit a lamp and then just extinguished the lamp without her usual prayer, she asked me if I could fetch her some food from the kitchen, I went out to the kitchen where my mother was waiting for me. I asked her to put food for two people in a thaali. She put two katories (Brass bowels) and seven chappaties (flour pan cake) cooked on hot plate, some purified butter milk splattered on it) and gave it to me, I took the thaali of food to my room put it on the bed and asked Sulakashni o have the food, she sat on the floor and tore a morsel, dipped it in the vegetable in the Katori and brought the same to my mouth, I took it in my mouth, she also had a bite of the chappati dipped in the vegetable and started eating the food without coaxing, when the food was over, she went out and brought water for me. She said she will like to have a nice nap and when she gets up then she may talk to me at length, if I did not mind, I should leave her alone as she is not as yet ready to face every one. She came out of the bed and closed the room without bolting the door.

I went to the court yard, patted the cow and fed her a chappati, and looked for the street dog who was a regular visitor but did not see it.

I called for my children, Kaka Nikoo, Chhotti and Didu, put my hands over their head by turn and asked them how were the things and are they enjoying their school holidays, they said they missed me too much and did not fled any enjoyment in my absence, and did not like their grandparents scolding them every time they had sweets but Dada(grandfather) did give them a Paisa each every day (a paisa is sixteenth part of a rupees) a paisa at that time could buy eight lollipops at a time) I told him that since I was back I hoped that now they will enjoy their holidays but they must give some time to their studies every day. Kaka asked me if I could buy him a hockey stick so that he could practice during the holidays and as such he may get into the school hockey team. Nokko said she wanted two ribbons one red and one black, Chhotti said needs to buy a new pencil as she has to do her homework, Didu said, he wanted a pencil and rubber apart from kulfi (ice cream on a stick) I spent some more time with the children and then I told them to go and play in the court yard.

I went to the room of my parents; my father got up and told me to sit down, my mother kept lying. I started telling my father about my visit to Dobh and the curtsies showered by Bhanna Ram and his wife, that I had opened the bank account in the Imperial Bank Rohtak and has deposited rupees one hundred in my new account, and that Bhanna Ram had given him rupees two hundred and also had promised to lend me more money if I needed it, that I have made up firm arrangement for renting out a shop on the main railway road form first of July and the monthly rent has been agreed upon at rupee three and eight annas per month. That I did not find any good land which I would have agreed to purchase and I did not look out for a house on rent. That Rohtak was of a course a district town and had a railway station, but it was not as big as Multan or Lahore and the people there were mostly poor and unfriendly except Bhanna Ram and Leku Ram. I told my father that I had gone to Delhi, the capital of the contry and had visited Gurdawara Sheesh Gunj, on hearing this my father uttered

DhanDhanNasanak (Oh Great Nanak) and Gauri Temple and Hanuman Temple, my father bowed his head and said, oh lord Shiva, MaaPaarvati, Lord Hanuman, please do have mercy.

My father was silent for some time and told his wife Ram Payari to go to the kitchen and cook some Masala tea, when mother went out and was out of ear shot my father said in a very low and agony full, voice it was Salaluddin, my friend who defiled my wife, it come to me as a rude shock and I made up mind that I shall have to revenge this wrong deed and for this Salaluddin will have to die, I had made a plan to achieve this revenge, but I kept my quite so as to not to give any clue to my father. After while I asked my father what was the information available to him and what kind of plan he has made. My father told me that he will sit in prayer before the God and will tell me the future course of action on the basis of information he had received from his few good friends, which may be relied upon or discarded, depending on the plan we make, and told me that both my elder brothers and their wives will to here on Saturday evening and his two brother will be here at the same time and they can sit and decide as what needs to be done in the given circumstances. My mother Ram Payari brought the tea we had the tea in silence and then I got up and said that I was going out to my shop, and may meet some people on the way. I reached my shop at about four O clock, all the neighbors came, said Ram Ram, and asked me where I was to for about a week, I told them I had gone out on an errand I opened the shop swept it, dusted it, lighted the incense stick, brought fresh water in the pitcher sat at the appointed place, said my usual shop prayer. Two customers came, bought a book, a pen and six copies, paid money and went away. I took out a small copy and a pencil and started noting down the stocks in the shop.

First I went to the shelf where good quality fountain pens were stocked, I counted Parker silver 36, Parker gold 16, Waterman superior 47, Waterman student 66. I calculated the values of every type of pen and then made the grand total of all the pens. Total value of which came to rupees three hundred twenty. I counted all bottles of ink pots and valued then of rupees one hundred sixty. Then I counted registers and note books, they were valued at Rupees one thousand two hundred fifty. The total value all off goods in shelf numbers one came to about seventeen hundred only.

The shelf number two had all small things like rubber, pencil, rulers and slate pencils, slates etc, it was valued at rupees five hundred eighty.

It was six by now and the counting of books would have taken a very long time, so he got up went out and shouted for a cup of tea from an adjacent tea shop, and looked into his note book in which he kept his shop account. He owed rupees seven hundred to various suppliers, and few sundry customer owed him rupees two hundred sixty rupees.

After having tea he went around the three book shelves and made and estimate of the value of all books, both new and old and about twenty four thousand and he correlated in his mind that the total values of the stock in shop was not more than thirty thousand in any way and adding the cost of shop the total would amount to rupees nothing more than forty five thousand, and he was ready to dispose of the whole business for rupees forty thousand on down cash payment and he started planning, as to how to go about it without causing panic in the market.

He closed the shop and started moving towards the Hindu cremation ground to look for Aghor Tantric Bhootia

Baba on the way he bought one paav of Jalabi (one paav is equal to one fourth of a one ser- about 910 grams. Jalebi is sweet meal made up of fermented fine floor deep fired and immersed in sugary syrup). He also bought one paav of Pakoras (Pakoras are made up of batter of gram flour powder called Besan to which salt, peeper, peeperica and all kind of vegetables are added and then a lump of the mixture is fried very deep in oil until it becomes crisp).

Bhaagmal found the Bhootia Baba at his usual place puffing upon a chillam (In earthen cigar type pipe in which tobacco is burnt on wooden coal). Bhaagmal touched the feet of Bhootia Baba, who was bare chested with lot of ash paste on his body and hair, and was wrapped in lungi (A wrap around loose cloth put around the waist, and folded a the knee). The baba asked him to sit down and accepted the offerings of Jalebis and Pakoras, he started eating Jalebis first, after few of it he started eating pakoras, when he felt somewhat started, he looked at Bhaagmal and asked him as to what has brought him to the Baba even though they were classmates in the school up to class six and then Bhola Ram now Bhootia Baba, had left for Himalaya as his father, mother, two sisters and here brothers were killed in broad day light by an English Judge, who was furious because Baba's mother who was extremely beautiful with a very supple and levisous body had refused to sleep with that Judge on demand and the very next morning his entire family was murdered, he was alive because he had done to the market to fetch onions as asked by her mother and he was hidden by force by one of his neighbour, though the people of the locality made a lot of noise and protest nothing came out of it, and the Judge was promoted as District Judge and was transferred to Multan after few days of this incident.

Bhaagmal was in great pain while narrating the event of defilement of his wife by one of their common class mate Salaluddin, on hearing the name of Salaluddin, Bhootia Baba went into a rage because he recalled that the father of Salaluddin was private assistant of the Judge for explaining the Urdu petition made before the judge and the PA hadblatantly refused to help in any way and had refused to recognize Bhola Ram when he met him after two years, though they were neighbours and Bhola Ram used to go to Salaluddin's house every day when his father was around.

Bhootia Baba took more jalebis and pakoras and asked Bhaagmal as to what he wanted to be done and the Baba will do anything and everything for him, as Baba had eaten his salt and the salt can not be disrespected. Now Bhaagmal said he wanted revenge and do revenge which lives for long time and suffering is unbearable and is for the total life to be lived.

Bhootia Baba told him to go and fetch some ash from a pyre which is still on fire. Bhaagmal went to cremation ground, found a burning pyre, collected some ash put it on a Tasla(A curved Platter) and brought it to Bhootia Baba.

The Baba took some ash and put it on his head, threw few to his left side and few to this right side and then started reciting some Sholokas (Hymen's). Invoking the God of Destruction and prayed to him to full fill the wishes of Bhaagmal and then told Bhaagmal to go back to his place and not to sleep with his wife for eleven days and come back on the twelthday with some burfi (A sweetmeat made of thickened milk with sugar) and Jalebis along with the confirmed news of complete paralysis of Salaluddin and his father.

Bhaagmal was told to have his bath at the crematorium well before he went back to his house. Bhaagmal had his bath and walked back to his house and on the way back home he bought some candies for his kidds, when he was at his house, he again had a bath and asked his wife to bring food for him, instead his mother brought food for him and told him that his father has as yet not taken his food. So they both should sit together and have their food which she will serve soon and informed him that kidds had their food and his wife and she will take their food when the gents had eaten their food.

Bhaagmal went to the room of his father and told him that he has evaluated the stock in his shop and the value of the shop along with the total stocks and furniture is roughly around forty five thousand and in the given depressed atmosphere he will be very happy to settle for rupee forty thousand paid to him in cash down payment. His father told him to start looking for a buyer and as far the land they shall decide on Saturday when the other boys and his brothers meet and sit together.

Ram Payari brought two thaalis with food on it, it was plain Daal, Papad and achar, and they both ate silently, Ram Payaritook the thaalis and brought water for them and then went out, took a thaali of food and went to Sulakashni's room both had their food and thaali was brought out by Ram Payari which was most unusual but was acceptable in the given circumstances.

Bhaagmal came out of his father room went to his room, saw Sulakshani sitting in a prayer, he changed his clothes, spread a cloth on the floor, lighted a lamp and sat in a prayer and started singing in very slow voice the prayer song was

> My lord you are very merciful
> My lord you are ever merciful
> On occasion you do not show mercy

May be it is a part of your design
Who so ever has ever know your design
You make the design and you read the design
Man dare not and cannot know your design
Oh Lord please have mercy
I do not want to learn your design
I only wish to live by your design
Your mercy, your mercy only.
Oh Lord be a God and show mercy
Shower mercy, and shower mercy
Oh Lord I am a greedy man
My greed knows no bounds
And do not want any bounds for your mercy
Oh Lord I pray to you to be my protector, my mentor,
my benefactor my real mother and father and the God
The God does not and will not and should not desert
his son, his subject
and his pariah
Oh God I am your pariah and beg for your mercy
Oh God do give me alone life by your mercy
Your mercy
Your mercy
Oh God your mercy
Amen Mercy
Amen Mercy

His prayer over he got up went out relieved himself cam
back, had a glass of water took his bedding, went out and
spread his bedding on a cot lying in the verandah and in few
minutes he was snoring loudly.

Sulakshani was lying awake in her bed, she had seen
her husband sit in prayer, recite a prayer in song form, take
his bedding out and having slept in the verandah, and nor

trying to address her at all or to say anything to her or ask her anything, about her worst event and accident having happened to her when she was molested, raped and bruised by her husband friend of long standing and one of her husband classmate for ten years. But she had one consolation in her mind howsoever trivial it might have been that she had chewed and mauled the number of Salaluddin, just like a bitch on remp age. She was sure in her mind that, Salaludin having her number fully bitten off and incapable of repair even by the best of surgeons in London will not dare to try and repeat his ghostly act of raping a woman, of course he will not have his number any more she wished she could have and should have chopped of his number and saved it as a bad savinouor. Also she could not achieve it, because no knife was handy enough to achieve her least felt desire.

Sulakashni could not sleep as the train of her wild thoughts kept running directionlessly and now she was thinking as to how she will explain her defilement and her shame to her husband, and how her husband will take the narration of her defilement, her husband think that she enjoyed and willingly participated in her rape, and all the bruises were just to disguise her silent willingness for the rape and its consequential enjoyment and will her husband believe in her saying that she had badly mauled and completely chewed the number of her husband's friend Salakuddin and she would have chopped off the number of Salakuddin if she had a knife handy or her husband will think that the story about the chopping off was made up only to show her in better position to gain sympathy. She could make herself sure about the reaction of her husband, she got up from her bad, want to the bath room relieved herself, came back had a glass of water and again went to her bed and lay on it, she again got up came out and looked out to see where was her husband sleeping though she already was in know that her husband was sleeping in the verandah, but she would have to make herself very sure about it. She was curious to know about the journey of her husband his stay at Dobh in Rohtak, and had he been able to open the bank account and rent a shop and a house, and had arranged the purchase of planned piece of land and if the land was fertile and irrigated. She wanted to find out if the area had schools for the boys and the girls and the area had some good seamstress, who could sew clothes for her and the girls of course gents teachers will be there, no question about it, but for now she had no way of satisfying her curiosity, it shall have to wait till her husband came near and told her everything she wanted and was eager to know will take some time her husband told her the facts, she will have to live with her curiosity and questions, but she was sure that her husband will not take long to come to her and spill the beans on being patted with little cajoling and some good touches at the right places. Now she went into a deep slumber and slept till six in the morning.

She got up in hurry and went to the bath room, had her bath, washed all clothes in the bath room, put the wet clothes on overhead strings in the open court yard to stay and dry, came back into the room, changed her clothes, combed her hair, put on a Bindi on her fore head, took out a Duppatta put it on her head, lighted a lamp and said her prayer before a photo of the God, bowed her head touched the feet of the God, in the photo, and then touched her head. She went to the kitchen, where her mother-in-law Rampayari was already making tea. She touched the feet of her mother-in-law, but mother-in-law did not bless her as usual in the past. She heaved a sigh and asked her mother-in-law, if she can also have some tea, she was asked to wait when the tea was cooked, it was passed in three glasses and she was given a glass of tea with two pieces of bread, Rampayari put two glasses of tea and few slices of bread in a thali and went out of the kitchen. Sulakshani kept sitting in the kitchen taking her tea and bread. when she was done with the tea, she got up, washed all dirty utensils from the overnight, scrubbed the kitchen with a wet rag, all done, she started preparing the breakfast for the kids and everybody else in the house. She decided to cook daliya (wheat porridge) with milk and salt, daliya was supposed to be sumptuous easily digestible, tasty and took much less time, then pranthas and everyone liked it very much, except her but she could take more bread in breakfast

She started waiting for her husband to wake up so that she could offer her tea in a bigger brass glass which he preferred in the morning. She looked up as to what vegetable was there in the house which may be peeled and chopped for cooking. She saw a big Ghiya (green bottle groud). She took the Ghiya washed it and peeled it and then chopped it into small pieces. Then she took some ginger, chopped it and then chopped the garlic, put whole chopped vegetable in a big bowl of water and let it soak for some time before the vegetable could be cooked. Her husband kept sleeping. She did not want to wake up him as she was sure that he must have be very tired and that is why he is still sleeping till such a long time. The kids were already up and about and had already asked her to give them something to eat. She put daliya in four bowls and brought them out of the kitchen to a corner of verandah and gave one bowl to each kid and told the kids not to make any noise as their father was asleep there as he must have been very much tired. Sulakashni went back to the kitchen took two big bowls filled them with daliya put the bowls in thali and took the thali to her father in law's room, knocked on it and was asked to come in. She put her dupatta on her head went inside, kept the thali on the side table touched the feet of her father in law and placed one bowl of daliya before him and the other for her mother in law waited there for a minute then came out of the room, her husband was still in deep sleep. She went into the kitchen and started cooking the ghiya vegetable. Then she heard some commotion in verandah and peeped out. She saw her husband playing and chatting with the kids. She called for Nikko, when Nikko came to her she told Nikko to go to her Pita Ji (papa)and tell him that Mata(mummy) will bring the tea very soon and gave Nikko a glass of water for her father.

She cooked the masala tea put it in big brass glass, it was very hot. She wrapped the glass with a cloth and took it on to her husband who took the glass from her and asked her if she was alright and said that he has over slept but he was still feeling tired and sleepy. She went back to the kitchen to take care of the vegetable.

Bhagmal sipped the hot tea, relished it and got up went to toilet to freshen himself came and asked kaka to go and asked her mata ji to give his clothes. Kaka went into the kitchen and asked his mata ji that pita ji was asking for his clothes as he wanted to have his bath. She said to kaka that he may tell his pita ji that his clothes have already been put in the bathroom. Kaka came back and told his father that the clothes are already there in the bathroom. Bhagmal went into the bathroom and had a long and refreshing bath, changed his clothes and came into and went to his room lighted a lamp and fired the incense sticks and prayed before the photo of the God.

Sulakshni came out with his breakfast of daliya and placed the bowl before him, he had a look at Sulakshni, wanted to say something, but decided against it and started taking his breakfast, the breakfast over he got up and called in the direction of Sulakshni, that he was going to his shop and his lunch be sent to his shop and then he went to the room of his parents touched their feet, told them that he was leaving for his shop and his lunch be sent to his shop, came out of the room and went out of the house and started walking down to his shop.

When he reached to his shop it was thirty minutes past nine, he opened the locks on the shop door, opened the door, went in, took a broom and swept the floor of the shop after that he picked up the water tumbler, sprinkled some water on the floor, scrubbed the we floor with a rag, then he lit a lamp and stood before the photo of the God, said a prayer and then he sat at his seat at the shop.

After some times, there came a customer and asked him if he can supply him his requirements and a list of the requirements was given and Bhagmal took some time to read the long list and found almost more than ninety percent goods in the requirement list were readily available at his shop and the remaining could be arranged without difficulty the customer was one Mr Khawaza Ahmed Principal of Govt Inter College at Maghiana a nearby town. Bhagmal informed the Principal that he will be able to supply his requirements on hearing this; the principal said that the price charged should be competitive and fair and he will take a cut of ten percent of the total bill, and the Principal has the cash ready to settle the bill.

Bhagmal made out a list of items which were not available with him and told the Principal that it will take about two hours to make the supply and he should sit there, have some tea and snacks by the time his supplies will be packed and ready for payment. The Principal said, thanks for the tea and that we will be back in about two hours and left. Then Bhagmal came out of the shop, told his neighbor shopkeeper to keep a watch on his shop and he will be back very soon. Bhagmal walked very fast towards the Tonga bazzar, on reaching Tonga bazzar he went to the shop of Safi Bros, the junior Saife welcomed him and after the pleasantries looked at the list of goods from Bhagmal, and asked the one of the shop assistant to pack the goods and in about twenty the goods were packed the bill raised and given to Bhagmal, when checked the bill and tallied the bill with his list, he paid the amount of the bill, the senior Saifi saw him and came towards him, putted him on the shoulder and asked about his father and asked the junior Saifi to returns rupees ten from the total amount received from Bhagmal. Bhagmal collected the goods and moved back briskly to his shop. Once he reached the shop, he ordered a cup of tea as he was about two hours late, he opened the package, he had has bought from Safai Brothers and arranged it, then he took his tea and started bringing out the goods and put them on the counters, when the entire goods as per list of requirement, he started packing them into a bigger bamboo and jute box used mainly for packing Beeris, when he was satisfied that the total requirement has been duly packed in the box, he look out a cash memo, and stared making the bill keeping in mind that the ten percent of the total bill has to be paid by the Principal, finally he completed the bill, and totaled it and found that the total bill amount was rupee five thousand six hundred eighty only. The Principal came in and asked if the supply and the bill were ready. The bill was handed over to the Principal who want thorough it checked the total and asked Bhagmal to put a ten paisa revenue stamp and write that the payment has been received in full and cash, the Principal than paid him rupee five thousand and two hundred rupees, asked the Bhagmal to put the package of goods outside the shop so that Tangawala (Horse driven Cab's driver) could take it, he harked the Tongawala and asked him to load the package on his tonga, the Principal said fare well to Bhaaagmal and left. By now it was one in the afternoon, he come out of his shop and moved towards Sunehari Masjid (Golden Mosque) nearby to see if Salaluddin or his father were there for the one clock Namaaz (afternoon prayer time). He remained standing nearby, but did not see Salaluddin or his father since there were only five or six Namaazis there. So he had no doubt that both the father and son was not there it gave him lot of satisfaction because it was most unusual for them to miss out the afternoon Namaaz but he wanted to be hundred percent sure of the success of Bhootia Baba, then Bhagmal told himself that he was a big fool to expect the results in less than twenty four hours, being dismayed he walked back to his shop. At the shop his son Kaka was waiting for him with his lunch and lassi, he gave a Chavani (four anna's) to Kaka and told him that the same had to be equally divided between four of them and there next chavani will be given to them only after a week. Kaka touched the feet of his father and darted out of the shop.

Bhagmal washed his hands and went behind the main counter, spread on old paper and opened the lunch pack and started eating his food slowly, the food has filled karela's (filled Bitter Gourd), he relished the karala's and gulped the lassi from the tumbler it was brought in, the food over, he got up, went out to a nearby open drain and relieved himself came back washed his hands, rewashed his mouth, and went behind the counter, cleaned the space where he had his lunch, and lay down on the ground to take a nap, he had hardly dozed off, when a customer came and asked for a dozen of a Parker Gold pens, when the pens were given to him and was asked to pay rupee one hundred twenty he said he will pay only rupees on hundred ten only, Bhagmal said for rupee five more but he paid rupees two only look the pens and went out.

Bhagmal once again lay down and tried to doze off, but simply could not doze off so he got up and sat up right at his appointed seat. His head was so much muddled up that he could not think anything straight. He took out a book and randomly opend the book where he read.

"The man is a wise fool, his wisdom is the biggest problem which hinders his progress, because of this professed wisdom he doubts and questions every act of the God but he cannot do anything to prevent or alter the acts of God. Since he cannot in his so called wisdom and cannot prevent any act of the God, he accepts the acts of God, but continue to doubt the wisdom of the God, and the man feels he is definitely more wise then the God, because he acts according to best of his interest, and the God does not always acts according to man's interest"

On reading the above given para in the given book, he started thinking that if he is held as a wise man it is because he acts in the interest of the people concerned in the matter, and he has an interlaying of the interests of people involved in the given circumstances and situations and not being fully satisfied with his own explanation of his wisdom, he decided not to think any more about the wisdom and told himself very loudly, that no one should and no one can doubt the wisdom of the God.

His train of thought was broken by the loud voice of a customer standing at his shop and trying to draw his attention. Bhagmal welcomed the customer and asked him how he could help him, the customer gave him the list of supplies required, he looked at the list went around the shop and brought out the goods listed, made a total of their prices on a piece of paper, told the customer that it was rupee two hundred sixty, the customer asked for a Cash Memo. Bhagmal made out a Cash Memo and handed it over to the customer along with the supply in a packet, the customer paid rupees two hundred fifty collected the packet and walked away. Bhagmal thanked the God very loudly for the very good sale during the day. It was getting dark, he lighted the Gas Lump, said his evening prayers and ordered a cup of tea, after sometimes the tea arrived, and he sipped the tea at leisure and sat there waiting for more customers. After half an hour a customer came asked for an Ink Pen and a dozen of HB Pencils, he paid the value of the goods and went away taking the supplies with him. At half an hour past seven Bhagmal closed the shop, and went to Sabzi Mandi (Vegetable Market) he bought two seers of potato and onion each, one seer of Tomoto, Ghia, Touri (Leek), Palak (Spinach) Aarbi (Root Potato) and four Kharbuja's (Musk Melons) some green peepers and coriander and mint leaf and unripe mango, his Thaila (Bag) was full to the brim, he decided to buy Daal etc. the next day. Next Bhagmal went to the shop of Mukandi Halwai, bought some Jalebis, Burfi and Namak Pare (Namak Para is made of fine floor, which is rolled on a wooden board and cut into very small pieces and then deep fried).

He walked back to his house, when he reached the house his parents and kids were sitting ideal in varrandah fanning themselves with hand held fans. He look the thaila to the kitche. Where his wife Sulakshni was preparing the dinner, he left the thaila of vegetables there only, brought out the

Burfi and Namak Pare, and two jelabis and handed them over to his wife and told her that she should eat away the jalebis, the balance jalebis each to his mother and father and gave two jalebis each to all his four children. And he was left only with one jalebi for himself, which he too ate with hurry. Jalebis over, he told his father about the very good sales at the shop on the day, and how even the people like college Principals of have become dishonest and making people like him dishonest also, but he justified his dishonesty by telling that after all he has to dispose of his stocks and if a little enforced dishonesty could help him in disposing off his stock, he will do it and simply ask for the forgiveness of the God and God is merciful and will understand and forgive his little dishonesty.

Sulalkshani came out of the kitchen and announced that food was ready and they should get ready for the dinner. Bhagmal went to the bathroom, had a bath, wrapped his tehmat, put on a fresh Bundi came out, went to his room lighted a lamp and prayed to the God, then came out sat in the varrandah Sulakashni first brought food for the kids in two thalies, then she brought a single thali, for Ram Payari, and then she brought two thalies one for his father-in-law and one for the husband, after some times she again came out and asked of everyone if anyone would need anything more, then she sat on the floor, when the kids had their food. Nikko and Chhotti took the empty utensils to the kitchen than kaka collected empty utensils of his grandparents and his father and took it to the kitchen, no desert was served. Sulakashni got up went to the kitchen had her food, collected the empty used utensils. After washing the utensils, she came out with the milk, gave a glass of milk to his father-in-law, mother-in-law and her husband and told him that she wanted to speak to him that night and then she went away.

When Bhagmal reached in the room Sulakashni was sitting on the bed her feet on the ground, she get up and asked her husband to sit, he sat on the bed and then Sulakashni sat on the floor, at the feet of her husband. She kept her head at the feet of her husband and tears were flowing like a stream from her eyes wetting the feet of her husband. Suddenly Bhagmal stroked her hair and told her that he knew and was very sure that she is pure and chaste even though she has been defiled by Salaluddin and as penance for his and her sins and their attonment he has vowed that he will not sleep with her for eleven days and hopefully the God will be merciful and shower his mercies upon both of them and they again will live as good man and wife. On hearing her husband talk of attonement of her sin, she wept loudly and then settled down sobbing regularly for few minutes and then got up and went to her bed and tried to sleep.

Bhagmal took his bedding and went to Varandah, spared his bedding on the cot lying there, went out relieved himself, took a glass of water and sat on the bed in lotus position and stared praying to the God, he was muttering Oh my God, today I acted dishonestly but oh God, how could I not be dishonest, when even well placed people were behaving dishonestly and inducing people like me to be dishonest. My only fault is that I could not resist the temptation but I accept my guilt that I did not try and resist the temptation thought I should have and could have rejected the temptation. But Oh God, whatever I do is as you gave to it to my mind I went ahead as I dare not doubt your wisdom please forgive me my temptation as I am capable of resisting everything but temptation Oh God, be merciful and never let temptation come my way please stop me from being dishonest and forgive my dishonesty Oh God, be pleased be merciful Oh God the merciful be merciful.

Prayer over Bhagmal folded his hands and lied down to sleep, and soon he was snoring happily. Sulakashni came out touched the feet of her husband went back and went to her bed and after a minute was snoring loudly.

She got up at five O' clock in the morning swept clean the kitchen, rubbed the floor with a wet rag, took out Aarbi started peeling it than chapped it, washed it and spread it in a cloth to let it dry before it could be cooked.

She put some water in the tea pan, burnt fire in the hearth and put it on the hearth and let it boil to cook tea. When the tea was cooked, she strained the tea into three brass glasses, took two of them to his father-in-law and mother-in-law who were expectantly waiting for the tea. She went back to the kitchen, had a glass of water and she started sipping the tea, having done with the sipping of tea, she got up and started preparing for the cooking the vegetable. She started cooking Aarbi, in about forty minutes, the vegetable was cooked.

Now she started preparing for the breakfast. She took a big bowel put some floor into it, put salt cummies seed, broken black pepper and thyme, added water stirred the mixture to make it thick batter, batter will be spread on the hotplate on hot oil and the dough will be well spread and allowed to fry till it became brown and crisp.

She was so much engrossed in her cooking plans that she did not hear the voice of her husband, who was standing at the door side of the kitchen asking for tea, he had already asked for the tea twice over, than he thumped on the door she craned here neck to see who was there saw her husband and told him that she will give him the tea in few minutes. She started cooking the tea, and it was done, strained the tea in a big glass, put a cloth around it and brought it to her husband, he carefully took the glass and started sipping the tea, once the tea was over he went to the toilet and then to his room to bring his clothes brought his clothes and went to the bathroom, had his bath, put on the clothes and then came out to his room lighted a lamp and an incense stick and started praying before the photo of the God.

After having given the tea to her husband she started cooking breakfast, the first two round floor purries (fried Pan Cake) She gave it to her father-in-law and the next two to her mother-in-law. She asked the kidds to be ready and seated for the breakfast. She gave one puree each to all the four and repeated it, in the meantime her husband was ready and was given the breakfast and then she cooked two more purees for herself.

After taking his breakfast Bhagmal went to the room of his parents touched their feet and told them he was going to the shop, he was asked to be back by five that was the time his brothers and his uncles will be home and was asked to bring some three seer of Aam's (Mango) and four Nimboo's (Lemon). His mother said, she and his wife will manage the kitchen, send his lunch and cook the dinner and they will start preparing for it in good time, so that when the guests arrive they would be well attended and given a good company, hearing all this Bhagmal came out and walked towards his shop on the way changed his mind and took a detour and went near the house of Salaluddin to gather the desired news, but he told himself that it was too early to expect any news instead of going towards Salaludddin's house, he took a turn and walked straight to his shop.

Once on his shop he opened it, swept the floor and scrubbed the floor with a wet rag lighted a lamp and a incense stick said his prayer and set on his appointed seat to wait for customer. After sometimes a small boy came to buy a lead pencil and then for half an hour there were no more customers. At eleven a customer came and paid rupees twenty owed to the shop. Then a supplier came and was paid rupee two hundred only, the supplier asked for an order of goods, was told that at present there was no demand for his goods as they have sufficient stock of the goods. Then a tea was asked for and when it came was sipped greedily

Kaka came and brought his lunch and said to his father that he wanted to have a Chuski (crushed ice molded to a shape and then a cloured Sugary Syrup is to poured over it) Kaka was given one Aanna and was told to buy four chuskies and take them home and have one for himself. Bhagmal was not feeling hungry and did not wish to have his food, he went out to nearby Soda shop, had a Masala Soda and came back and lied down on the ground behind the counter, he had hardly laid down when a customer came with two child, and asked for a dozen of Note Books two Waterman student pens four HB Pencils and two erasers the requirement asked for was given to them and money for the same collected the customer left, once again Bhagmal lied down on the floor and tried to doze off but could not after about ten minutes, he got up took the tumbler of water, came out of the shop washed his face, wiped his face with his handkerchief, though Aarbi was his favorite vegetable, he left like having his tea, he came out and shouted for a cup of tea, after some times the tea was served before him, he sipped his tea very slowly not enjoying it much then he got up and decided to close the shop for the day and go to his home, he closed the shop locked it and started for his home, he felt tired and drained out and walked very slow. When he reached near the Subzi Mandi he looked around for Mangoes spotted some good looking variety, went to the Rehri (Hand cart) and asked for the price and was told that the mangoes will cost him rupee two per seer he told the reheri wala that he will buy five seer but will pay only rupees eight only, the reheri wala said, he must pay at least rupees nine, only than he will be given the mangoes he agreed and selected the mangoes, weight was done and the mangoes were put into his thaila (Handbag) he paid rupees nine to the seller, and went to the sweet, shop and asked for one seer of Jalebi, was told to wait so that he could have fresh and hot Jalebi he agreed to wait, paid the price, after some times he was handed over the Jalebis in Lifafa(Paper bag) he put the paper bag in his thaila and walked towards his home.

When Bhagmal reached home, his both uncles were already there and soon his both elder brothers and their wives arrived. He went to his father's room and saw his both uncles touched their feet and asked them if everything was good at home than his both brothers came there, he touched their feet and embraced them, they asked of him, if he was good, he replied in the affirmative, then he came out of his father's room and went to his room, where he met his Bhabhi's (brothers wife) touched their feet and sought their blessings then came out of his room, then re-entered the room and asked his wife if the sherbet (Sweet Water) was ready, he will take it, his wife told him to wait for some time and the sherbat will be given to him. So that he could take it with them, he told his wife that he was brought Jalebis which should also be served, his wife said she will serve the Jalebis along with Namak Para (salt and fired chipps made of fine flour.

He was given a tray with six glasses Jalebis and Namak Para, and was asked to take them to his father's room, come back and collect the Jug of Sharbat, he did as was told by his wife. He went to his father's room served the sharbat and offered Jalebis to his father, his uncles and brothers. His father told him t go and fetch Lala Shivan Ditta from his home and ask him to have his dinner with them. Lala Shivran Ditta, was the younger brother of Purshattam Ram's father who had died since long back.

Bhagmal came out of the house and started walking to the house of Lala Shivan Ditta which was at least a mile away, when he reached the house of Shivam Ditta he met his wife, touched her feet and asked if she was fine and will she give him some Pinnies (A round ball made out of sugared fine flour, deep fried in cow milk butter oil with lot of dry fruit added to it). She told him to wait so that she could give him some pinnies. She went in and came out with a bagful of pinnies. Bhagmal asked her about Shivan Datta and was told that he has gone out for an evening walk and will be back any tine now. So he should wait for him. In about five minutes Lala Shivan Ditta came saw him touched his head and asked him if everything was fine with him and how was his father mother and wife, while answering his questions, he got up and touched his feet and told him that his father has requested him to come to his house and have his dinner there, as both his uncles and brothers were also at home. Lala Shivan Ditta asked again, was everything fine and there is nothing to worry about to which he said that the things were fine, his father just wanted to see him along with his brothers and sons on a family matter.

Lala Shivan Ditta told his wife that he was going to the house of Purshattam and may have his dinner there and may come back late. She should eat her dinner on time, and before going o bed both will have milk together and told Bhagmal to go and fetch tonga as he was in no mood to walk to his house. Bhagmal came out and harked a Tonga settled the price at Takka and paisa, and the Tonga came with two more passenger. Lala Shivan Ditta came and sat on the Tonga, after some distance two more passengers boarded the Tonga, when the Tonga approached the locality, where Bhagmal and Shivam Ditta had to get down, the tonge wala brought the tonga to stop, they both got down. Bhagmal paid the Tonga wala and they walked towards the house and finally reached the house where Shivan Ditta was welcomed well and everyone touched his feet, sharbat and Jalabis were served to him, then Ram Payari enquired about his wife and was told she was fine but for her gout.

The man flock sat together. The door was closed and Purshottam told them about the information he had received from somewhat reliable sources about the partition of India and he personally thought it was a very serious matter and they need to chalk out a plan to meet the situation as very soon they may have to migrate to a distant place which is not known to them and will be very unfamiliar to them and there was the question of houses, property, business, employment, children and the women flock. Everyone was listening attentively and at the sometime everybody thought and felt that nobody could suggest any thing and it was decided that they should meet again tomorrow after lunch time and should also ask other relatives like husband of their daughters and their father in laws, and fathers of their daughter-in-law. Everyone agreed upon it and took the responsibility of inviting his relative. The meeting was fixed at three in the afternoon.

Bhagmal was asked to ensure dinner for Lala Shivan Ditta first, so that he could leave in time.

Bhagmal went to the kitchen and told his wife to get dinner ready at least for one person ready at the earliest, he was told that the Daal and Subzi (vegetables) is ready and Rotis (Pan Cake) will be cooked in few minutes. After ten minutes Ram Payari came with a thaali of food kept it before Lala Shivam Ditta and requested him to take the food, he was given a tumbler of water, he got up went out of the room washed his hand, came back and started eating his dinner in silence, more chappati's (Pan Cake) were brought, he look only one chappati and said he will not have any more. Nikko came with mangoes, folded her hand and put her forehead on the lap of his grandfather who touched it with affection and blessed her.

Lala Shivan Ditta asked for leave till they met the next day, and Jeevan Dass the younger brother of Purshottam Lal offered to drop Lala jee at his house. Both of them came out, looked for a Tonga but did not find any and then decided to walk over at Lala Shivan Ditta's house. Jeevan Dass went inside the house touched the feet of Shivan Ditta's wife, who asked him about his wife and children and offered to bring some sharbat for him which Jeevan Dass declined very politely and then came out of the house and walked back to his house where he was staying. When Jeevan Dass reached back at house the food was brought by Kaka and Nikko. Every thali had two katories (Bowels) one of it had fried daal and the other had fried tindas (Tinda is green ball shaped vegetable with very soft eatable seeds and thick white mass around it) and Chhapatis one thaali each of the food was placed before all the six men then Kaka and Nikko was back and came with dry grilled Pappads and aachar. Pappads and aachhar was put in each thaali, but the bowel of aachhar was kept in the centre with a spoon in the bowel, so that anyone who wanted to have aachar could help himself. At least six glasses of water and tumble full of water was brought for desert slice and peeled mango was brought and everyone was urged to have it the food over now it was the turn of kidds and ladies when Kaka and Didu brought out the used utensil. Sulakshni was quick to wash them and then rub them dry by a cloth. The kidds were seated on the ground and were served the food then all the ladies sat on the floor, two bowels of daal and one bowel of vegetable and a thaali with chhappati was kept in the centre, every women was given a katori for the dal and a chhappati was in their hand, vegetable was put on the chhappati itself and everyone started eating the food, chattering among themselves, they all had the left over mangoes as the kernel of the mango was given to the children. Once the food was done, he three older ladies came out of kitchen and Sulakashni, Kunti and Amrit remained in the kitchen and starting cleaning and washing the kitchen used utensils. Utensils were washed and put in a Tokra(A round big bowel made like a grill) so that the water may drain out, and then the utensils were sorted out and put at their appointed place. Kunti swept the floor and Amrit scrubbed the kitchen floor with the help of wet cloth, having done the routine chart they started chattering between themsalves. When Ram Payari called in and said that milk should be served in one hour's time.

After having their food Lakh Raj and his brother asked Bhagmal to accompany them for a walk. When he three of them come out of the house and were at some safe distance Lakh Raj lighted his Star cigarette, Brij Bhan who simply said no because he need to smoke another brand Light house. Hence he brought out a cigarette and lighted, Bhagmal was not offered any cigarette because they both knew that he did no smoke at all. Then Lekh Raj asked to Bhagmal as how his trip to Rohtak and did he scout for some good land to buy and was told by Bhagmal that he could not find any good land but Bhanna Ram was put on the job and as soon as he finds some good land, he will then send a telegram in this regard. Bhagmal told both of his brothers his impression of Rohtak and people in the area and his meeting with a Police man who did not wish to serve the Kala Angrez (an Indian who tries to speak and behave like an English man)

Bhagmal told them that he had tied up an agreement to rent out a shop on the main Railway Road from one Lala Ghasi Ram, at a monthly rent of three and a half a rupee per month from 1ˢᵗ July of the year and Bhanna Ram had stood surety for him.

Lakh Raj told him that he has a definite knowledge that the partition is imminent as Mohommad Ali Jinnah, had refused to agree to any other formula, which did not create Pakistan in which only the Muslims will enjoy the civil rights, all other communities will be only second class citizens and Jawahar Lal in his hurry to be the Prime Minister had agreed upon the division and Mahatama Gandhi did not wish to displease either Nehur or Jinnah the partition scheme will be disclosed to the public on approval of the Royal Crown, when communicated to the Lord Mountbatten the Last Viceroy of India and Lord Mountbatten will execute the scheme of partition, which has already been drawn up according to which all Hindu's living in the areas going to Pakistan will have to migrate to new India by a given deadline and date and so will all the Muslims will migrate to Pakistan. The division of the state assets will be worked out by a team of bureaucrats having been assigned this job, so they must immediately decide their course of action for migration to new India. He was a firm opinion that they should not be swayed up by the sweet talk of full safety of every citizen, who adopt the newly carved out Pakistan. Brij Bhan said his appreciation of the situations that their father, mother and Sulakashni and all the four kidds and their wife should leave for the new India with all their gold and valuables, and settle temporarily at Rohtak with the help of Bhanna Ram, rent out a big house in densely populated

Hindu locality, so that at least they are safe, the brothers will follow them as soon as the situations permit their shifting to Rohtak and mean time both Lekh Raj and Brij Bhan should apply for their transfer to Rohtak at the most earliest, as Bhagmal has already opened a bank account at Rohtak, they should on transfer their maximum deposit to Rohtak branch through telegraphic transfer, both Brij Bhan and Lekh Raj transfer their money from their bank accounts by a telegraphic transfer to the account of Bhagmal to his Rohtak branch account, and they should also transfer all their certificates and other important documents to the safe custody of Bhanna Ram, however, if possible they should dispose of will their immovable property through they may not get a very reasonable and fair price in these troublesome times but it will be for better to wait for it award of claim if compensation after the partition, which might be less than thirty percent of the claim as is done by the revenue department, when they acquire some body's land, and it takes a long and very tedious procedure time energy and some bribe to get the claim settled even in long time. The three brothers realized that they have come a long distance away from the house; they turned back and walked to the house.

Purshottam Lal and his brothers were discussing the various scenarios propped by up the impending partition and the available options for them, they did not and could not see beyond the pail of gloom looking large, as they believed shifting to new place will not be easy or comfortable and how about their possessions social set up, their houses and the way of life, will they have similar set up, social standing and comfortable houses in New India and they were not safe in place where they have their roots since the times of their forefathers, how they can be sure or hopeful of any kind of safety in New India, which will be ruled by the congress through Nehru and many Kala Angrez, who show lot of contempt for low middle class of people, who ape the British in their dress, mannerism, language and eating habits but struck with old die hard habits of sitting and lying on the floor, and keep their woman folk is in deep purdah, don't send their girl child to school and groom boys to attend colleges or professional courses have no literary task and observe too many fasts. When the three grown up boys reached home they all went to the room of their father, Purshottam Lal for their wandering and loitering late at night, then they all were asked to sit down and to listen very carefully to whatever is being told to them.

They were told that on the coming Saturday they will have a paath of Sunder Kaand at four in the evening at their house, the path will be done by Baba Mool Chand Ji Maharaj and his disciples, and every one presence here should ensure that his close relatives like father-in-law brothers- in-law and other close relatives should present themselves at their house at lunch time and have their lunch and modalities of migration will be discussed.

Bhagmal was asked to arrange for Halwai Kada Ram who will cook Alloo (Potato), Puri (friedpan cake) and Suzi Halwa (Flour extract pudding) the food will be served on Pattals and a tent will have to be erected and everything should be perfect and on time.

Then Ram Payari came with three glasses of luke warm milk gave one to her husband two to his brothers and asked the three boys to come to other room, as she had to discuss with them, the three brothers followed their mother to the guest room.

Ram Payari was sitting on the floor alongwith the wives of Lekh Raj and Brij Bhan. Kunti the wife of Lekh Raj was looking tired and anemic, while Amrit the wife of Brij Bhan had started looking very old though she was not even twenty five, due to the impotence of her husband.

Ram Payari scolded Kunti for having lost child during birth and infancy, and told her that she must try again and at least should have one kid, a boy if not then even a girl child will do, then she addressed Amrit and said she was not proving to be a very good wife, as she has not produced a single child in her three years married life in reply Amrit started sobbing loudly, water was bought to her by Sulakashni, she cried once more and looked stately at her mother in law, Ram Payari and told her that she was not at fault in any way and his son Brij Bhan was stone impotent and how could he help or manage without seed which her husband cannot sow. Ram Payari was surprised blind and was aghast on haring her daughter in-law and said to her why did she tell her earlier and was told that her husband did not allow her to tell anyone about his impotence and rather compelled her on oath never to tell anybody about since he was trying to get some good medicine and treatment to cure himself from this impotence and soon they will have a child of their own, after this revelation Brij Bhan left the room feeling ashamed before ladies, his mother went out and brought him in and asked him to sit down and explain his treatment so that something could be and should be done to get him rid off his impotency. Then she addressed Bhagmal and told him to go and fetch his friend and classmate Bhootia Baba from the Shamshaan(Hindu cremation ground) the next day for sure after the breakfast. She will touch the feet of Bhootia Baba and ask for his blessings and miracles so that she may have more grandchildren and both daughter in law do not die barren or have to go wayward. The meeting was called off and Ram Payari said she was ready to sleep.

All but Ram Payari came out of the room and then they went to Bhagmal room, they sat there talked and gossiped.

Bhagmal took out three beddings and went to the verandah and spread the beddings on floor. Kunti and Amrit went to the guest room where Ram Payari was sleeping; they went and lied upon the bed on floor.

Lekh Raj and Brij Bhan went out of the house and smoked and came back and lied down in the made out beds and soon started snoring

Bhagmal was not feeling sleepy, so he sat on his bed and started praying to the God; of course he did not light a lamp and incense. In his prayer he was saying

Oh Lord of the universe
You are said to be Omni potent
Omni present and Omni secent
If you are Omni present, then
How can you let bad things happen
And if you are Omni potent
Why don't you stop bad things from happening
And if you are Omni sicent
Why do people then do it ignoring you
Please God, do punish those who
Ignore you and do wrong, but you
Must reward those who acknowledge
Your might and always try to do only the right
Since you do not reward easily and
Freely people get disgusted and start
Doing, wrong acts.
Oh God, please Act Must you Act
To prevent wrong Acts
Sinful Acts
Let people do only the Good Acts

Let Good Acts be rewarded fairly
Let Good Acts be recognized
Let only Good Acts prevail
Oh God you are the only Just
Oh God you must stop the unjust
Let only the just happen
Oh God let no unjust happen
Oh God, Oh God, Oh God.

After breakfast in the morning, the three brothers came out of the house, Brij Bhan and Lakh Raj lighted their cigarettes and puffed on it they all went to the Kirayana Shop (Grocery Store) and bought their requirements and then they went to the Subzi Mandi, bought Subzis and fruit. Lekh Raj said he will take the goods to the house, and Brij Bhan and Bhagmal should proceed for the Shamshan Bhoomi, as he did not wish to go there.

On way to Shamshan Bhoomi, Brij Bhan told Bhagmal for last about three years he is having himself treated for his impotency but without any success, and he is fed up with the taunt of his wife but is very thankful to her, as she has never revealed this to anybody till the last night, when she blurted out the secret in response to the scolding of her mother-in-law and it was very spontaneous and natural and Amrit did not intend any ill will but only the stigma of being barren, which of course was not her making at all, but she has lived long enough to the taunts of every woman she met. Brij Bhan he was getting very impatient to present himself before Bhootia Baba and expected a miracle from the Baba of course the Baba was not a God, but the Baba must help him for his sake and he can for sure make a miracle when they reached the sweetmeat shop Brij Bhan bought some Pakodd's and Jalebis and some Rabbari (Rabbari is long boiled and thickened milk added with sugar and almonds). When they reached the Shamshan Bhoomi Bhootia Baba was standing on one of his leg, his both hands folded and his chin resting on his chest, before the large image in stone of the Lord Shiva and mumbling some Shalokas (Hymnes)

They both sat down on the floor to one side to wait for Bhootia Baba to adopt a normal position, after about half an hour Bhootia Baba lay prostrate on the ground, got up and loudy said Har Har Mahadev (Let Mahadev the Lord Shiva be forever) and then walked to a corner of the ground without even glancing towards them, he set down on an devoted square stone in crossed leg position both the brother got up went before the Baba, touched his feet, he looked up and saw Brij Bhan and recognized him and asked him, how came he had come to meet him and where is Lekhu (Lekh Raj) and Bhagmal, without answering the questions, Brij Bhan made the offerings, Baba looked at the offerings and asked him, has he brought the offering because he has been blessed with a promotion in his job or the God has blessed him with twin sons or hearing the Baba, Brij Bhan could not stop himself and started weeping and sobbing profusely, the Baba saw Bhagmal, who had just now touched his feet, he got up and told both of them to follow, but they should not forget to bring the offerings with them.

The Baba walked briskly to his hut which was situated in a distant corner of the Sham Shan Bhoomi. He sat down in crossed legged position on a uneven raised platform, and took a Chillam, lighted it puffed it for a long time and then asked both of them to sit down both the brothers sat down before the Baba on the ground placing the offering to the side of Baba, Then the Baba addressed Brij Bhan and asked him as to what bothered him Brij Bhan told him that he was married a long time but had no child as he was declared stone impotent and no treatment has worked so far. On hearing him Baba told him to sit a little aside and wait till he had moved away to some distance and then the Baba asked Bhaaagmal said he did not have any news, but his mother will be highly obliged if he could came to his house and bless her, Baba said, he will be at his house today itself but tell your mother to give the baba some Maal Purrras with Kheer (Mal Purras made from floor with sugar made into a batter, than deep fired in oil till it is brown and crisp Kheer is milk and rice pudding).

Baba signaled to Brij Bhan to come back to him and told him that he should come back at five in the evening and collected his medicines and hopefully with the help and grace of God, he will not remain impotent anymore and may have a child in about six months, but he must bring three Chhatak, Kali Mirch (Black Pepper) and three Chhattak long (A seer in India has sixteen Chhattaks and Kaali Mirch is black pepper and long is a clove) The Baba told them to go back home and prepare for his arrival.

It was ten O' clock when Bhagmal reached his house he told her mother that Bhootia Baba had agreed upon to come but had said that he will eat Mall Purras and Kheer, so please keep it ready.

Brij Bhan went to his father's room where his brother Lekh Raj and his uncles Sham Lal and Kale Ram was also sitting and were discussing only God knew what not. He listened to their chatter but could not make any head or tail of the same and come outside. Saw Sulakashni outside the kitchen and requested her to cook some tea for him and may be for her husband also if he was nearby. He went and sat in the verandah, was joined by Lekh Raj and later on by Bhagmal, Brij Bhan shouted for Kaka who came running and asked what is wanted of him, and was told to go his mother that all three people in the verandah will have tea. The three brothers again assured themselves that they will be able to draw a good plan to meet any exigency imposed by the impending partition and the aftermath, especially Brij Bhan do much more being in the revenue department and being known to the Tehsildar, SDM and other important govt officials who matter the tea came, they all sipped it hot, Lekh Raj and Brij Bhan went out lighted their cigarettes and puffed on it, Lekh Raj asked Brij Bhan as to whatever had happened at the Shamshaan Bhoomi he was told that Bhootia Baba has agreed to come today it self to have Mall Purras and Kher, and he has to go back to the Shamshaan Bhoomi at five in the evening. Lekh Raj asked him did the Baba asked about him also and was told no, he was not mentioned at all.

The lunch was served in the verandah and all the six males and the four kidds sat on the floor, thaalis were laid, and katories were stocked, glasses were placed as a pile, a big water tumbler was kept there. Ram Payari brought a Pateela full of vegetable, and then went back brought another Patila filled with Raita Pakodi (Churned Curd with fired gram floor balls).

Lassi was brought by Sulakashni (she had covered her head and face with her dupatta) later she brought cut out Kharbooja (Musk Melon) Ram Payari had brought a bunch of Chappattis. She spread the thaali by keeping a thali each and two katories before everyone put two chappati in each thaali and then served vegetable and raita to everyone, and were told to help them with more chhappatis and vegetable etc and they should also partake Lassi and Kharbooja when men had their food, the used utensils were removed by Kaka and Didu and taken to kitchen for washing. Sulakashni sat down and washed all the used utensils, Kunti rinsed the utensils to dry then, when the utensil were done and ready all the women sat down except Sulakashni., who served them with vegetable, Raita, Chappati, Lassi and Kharbooja they had hardly finished, when Bootia Baba appeared at the door and loudly said Alakh Niranjan (Long live the Omnipotent GOD and Glory to Him) Ram Payari rushed to the door, followed by the other ladies of the house, Ram Payari bowed down and tried to touch the feet of Bhootia Baba when she had touched his feet, he bowed down his head before Rampayari and said please do bless me, I am also your son, Ram Payari touched his head with her both hands, all the other ladies touched the feet of Bhootia Baba and were blessed.

Then all the men flock came out and touched the feet of Bhootia Baba, when Purshottam had come forward to touch his feet, he said wait Pitajee (Father) let me touch your feet first and you bless me and then you may touch my feet. Bhootia Baba touched the feet of Purshottam Lal and was blessed and then Purshottam Lal touched the feet of Bhootia Baba, the Baba took him aside to a distance and told him that the partition was not very far away, rather it was round the corner and when they plan to migrate to New India, they should take him along so that he may be of some use to them.

Then Bhootia Baba sat on the wooden cot lying innthevarandah, and asked Ram Payari to send the wife of Lekh Raj first and no one else should be any near or in the ear shot of him. Kunti came and once again touched the feet of Bab, he put his right thumb on her forehead and put lot of pressure and gave her some ash and told her to swallow it at once and go to the kitchen take one sip of water and come back but she should not speak a word till she came back to him. Kunti did as she was told, Baba brought his mouth to her left ear and said OM and told her that her next child will live long. Kunti touched the feet of Baba and went away.

Then the Baba asked Ram Payari to send the wife of Brij Bhan, Amrit came and touched the feet of Baba, Baba put his both hands on her head put good pressure on her head, removed his right hand and slapped strongly on her back, she minced in pain, then put his mouth to her left ear and told her that she will conceive within six months and will have twin children and was asked to leave Amrit got up touched the feet of Baba and went away. Ram Payari appeared and the Baba asked her to sit down, hey mata (mother) what her son could do for her. She replied please take care the partition is coming and she was scared of it and wants his son the Baba to help his mother. Baba said Oh mother you don't worry, whatever your son Baba could do he will do it for sure, but GOD's will only prevails and he will be helpless before God, but she need not worry, because except for some bad news things will turn out to be good and she should have faith in his sons and asked her did she cook Mall Purra's and Kheer for him and if they are ready, please go and bring it but before that d send Sulakashni to him on hearing the name of Sulakashni, Ram Payari got worried at the moment the Baba told her not to worry at all and send Sulakashni and everything will be fine. Ram Payari went to the kitchen and told Sulakashni to go and seek the blessing of the Baba, while she brings Mall Purras and Kheer for the Baba. Sulakashni went to the verandah, touched the feet of the Baba and sat before Baba on the ground, Baba shared at her hand and then said very slowly Hey Sulakashni your wish in regards to Salaludin will be full filled and you need not curse yourself anymore and to have faith in the justice of God, and she can be very sure that her husband will be have only as her beloved husband after nine days, he put his right hand over head and asked her to leave and send Ram Payari her mother-in-law as he is very hungry and she has promised him to give him something good to eat. Ram Payari came with Maal Purras and Kheer he Baba mumbled something took two mall purra's out of the thali and gave it to everyone and Baba started eating.

When Baba felt satisfied he asked for water and Bhagmal. Bhagmal came with a tumbler of water, Baba took the tumbler gulped some water and told him that he will have the awaited news within next two days, but he must remember to bring him the Burfi on twelveth day. The Baba got up and said Alakh Niranajan again and left without waiting for anybody to bid for well, Ram Payari came running and gave him rupee twenty one, the Baba returned her rupee one and said this rupee you must save and keep it safe and left.

When Baba left it was almost four in the evening, the tea was brought every one sipped the tea, Purshottam Lal's two brothers said they must go to the Bus stand as the last bus left at five in the evening and they will attend the Paath with other members of the family, farewell was said and both of them left with their bags.

Brij Bhan said since he has to go to the market to buy few things, he will go and came back soon and he left. He had to be at Shamshaan Bhoomi at five in the evening on his way he bought Kaali Mirch and Long, both in a small paper bag. He was before the Baba by five touched the feet of the Baba and placed the paper bag before, the Baba opened the paper bag brought out the two puriyas (Puriya-Hand wrapped paper pack) took a handful of Raakh (Ash) from the Dhuni (Smoldering fire without smoke) and told he should divide the Raakh into one hundred eight parts and should have one part every day with milk and his problem shall be taken care off by the God. After taking the Raakh, which he put in his side pocket he walked back briskly to his house on the way he bought some Ganeris (Peeled and cut prices of the sugar cane) for the house especially for the kidds. He reached home by five thirty and went and sat with his father. Lekh Raj and Bhagmal were not there and probably had gone out to smoke.

At six Lekh Raj and Bhagmal came to the room of their father. Lekh Raj said he plans to leave at six in the morning tomorrow, but he will leave his wife here and will go out and tell his wife to cook for him some food which he could take with him to serve him as breakfast, lunch and dinner he went out sought out his wife and told her to prepare enough food for him to last three times as he will leave very early in the morning, and she will stay here only till be comes back for the paath. Brij Bhan said he will ask for a leave of five-six days and send a telegram to this effect tomorrow morning and try and meet people in the revenue department to get some worthwhile news and information which they could utilize in their planning. Purshottam Lal just listened to everything being said, but he did not say a word by himself.

Bhagmal said he was going out to arrange for Halwai and the tent, and the other things he will arrange the next morning, but they may need some bedding for the guest, which they can borrow from neighbours but he will prefer to get it on rent, his father said you rent it, but be discreet about it. It is good that we live at little distance from the main locality, it has its own advantages and disadvantages, but at the present moment it seems to be an advantage, as they are no prying neighbours, snooping around. Bhagmal went out and left, an hour later he was back and confirmed that the necessary arrangement had been done. As far the Parshaad (free offering to be distributed to those who attend the function) he will buy it readymade from the Halwai shop.

The father and sons started discuss again the options they have and the best course of action should be adopted to tackle the vagaries of the position. Brij Bhan said he will talk to the SDM and request him for an immediate transfer to Rohtak so he could officially shift to Rohak before the partition is announced, this will help him and everyone in the family to settle easily at the new place as he will make all necessary arrangements. Lekh Raj said he will meet his XEN (Executive Engineer) to transfer him to Rohtak or near about and they both can definitely do wonders for everybody while he migrates to New India. They both said in unison, that since there going to Rohtak is not very sure at the present, but let father transfer his funds in the Imperial Bank Account to the account of Bhagmal at Rohtak in next ten days and for this Bhagmal should go once again to Rohtak and take all jewelry to Rohtak deposit it in the Bank Locker, which he may rent out there and take all other important papers like educational certificate etc and put those also into the locker at Rohtak. As far land and shop and house related papers, they may be needed here if they could find some customers for their property and Bhagmal should also sell all stocks at his shop even if has to make a small loss and find a customer to buy his ship for a reasonable price on the given circumstances, and Lekh Raj and Brij Bhan should also try and sell their houses at the earliest if they could find some good customers. Purshottam Lal had listened intently to the whole conversation and said he found their plan good but he will finally tell them tomorrow. Ram Payari came and told them that the food is being laid in the verandah and they should go and sit there in the verandah and have their food, they all went out and sat in the verandah, Bhagmal washed his feet and face, went to his room lighted a lamp and said his regular prayer and came back to the verandah. They all were served food by Kaka and Nikko, they all ate in silence, and the used utensils were removed by Didu. Then the kidds were given their food.

All the women sat in the guest room and ate their food. Sulakashni and Amrit collected the empty utensils to the kitchen, where they washed all used utensils, scrubbed the kitchen floor with wet cloth, when all done they went back ton guest room and made beddings for all the ladies and kidds. Today they had no spare milk, so they had not to wait for the milk to be served and this fact was made know to everyone by Nikko.

Purshottam Lal called all his sons to came and sit with him for some time, so that they could have a plan to work out before the Paath ceremony, so that their individual plan will not be affected by the outcome of the wider joint meeting.

Purshottam Lal said Brij Bhan should not take leave for now and should go back to his work and gather all kind of relevant information however he may leave his wife here, he should also submit his request for transfer to Rohtak the same thing should be done by Lekh Raj, and both should come back on Thursday evening with whatever information they have especially Brij Bhan should find about the feasibility of selling their land holdings of five killas(acres), if it can command a value of rupees ten thousand he should accept the bayana (advance). Both Lekh Raj and Brij Bhan should obtain cheque books from their bank.

Bhagmal and Purshottam Lal both will go and meet the agent of the Imperial Bank to explore the possibility of stowing two trunks in the bank's safe deposit vault,

Bhagmal should once again go back to Rohtak to have the fact of the area independent of Bhanna Ram, buying or renting a house will not be any wise in he given disturbed atmosphere, rather Bhagmal should have the feel of town, should memorize its topography, economic conditions and opportunity the behavior of the local muslim and non-muslim population, the main business in the town especially owned by the muslims, the kind of land within fifteen miles radius of Rohtak town and also find out about the most densely populated muslim localities in the town and also the most populated muslim villages around Rohtak and the type and quality of land there especially the availability for drinking and irrigation water through canals of any or all weather deep wells, the eating habits of the local population especially the non-muslims. He should also find out the accessibility of Rohtak to Delhi or major sub towns near Rohtak, the local dialect, people, women flocks and cattle etc. It was decided that Bhagmal will leave for Rohtak as soon as possible after the Paath for this he must get a bank draft payable at Rohtak in his name to be deposited in his Rohtak bank account, take all important papers and hand it now to Bhanna Ram for safe keeping, and he must be back home before 30th May definitely. Purshottam told all of them to go and have a sleep.

They all got up and went out of the house, walked some distance from the house both Lakh Raj and Brij Bhan lit their cigarettes and puffed on it in hurry, they all spoke at once saying the plan seemed to be good and practically and hopefully it will work but what a great joke is the proposed and planned partition is. Simply to humour the power mongering politicians who have no regrets for the sufferings and uprooting of the millions of Hindoos, of course Muslims will also suffer, but with the appeals of Mahatama and

Nehru to muslims to stay put in undivided area, as only the, Punjab, Sind, and Bengal are to be partitioned.

It will be mammoth and unmanageable task to divide the Great Indian Nation, its Army, Navy, Air Force, Postal and Telegraph services, Railway, The Reserve Bank, the Impearl Bank and Indian Civil Services disorder and anarchy will prevail consequent upon the partition and there will be an imaginable loss of life and property and the cattle and great mistrust will crop in the society on both sides of the divided nations but who cares the British will ensure that both the new countries are ruined and fail and would approach them to protect them from the anarchy they have created with the help of the congress and the Muslim League, but also people never mattered anytime, not at the time of Roman Inquest or French Revolution, Landon Fire or during the First and Second World Wars or when USA bombed Hiroshima and Nagasaki in Japan or killing of millions of Jews by the German Nazis. People never mattered and never will matter, be it an Autocracy, Plutocracy or Democracy or Dictatorship people or born only to die for the sake of greedy politicians who rule over people in different grabs.

Suddenly Brij Bhan started singing loudly in a low coarse voice "Bhagwan do din ke liyea insaan ban ke dekh or Dharti per do din ka mehmaan ban ke dekh" ("Oh God be a man on the earth for two days and be a guest for two days")

But Brij Bhan cighter did not know the next santeza or did not wish to go on with the song.

Now everyone was feeling sad and trying to visualize the happening of coming days this depression was mind boggling and rampant and produced only the horrified visuals and threatening voices hunger, violence, blood, looting rape and man without compassion who was taking pleasure in torturing his friends and neighbours. On the very early morning of Monday, there were rasp knock at the door of Purshottam Lal, Lekh Raj who was getting ready to go to the bus stand, he went near the door and asked in a loud voice, as to who was there knocking at the door, the man at the door identified himself as the servant of Sabahuddin. Lekh Raj opened the door and let the servant in, the servant told him that the mother's Salaluddin was sitting outside the door and wanted to have a small talk with Ram Payari the mother of Bhagmal the servant was told to go and bring the woman inside, mother of Salaluddin came in she was the Burqua (A Burqua is whole body coverlet worn by muslim women and Burqua has two eye holes to see around), She was asked to sit down, she sat on the floor, Lekh Raj asked her to sit on the cot, but she continued to sit on the floor., when Ram Payari appeared, she got up and started weeping very loudly and removed a flap of the Burqua which bared her face. Ram Payari called out for Kaka to bring a glass of water, when Kaka appeared with glass of water, he was told to ask her mother to cook some tea, to which the other woman said sorry but she does not to drink tea. She said that she has bothered Ram Payari that early in the day, because his son Salaluddin and his father have been paralyzed and hardly could see around, and she has been told that only Bhootia Baba of Shamshaan could help and being a muslim she cannot go to the Hindu cremation ground, she has come to take her help in the metter. So that his son and husband could be cured and for that she would have to go to the Shamshaan Bhoomi and plead on her behalf before the Baba of course she will bear all the cost involved and she is willing to pay rupee one hundred one to the baba for showingfavours Ram Payari kept silent for some time and said that her son and husband have been punished by the God, and she does not think that Baba will agree to do anything to defy the acts of God, and if requested he may get angry and curse the favour seeker at this, Salaluddin's mother said in that case she will not be left any alternative but to defy the dictates of the Mulah (The Priest of a Mosque) and visit the Baba herself at the Shamshaan, but Ram Payari must send a message to the Baba to come outside the Shamshaan and sit outside where she will seek his favour, Ram Payari agreed to do it. Then Farzana Bibi, the mother of Salaluddin left.

Purshottam Lal come out of his room and saw Ram Payari sitting in the verandah in a deep thought, he touched her shoulder and asked her in a tender voice if everything was well. Ram Payari took a deep sigh and told him as to what has transpired just now. He was also astonished, but recovered in a second and said well you did the right thing, now let the Baba know about her visit. Soon Lekh Raj and Brij Bhan were ready to leave but for waiting for the food, the food was brought in two packet and one pack each was given to both of them, they touched the feet of their mother, went to their father room and touched his feet and assured they shall be back as discussed and they both went away out of the house and walked briskly towards the bus they were in hurry lest they miss their bus, when they reached the bus sand, the bus was almost full and ready to leave, they got into the bus bought two tickets and occupied the vacant seats.

Ram Payari woke up, Bhagmal and told him to go and inform Bhootia Baba about the impending visit of a Farzana Bibi, the mother of his friend and classmate Salaluddin, who himself and his father have been paralyzed and have lost much of their vision. The information came to Bhagmal as about from the blue and he wondered as to how and why he should go to the Shamshaan Bhoomi and inform the Bhootia Baba about the visit of Farzana Bibi, the mother of his victim and the wife of his victim and his culprit, but Bhaagram dare not refuse to obey his mother and reveal the truth about the paralysis of Salaluddin and his father, and his complicity in the whole thing and how and why had the Bhoota Baba had carried out his request and his own deep rooted wish of averaging death of his mother, father and sisters some years back by a British Judge and refusal to help by the father of Salaluddin what was perplexing was that the twelth day was little far, and should he take Burfi for the Baba, he decided against buying the burfi and seek the advice of Baba in the matter.

After completing his morning chores, he prayed and had his breakfast and was informed by Sulakashni that he should bring some vegetables before going to his shop. He took a thaila and went to the Sabzi Mandi and bought some vegetables, when he was returning home, he saw Bhootia Baba standing before him with his chillam in his hands, he touched the feet of Baba and informed him about the visit of Farzana Bibi this evening at six, and he should make himself available outside the Shamshaan Bhoomi. Baba did not said a thing and moved, soon Bhagmal was back at home with a bag full of vegetable, which he kept in the kitchen and informed Kunti to inform Sulakashni that he has brought the vegetable and asked where was his mother, Kunti told him that she probably was sitting with Pitajee, he went to the room of his father and found his mother and told her that he met the Baba at Sabzi Mandi and had informed the Baba about the visit of Salaluddin's mother this evening at six and that the Baba should meet the lady outside the Shamshaan as desired by his mother. Baba did not reply and simply walked away. Bhagmal then walked back to his shop, opened the shop swept it and scrubbed the floor with a wet rag, lighted the lamp and prayed to the God, and then sat in his appointed seat and waited for the customers to come, for about an hour no customer came, then two customers came to make sundry purchases for rupees twenty and then for the next one hour, there was no customer to attend, so Bhagmal asked for a cup of tea when the tea came, he started sipping the tea, but his mind was immersed in stray thoughts.

He was thinking about all his faith in the presence of Bhootia Baba have proved right and the Baba had been able to punish Salaluddin for his sake or rather for the sake of his wife a woman who was molested and Baba has also avenged his long carried burden of injustice met to all at the hands of Salaluddin's father, both Congress leaders of area and supposed to be Allah's Namazi. Now he was afraid of the power and reach of the power of the Baba and resolved never to cross the Baba, but a thought came in his mind that whatever Baba did was for the sake of their childhood friendship, both having been class mates in the same school and same class for six years and both were the players in the same hockey team. So, there was nothing to fear of the Baba moreover the Baba was a gentleman, an honest man who will be willing to help anyone who sought his help the Baba was doing the work of God by helping the people in need and in distress, who came to him for his help and they had a genuine cause for his help. Suddenly two policeman a Hawaldaaar (Corporal) and an ASI came and said they wanted to purchase thirty six ink pens, twenty four lead pencils, twenty erasers and forty eight full size ruled sheets, but before they paid the bill in cash, they must be served hot milk some burfi and samosa. Bhagmal said they will get what they have asked for and then he went to the tea shop nearby and told the shopkeeper to send two glasses of sweetened milk, one paav of Burfi and three samosa with chutney and came back to his shop, and started filling the order, the tea man came with the ordered supplies placed it on the counter and left. Bhagmal asked the policemen to help themselves and meanwhile he will pack up the supplies and prepare the bill, he took a samosa and cup of tea, and started eating the samosa and sipping the tea. He calculated that milk etc will cost about rupee three, which he must recover. So he proceeded in a manner that not only did he recover rupee three he had spent, but he also made rupees three extra. The policemen having feted themselves paid his bill, took the packet of their supplies and left. Bhagmal felt happy because he had hoodwinked the dishonest policeman, but at the same times he felt gloomy for his own dishonesty, he prayed to the God to forgive him for his greed dishonesty and prayed the God to not put him to such dishonest occasion, because he does not have the strength to shun such temptations. At home Ram Paryari was trying to have a chat with other ladies of the house. She wanted to pass on the news of the visit of Farzana Bibi the mother of Salaluddin, who had lost his vision and is half paralyzed and Farzana Bibi's husband has also been paralyzed and has lost his vision and Farzana had come to her that she go to Bhootia Baba and plead on her behalf, and she has excused herself and now Farzana Bibi will go by herself to the Shamshaan Bhoomi' and meet the Baba outside the Shamshaan, and this message has been conveyed to the Baba by Bhagmal and Baba was agreed to meet Farzana outside the Shamshaan this evening at six.

This information was not of much value to Kunti and Amrit, though they felt sorry for Farzana Bibi, who had given them a Chhunari when they had come to this house as brides. Sulakashni also did get such a chhunari, but that was no more of value to her after the humiliation she had suffered at the hands of Salaluddin and she felt a satisfaction from the fact that she had almost chewed off the member of Salaluddin, but she had many regrets for her failure to chopp off the member, but Alas God was great. So was the Bhootia Baba whose assurance has proved to be true and now Salaluddin will suffer forever till he dies and may the death not come to him for next hundred years, but how could this information be passed into her husband who probably will understand. Bhagmal was eager to find out what has transpired between the Bhootia Baba and Farzana Bibi, he decided that he will be present outside the Shamshaan Bhoomi when they met.

By now it was two clock but his lunch had not arrived, he got worried as usually it did not happen because most of the time he brought his lunch with him in the morning and since at present schools were closed for long summer vacation, Kaka was bringing his lunch because Kaka wished to be rewarded with a sort of a tip, soon Kaka came with his lunch pack and lessi and told his father that the Dadi (Grandmother) had asked for some Pakoraas. Bhagmal went out of the shop and walked to the Pakorras shop, bought half seer pakoras, free chutenty was given to him he came back to his shop took out two pakoraas and the rest of it were given to Kaka to take home. Kaka left and Bhagmal sat down to have his lunch. Lunch over, he went out to relieve himself and then came back washed his hands and sat on his seat, then he got up and decided to lie down, he had hardly dozed off when someone loudly said "Alakh Niranjan" he thought it must be Bhootia Baba, but when he got up he saw another Saadhu (Monk) in Bhagva Clothes (Saffron Robes), Bhagmal folded his hand took out a chavani (one forth part of a rupee) went near the Saadhu touched his feet and offered him the chavanni. The Saadhu put his both hands on his heads and blessed him and said he would like to sit down and eat his food which he had with him and the food has been cooked by himself he will need only some water. Bhagmal asked the Saadhu, should he get his some Dahi(curd) or Doodh (milk), the Saddhu said no but he will be happy to have some sugar. Bhagmal had the sugar at the shop itself he brought out the sugar container and put it before the sadhu. Saadhu sat down and washed his hand, spread his food on a thaali which he brought out from his handbag sprinkled some few drops of water on the food, took some sugar from the container put it in his thaali and started eating in complete silence. When the Saadhu was done up with his food he got up gulped some water and washed his mouth, the Saadhu bent to pick up thaali but Bhagmal was quick enough and he picked up the thaali, went to clean it with some ash from the tea shop, washed it and brought the thali to his shop, took out a washed piece of cloth rinsed it and handed it over to the Saadhu. The Saadhu told Bhagmal that he could read his hand for just one rupee on an impulse Bhagmal extended his right hand in front of the Saadhu, the Saadhu took his hand in his left hand studied it over for few moments and said that he has a fine future but the present that means about next six months will be difficult and disturbing, causing financial losses and somebody in the near family is likely to die and there may be a separation in the family and he shall have to travel long distances and the travelling will be cumber some and problematic, but he will not be able to prevent the situation. The good news is that he will get some good offer which he must accept without reservations.

The Saadhu got up and extended his right hand for the fee, Bhagmal put a two rupee note on his extended palm, the Saadhu, brought a one rupee coin from his bag and returned it to Bhagmal and walked out of the shop.

Whatever, the Saadhu had told Bhagmal, it made him very sad and perplexed as what the Saadhu did tell him was very worry some and disturbing his nerves became taut and he got restless he gulped some water, went out of the shop and asked for a cup of tea, when the tea came, he gulped it hotand went inside the counter and lay on the ground and dozzed off, when he woke it was five in the evening, he went out of the shop with the tumbler of water, then put the tumbler at the door of shop and went to relive himself, came back washed his hand and washed his face, went into the shop took out a towel rinsed his face, took some money from the Galla (cash box) and put it in his pocket, came out closed the shop and started walking slowly towards the Shamshaan Bhoomi, he bought some Namak Pare (salted fried chips) for the Bhootia Baba. It was forty five minutes past five in the evening when he reached outside the Shamshaan Bhoomi, he had just reached there when a Tonga (Horse Carriage) stopped apposite the gate of Shamshaan Bhoomi, a woman clad in a black Burqua got down from the Tonga the coach man took the Tonga a little away and the coachman got down and sat on the back seat of the Tonga, the Burqua clad woman sat on a big stone lying by the side wall to wait for someone, Bhagmal surmised that the woman should be Farzano Bibi who is sitting there to wait for Bhootia Baba he walked towards the woman, when he reached near the woman, he said in loud voice Salaam ammi (salutation mother) the woman answered in a whisper, who is there, he said it was Bhagmal, then the Bhootia Baba came, saw Bhagmal and asked him why was he there, then Baba addressed the Burqua clad woman and said Salaam Ammi. The Burqua clad woman said in unflustered voice Salam Baba, Salaam Baba, have mercy on my son and husband have become paralyzed and have lost their vision. She has not brought any offering as she was not sure whether he will accept her offerings she being a Muslim, the Baba said in a gruff voice that it did not matter if she has not brought any offering, but if a Muslim woman can come to him, he for sure could accept her offerings, any way he has heard her problem, and she has taken an extreme step of visiting a Hindoo Baba near Shamshaan Bhoomi, so the Baba will not dismay her and send her empty handed and Baba assures him that her husband will get back his vision but live with his paralysis, but her son will have no mercy as his crime is so grave and serious that no mercy is possible as he betrayed one of his friends and defiled his wife in his bad sense and that is unpardonable sin for which he must pay, and his advice to the mother is that she go to Ajmer Sharif and seek the blessings of the Khawaza and if Khawaza find it fit to shower mercy, he is the Lord of the world, saying this the Baba walked to the Shamshaan Bhoomi and beckoned Bhagmal to follow him. Farzana Bibi, shouted loudly for the Baba when he came back, she give five rupees to the Baba, which Baba took in silence once inside the Shamshaan Bhoomi asked of Bhagmal as to what has brought him here was it to find out as to what boons the Baba grants to Farozana Bibi, Bhaagmal touched the feet of Baba and asked for forgiveness and handed over the Namak Paras to Baba, who looked at it and laughed and said now you are trying to bribe me now you can go to your wife only after the pack only and that too if you bring Burfi for the Baba, Baba sat down on a stone and asked Bhagmal to sit down and listen to him carefully, be careful when you go down to Rohtak and be observant and not to sleep with Todomai in any case and if he gets some worthwhile offer be must accept it and he should return back within four days and now he should go back to his house and his kidds. Bhagmal got up and touched the feet of Baba and left for his house.

When he reached his home, he was called to appear before his father, he touched the feet of his father and sat before him. His father said he has been told by their Aradali of Police Kaptaan (SSP) that move is afoot to make arrangements for the movement of people across the partitioned areas and to ensure their safety and travel even the Army may be deployed especially for the safety of trains as there is strong apprehension of mass looting by muslim goons, who have organized to loot the Hindoos of the moov and the Aardali also said that special care will have to be taken of young women, girls and small boys as they will be easy targets for the goons and as and when we moov we must have arms with us especially the pistol for protection and he can readily help us to buy few pistols for the right price, of course the arms will not be licensed and we should tell him at the earliest and should keep the money ready and he expects a Baksheesh (Tip) of at least five rupees for each pistol, he is also ready to help us procure the single Barrel Gus and its ammunition at a very reasonable price and he will be here again on Wednesday evening to have our answer and some advance money. The news was good and exciting and threw some good possibilities. His father said if he has any news, he told his father about the visit of a Saadhu, who read his hand for a rupee and told him that he will soon have a good offer which he should accept, but he may have to face difficulties and calamities which cannot be avoided at all, so he must try and live with the will of the God.

Bhagmal went to his room, came out with a towel and went to the bathroom washed his face and feet, then back to his room, put on a Tehmat and Bundi, lighted a lamp and said his prayer before the God, his son Kaka barged in and said Pita Jee, Mata Jee says that the food is ready and served and he should go to Dada's room to have his food. Bhagmal went to his father's room, took his thaali of food and stared chewing his food in total silence, both of them were done with their food, Kaka brought water and took the used thaalis.

Bhagmal came out of the house and started walking slowly in a thought manner but he was not thinking of anything in particular rather he was trying to recall the events of the day. The mental state of Sulakashni and was trying to chart out his proposed visit to Rohtak to obtain knowledge of its social fabric, its economic position and his chances of establishing himself in this town among the unfamiliar circumstances., unknown people who do not seem to be very welcoming the stranger and the scope for his kind of business a town which almost looked as stagnant and without much life or social activity or life, he said to himself that may be his knowledge about this town its people or economics or dynamics was very shallow and his assessment very biased someone said Ram Ram and his train of thought came to a halt and he also said Ram Ram. Started walking back to the house, once in the house, he sat in the verandah and all the flour kidds came to him, and said they would like to play Ludo (Ladder and Snakes) and he should act as a judge, so that no one cheats, he agreed to be a judge of their game. Suddenly he asked the kidds that if they knew the game Ludo meant the kidds said it was just like any other game, he said no, the game of Ludi gave out a very strong and deep message and that is that the ladder means good acts, when you do good acts you rose up the ladder and reach higher goals of life, whereas the snake represent evil, the more evil you do the lower you, go down, the ladder let you reach the heavens and the snakes take you to devil in the hell. The kidds listened to him with rasp attention and when he closed the story, the kidds said they will always do good acts so as to rise on a ladder and will avoid all evil acts so that evil snakes do not send them to the hell.

Bhagmal got up went to his room and changed his clothes, put on a Tehmad and Bundi, took his bedding and came out to the verandah, spread the bedding on the wooden cot lying in the verandah, sit on his bed in crossed legs position and folded his hands and started praying to the God in audible voice, he was uttering,

Oh my God, you are great
Oh my God, you are most powerful
Oh my God, you are the most merciful
Oh my God, you are the benefactor of the poor
Oh my God, you are my father
Oh my God, you are my mother
Oh my God, can a mother forsake his child
Oh my God, how can a father not support a son
Oh my God, how can your child be orphaned
Oh my God, shower your benevolence
Oh my God, shower you mercies
Oh my God, forgive your son for his lapses
Oh my God, let your child re-deem himself
Oh my God, please guide your child
Oh my God, show the right path to your child
Oh my God, do bestow your favours on your child
Oh my God, Let your child back in your glory

Oh my God, Let your child live by your mercy
Oh my God, Lt your child be your devotee
Oh my God, Let your child devote himself to you
Oh my God, your child seeks your blessings
Oh my God, please do bless your child
Oh my God, Let your blessings last forever

Prayer done Bhagmal got up went inside relieved himself came back had a glass full of water and went to sleep and he was snoring instantly.

Pushattoam Lal woke up at four in the morning, had a stroll on the court yard of his house, and went near the guest room and called the name of Ram Payari, instead Amrit came out touched the feet of his father in law and told him that Ram Payari was taking bath and was told to ask her to get him his tea. Amrit lit the hearth and started cooking the tea when the tea was ready Ram Payari came and asked Amrit to put tea into two glasses. She took both the glasses to her husband's room, where she gave one glass of tea to her husband and kept one for herself. She took her tea, went out washed her mouth came back to the room, spread mat on the floor, and took out a small book "Manka 108" (one hundred eight couplets from the Ram Charit Maanas by Tulsi Dass). She was singing each manka in a melodious voice Purshottam was to listening in a rythmatic fashion enjoying the rendering of mankas

Sulakashni got up twenty minutes past five, went to toilet and then had her bath, lighted lamp and said her prayers, then cooked tea for herself and her husband, who was taking a bath in the court yard, she brought his fresh clothes and put them on his bed, and then decided to wake up Kunti and Amrit, but both were up, Kunti had gone to the toilet and Amrit was in the bathroom, she cooked tea for them also. When Bhagmal was ready she handed over the glass of tea to him and told that few items of grocery were required and maybe he should buy more onions and some kharboojas to which Bhagmal just nodded his head in consent

The ladies after having tea started preparing for the day's breakfast. Since cooking Daliya was the easier and was liked by everyone also, they cooked daliya, Kunti peeled the Karela (Bitter Ground) sprinkled some salt on the peeled Karelas and put it under the sun, Amrit cut out some onions to be added to Kerala, Sulakashni started preparing Boondi Raito (Boondi is around balls made of ground fine horse gram floor known as Besan and is deep fried in boiling hot oil until crisp)

Bhagmal who had gone out to buy items of grocery and onions and Kharboozas had come back with the stuff and had also brought some Khurmaanis (Peach), he called the kidds and gave them three Khurmanis each, and the balance he gave to Sulakashni, who was checking the grocery items, she told him that he has forgotten to buy Sooka Dhania (Dry coriander pods) to which Bhagmal said he will bring it in the evening and came to sit in the verandah to wait for his breakfast. The breakfast was served first to Purshottam Lal and Ram Payari then to all the kidds and then to Bhagmal he ate it with great attention and then asked for some more he was given more daliya which he ate, he was told to wait for some times till his lunch was ready, which he should take as Kaka was going to practice hockey with his school mates and will not be able to bring him his lunch.

On Tuesday evening Birij Bhan came he had brought lot of mangoes and Aloochas (Plums) with him, he asked for some tea and snacks, which were brought to him by his wife Amrit. She put the tray aside and touched his feet, she had brought a glass of tea for Bhagmal, who was sitting there, after taking his tea, Brij Bhan went to his father's room, who was sitting upright and praying, his mother was also praying, he came out of the room without disturbing them. Once in the verandah, he asked Bhagmal to accompany him outside, both went out of the house, once on road Brij Bhan lighted the cigarette, and told Baagmal that he has put in his application for his immediate transfer to Rohtak, but has been informed that at the present time there is a departmental ban on all the transfer till such times the scheme of partition is finalized and notified, but his application has been admitted and has been recommended for favourable action by the office superintendent and he hopes that the SDM will accept the recommendations. He asked Bhagmal what useful information he has to which Bhagmal told him the visit of the Saadhu and his forecast to which Brij Bhan said that most of the forecasts were never very true and as such should not be giving much attention and then asked him his plan of visiting Rohtak to which Bhagmal said he plans to leave on Sunday. Once the Paath is over and he has more useful information which he may put to good use while at Rohtak, Brij Bhan told him that he has a very bad and sad news which is that all kind of transfer of immovable properties including land and houses has been stopped till further notice and even Bayana's registration (Advance Payments and Commitment) has been suspended, however he has brought out the land revenue papers of ownership of his father's land, house and papers pertaining to his house and Lekh Raj's house, and tomorrow he will go to the Arzi Navves (official petition writer) and get two copies made and get them attested from Local revenue officer of course it will entail an expenditure of at least rupees twenty, then he asked if he had met the Bhootia Baba again and did the Baba said anything, Bhagmal told him about Salaluddin's paralysis and his father paralysis and the visit of Farzana Bibi the mother of Salaluddin with their mother, and the mother arranging Farzana Bibi's meeting with the Bhootia Baba and Baba's never refused to help Farzana Bibi and that she should visit Ajmer Sharif and seek the blessing of the Khawaza. When they reach back home, Brij Bhan went near the guest room and called his wife's name and said she should give his night clothes and his bedding. She replied that she will send the same very soon. Brij Bhan went to his father's room, met his parents touched their feet and he told his father that he has brought the property papers but as per available information all sales of every kind of landed properties has been stopped till the partition is finalized and notified. Purshotam Lal said that any plan to sell the house and the land is not possible with the new order in force and so no house or land can be bought at Rohtak, so the best thing is to sell all valuables at commendable and reasonable price and deposit the money in the bank and find out from some Hindu merchant bankers if he can issue a Hundi at sight (letter of credit at sight) at Rohtak by some reputable and honest Hindu merchant banker, as also they should explore the possibility of stowing some trunks into the safe vaults of the Imperial Bank here for safe custody till such times till the storm of partition settles, and this should be done by Brij Bhan as the agent is sort of his relative on his in laws side and Brij Bhan should visit his local office here to gather all good and bad news, which may be put to some kind of use at the planned meeting and Bhagmal and Brij Bhan should once again make a visit to the Shamshaan Bhoomi and specifically request to the Bhootia Baba to bless the occasion of thePaath with his presence and bless the Parshaad with the divine strength. Kaka came and said that the dinner is ready and will be served in the verandah very soon on hearing about the dinner Bhagmal, went and had a bath and put on a tehmat and Bundi, came back and sat in the verandah waiting for the dinner to be served. Kaka brought two thaalis one thaali was brought by Didu, the Aloochas were brought by Nikko and Chhotti brought the water then food was brought in one thaali having four Katories, twelve chhappattis and eight Aloochas. The kidds ate their food and asked for mango to be given. Nikko went and brought four serving of mango one for each of the kidds. Kaka was called into take water, he brought the water tumbler and three glasses put water in each glass and handed over glass of water to all the thee gents. When everyone had eaten Kaka and Didu, collected the used empty utensils and took it to the kitchen, where they were cleaned and washed by Kunti.

Ladies of the house sat in the kitchen and had their food, utensils were cleaned and washed by Sulakashni, Amrit scrubbed the kitchen floor with the wet cloth rag, Ram Payari went to her room and sat beside Purshotam Lal, Brij Bhan and Bhaagmla went out of the house, Brij Bhan lighted a ciggrette and puffed on it, they both walked to the market and had a meetha paan(sweet Beetal) for a Tekka (Tekka is thirty second part of a rupee) and went here and there and then came back to the house.

Bhagmal went in and brought out two bedding one bed he spread it on the wooden cot in the verandah and the other he spread it on the floor and Brij Bhan come and lay down on the bedding over the verandah and was soon asleep first Bhagmal sat on the bedding in a crossed leg position and folded his hands and tried to visualize the God and started saying his prayer in a whisper he was saying;

I am a sinner, you are my redeemer
I act only in greed, but why do you breed the greed.
I am an evil man but you made the evil.
I act foolishly, but why do not you pardon me in your wisdom.
I am foolish and greedy man but you can help me to shun my greed and foolishness.
I look forward to your help, your guidance and mercy
God only you can rid me of my foolishness and greed
Please God, be merciful and make me wise.
So I shall not act foolishly in greed.
Please God bless me with your vision.
Please God give me your attention
Please God cure me of my malice.

Once his prayer was rendered, he got up went outside relieved himself came back and had a glass of water and lay down on his bed but he could not sleep, his mind was wandering like a whirlwind, and he could hardly make out, as to what was he thinking, as so many different flashes were passing through his muddled mind that he could not comprehend a thing, he got up rolled in the court yard, but his mind remained in turmoil, again sat down on his bed in stiff crossed leg position and tried to meditate by trying to concentrate on the far way glimmer of light, which seemed to him a glimmer of hope and future events to happen, as fore told by the Saadhu and Bhootia Baba, he decided that since he has decided to board the train on Sunday night he must visit the Bhootia Baba offer him Burfi and tell him that he was leaving for Dobh on Sunday night, than he remembered that any way he and Brij Bhan have to go to invite the Baba, this thought enabled him to be serene, now he was mentally at peace and was ready to sleep, he laid down on the bed and started snoring instantly. When he got up in the morning the sun was very high and the heat and light of the sun was very high, he went to the toilet, came out, went to his room took his clothes and had a bath and came out and called his son, when Kaka appeared he told him to go and tell his mother that he was waiting for his breakfast in the verandah and after breakfast he would like some tea, when his breakfast was brought by his wife he was very much astonished, as it had rarely happened in the past, all during his ten years of married life, in the first six years married life the breakfast was served to him mostly by his mother or he was called to the kitchen to collect his breakfast. Sulakashni asked him if he was well and has no problems that made him oversleep; he assured her that he was very fine, he overslept because he dozed off only in the early morning and that is what made him oversleep, and there was nothing to be alarmed or worried, there was loud coughing sound at the forward of verandah, Sulakashni coverd her face, and went away, Purshottam Lal and Ram Payari approached him and asked in unison, if he was quite well and did not need any medical advice, he assured that there was nothing to worry, he simply overslept because he had slept only in the early morning, than appeared Brij Bahn with similar question about his well being and he gave him the same assurance. Brij Bhan told him to have his breakfast and be ready to go with him to the Shamshaan Bhoomi to invite the Baba; he said he will be ready to come along in fifteen minutes after having his tea, on mention of tea, Brij Bhan said he would also like to have some tea. Kaka was asked to go and tell his mother to give two glasses of tea, after about five minutes Kaka brought two glasses of tea and gave one glass of tea to each, they had tea it was luke warm, then they both went out of the house and started walking towards the abode of the

Baba, on the way Bhagmal bought one paav of Burfi for the Baba, when they reached the Shamshaan Bhoomi, Baba was taking bath, they sat down on the floor before the appointed seat of Baba. After about ten minutes the Baba came, they both got up and touched the Baba's feet, were asked to sit down, Bhagmal handed over the Burfi to the Baba, the Baba gave them a piece each, Bhagmal informed the Baba that he plans to leave for Dobh by Sunday night train and he has come to seek his blessings for his success and safety. Baba put his both hands on his head and said, go, the God will be with you, and ensure to return by Tuesday, and inform your contract at Dobh about your visit. Brij Bhan said to eh Baba that their father has especially sent both of them to invite him to come and grace the path and bless the parsaad on hearing this the Baba said he will be there without fail. They both touched his feet and left. When they both were out of the Shamshaan Bhoomi Brij Bhan lit a cigarette and told Bhagmal he will go first to the house to take papers for the Aarzi Navees for attestation, and he should go to his shop and if he is free in time then he will bring him his lunch at his shop, otherwise he will leave a word with the ladies that his lunch is sent to him on time without waiting for him to return or rather he will leave a word that his lunch should also be sent to the shop and he will eat his lunch with him only and that he is the best thing to be done, when he reached at the roadwhich led to Bhagmal's shop, Brij Bhan walked to next road to which would take him to the house

Soon Bhagmal was at his shop, he opened the shop, swept it, and scrubbed the shop floor with a wet mop, washed his hand lighted a lamp and said his usual prayer and sat on his appointed seat, he had hardly settled, when a customer who identified himself as an official of the DC office, produced a list of goods he wanted to be purchase. Bhagmal looked at the list and found that he could supply the goods, asked the customer to be seated and asked him as to what he will like to have, tea, lassi, milk whatever he preferred the customer said he will be happy to have some sweet lassi, Bhagmal went out of the shop and its neighborhood, he asked the shopkeeper to send one sweet lassi, one tea and two samosas and two ladoos (ladoos are made from gram flour batter made as small size round balls then fired in oil, which is put into a sugar syrup and brought out and then molded into a round ball by hands), when Bhagmal was back in the shop, he started filling in the order by putting the goods on the counter, when everything asked for put on the counter he started making out the bill, he was adding ten percent markup in the prices when the bill as ready, he started packing the goods, in the meantime the lassi and samosa etc were brought in, he took the cup of tea and a samosa (SAMOSA – is made from whole wheat fine flour the dough rolled out on a board and is cut into a triangular shape and is halved and is stuffed with boiled potatoes duly salted and other ingredients added to it, then it is closed at all the corner, and put into boiling hot oil and allowed to fry till it is brown and then brought out and is ready to be eaten with chutany) and asked the customer to enjoy himself with lassi and samosa and Ladoo, the customer partook everything placed before him, and thanked, asked for the bill paid it and then said he will like to have a waterman silver pen, was given one the customer collected his goods pack and walked off without paying for the pen, he said it was his Baksheesh (tip) and walked out without waiting Bhagmal did not mind much as he had already added the price of the pen and lassi etc in the bill and rather had more profit than the usual. Soon a boy came asked for two books, books were given to him and the boy paid the price, collected the books and went away. No other customer for another two hours then a boy came and asked for six HB pencils, pencils were given to him and he paid the money for it, than a supplier came and asked for an order of pens or pencil. Bhagmal checked his account and paid him rupees sixty due to him and told him that he hardly needed any supply, the supplier suddenly asked him if he is planning to migrate once the partition is finalized to this Bhagmal, he is yet to decide as he is not sure as how the things will transpire, the supplier said if he plans to migrate he shall be happy to buy out all his stocks at discounted price at a down payment, but he must have at least three days' notice, Bhagmal said thanks for his offer and said he will get in touch if needed. At about one Brij Bhan came and informed Bhagmal that he has got the papers attested in two copies of each document and he should take one copy of each document with him and keep it in safe custody, of bank at Rohtak and he will retain one copy with him. Kaka came in and brought lunch and lassi, and asked for kulfi (A sort of Ice Cream, made around a wooden rod known as Tila) Brij Bhan gave him two annaas (one eighth part of rupee) and told him to buy ten Kulfis and take them to house and give one to everyone and keep the balance if any. They both washed their hands and sat on the floor behind the counter to eat their lunch. They ate their lunch in silence drank lassi and got up to clean up and wash their hands. After washing his hand Brij Bahn said he was going out and will roam about in the bazaar and then will go to home.

Bhagmal lied on the ground behind the counter and was soon fast asleep, when he got up it was four in the evening, he went out of the shop, relieved himself, washed his face and asked for tea and came back to the shop, sat on his seat waiting for the tea to arrive tea was brought to him, he paid for it and started sipping therefore another two hours no customer came, he was ready to close the shop for the day, when Lekh Raj walked into the shop with a bag and told him that he would like to have some tea. Bhagmal got up to go out and ask for tea when a customer came and asked for some goods. Bhagmal handed over the goods to the customer and collected the money from the customer when Brij Bhan came into the shop; he saw Lekh Raj there and said Namestey (A form of Hello) to him and asked him, how were the things, Lekh Raj said first he will have his tea and then he will tell him what news he has. Bhagmal went out and asked for three cups of tea, came back and sat down, tea was brought after about ten minutes, they all had their tea, tea over Lekh Raj told them that his application for transfer has not been entertained as there are order that transfers will happen only after the notification of partition and whatever transfer have been done during the last fortnight stand cancelled, that he met his Executive Engineer Shri Yog Raj and have been assured that he will definitely help to get the desired transfer once the partition notification is done which is likely to happen every soon, and he also has to ask for his transfer to Karnaal, which is near to Delhi and has good schools and a government college and the land is good and irrigated but is very costly and in fact of it is not owned by the muslim population, but the major and minor trade is controlled by the muslim people. By now it was seven in the evening, the time by which most of the shops closed for the day.

Bhagmal said he will go to the Halwai shop and order the Parshad (sweet eatable distributed freely to all those who attend the discourse) which he will collect tomorrow in the morning, Lekh Raj said he will go to the house and have a bath, he was asked to take the lunch box also. Brij Bhan and Bhagmal went to the Halwai shop and placed an order for two seers of Boondi (The sweet fried gram flour small round balls) and Namk Pary (Salted fine floor fired chips). Brij Bhan asked of Bhagmal that has he sent the telegram to Bhanne Ram, Bhagmal said he will send it just now and they walked towards the telegraph office. Bhagmal took the telegram from and sent the following express telegram "Reaching Monday morning by Punjab Mail Bhagmal"

When Bhaagmal and Brij Bhan reached home they reached straight to their father room, touched the feet of their father, Lekh Raj was already sitting there, Brij Bhan informed his father that he had the property papers duly attested and it cost him rupees thirty to get it done and he has made out two copies, one copy will be taken by Bhaagmal to Rohtak for safe keeping in the bank if possible or with Bhaana Ram. Bhaagmal told his father that he has sent a telegram to Bhaana Ram informing him that he will be reaching there on Monday by Punjab Mail, and he placed the order for the parsad and Bhootia Baba has assured that he will be their to attend the paath. Kaka came and asked them all to come and sit in the veranda where the dinner will be served very soon, they all came out, Brij Bhan and Lekh Raj headed for the guest room to change the clothes and Bhaagmal went to his room to take bath and put on his Tehmat and Bundi. They all soon came back and sat in the veranda waiting for their food, Ram Pyari brought thaalis and put one thaali before everyone, Nikko brought chapatti, Ram Pyari puttwo chapatti in each thaali, Dindu brought out achhar and papads, Chotti came out with empty glasses and a tumbler of water was brought out by Ram Pyari, she poured water in each glass and kept one glass of water before everyone, soon there was a call for Kaka from the kitchen, he went there and came out with papads, he asked Nikko to go to the kitchen and fetch kharbooja. She brought kharbooja.

Ram Pyari brought two thaalis and asked the kids to sit and share the food and kharbooja was put in their thaali along with achhar and papad, the kids ate their food without making any kind of noise, when everybody had his food the were utensils were removed by Kaka and Didu, taken to the kitchen, where they were cleaned by Sulakashmi and Amrit and the kitchen floor was cleaned and scrubbed with a wet mop, mats were spread and food was put in a big thaali, daal in each katori, achhar and papad in the thaali. One kharbooja in a spare thaali, all the four ladies ate their food in silence, when it was done Kunti offered to clean the used utensils and Ram Pyari said that everyone must get up little early in the morning, Sulakshmi will sweep and wash aanagan (court yard) and scrub it clean with a dry mop. Amrit will peel and chop the vegetables and Kunti will cook daliya for the breakfast and she should cook somewhat extra daliya may be some guest come up early in the morning and if anything is required than Sulakshmi will ask Bhaagmal to bring it the earliest, then she recalled that tomorrow's lunch of Alloo Puri will be cooked by a Halwai, she called Amrit and told her not peet or chop off the vegetables as the lunch will be cooked by a Halwai. She asked Sulakshmi to check if they had enough of Aachhar to feed about sixty people, if not then told she should tell Bhaagmal to buy some from bazzar. She left for her husband's room, sat at her bed and said her night prayer and went to sleep.

Kaka went to his father's room to get beddings but was told that he will find three beddings in the guest room, he went to the guest room, where Lekh Raj told him that he will sleep in the guest room itself Kaka went away with two beddings, when he spread them, one in the cot and the other on floor, Lekh Raj also brought his bedding and spread it on the floor.

Sulakshmi was sitting in her room before going to the guest room to sleep, when Bhaagmal came to the room and told Sulakshmi that he will be leaving for Rohtak on Sunday for about three days to attend to urgent and important work and on his arrival back, he will find some time to sleep with her and she can forget the bad incident, as her wish has been fulfilled by the God, through the help and grace of Bhootia Baba and he assures her that he has nothing against her and the accident was not her fault, on hearing Bhaagmal she got up and touched his feet and started sobbing, Bhaagmal brought some water for her and gave it to her and started to move out off the room, when Sulakshmi told him that the he should buy some mixed aachhar for the guests at lunch, he replied that he will bring it for sure and came of the room.

Sulakshmi got up very early in the morning swept and washed the court yard and then took a big dry mop and rubbed it clean, then she went to the kitchen swept and washed it and then mopped it with dry mop. Since she did not have anything to do better, she started cooking daliya for the breakfast. She cooked Daliya for about twenty people, when she felt her mother was up and gone to the bath room, she started cooking tea for everyone. As she knew that in about next fifteen minutes except for the kids everyone will be up and tea will be asked for, when the tea was ready he poured it in a jug and then put into two glasses and took it to her father in law room, she knocked at the door, her mother in law came out and was given two glasses of tea. Sulakshmi came back to the kitchen, put some tea in more glass and started sipping it, in the mean time Brij

Bhan came to the entrance of kitchen and called for Amrit, instead Sulakshmi came out, she had covered her face and handed him over a glass of tea. He said, she should give him two more glasses of tea. she went in and brought two more glasses of tea in a tray he put the third glass in the tray and walked towards the veranda and gave the tea to the both his brothers. Kunti and Amrit had their bath and were in the kitchen to drink tea. Since Daliya was already cooked, so the women had nothing to do, so they started chatting among themselves. After sometimes Ram Pyari came enquired of Daliya will be ready on time, she was told it has been cooked by Sulakshmi and will be served very soon, then Ram Pyari told them to Dress well before the guests started coming and they should arrange for more milk and keep the water boiling for the tea, so it could be given to anyone asking for it and she left for her room.

The Tent wala came at seven in the morning and put up a big Shamiana (Tent) and spread Darries (Big Cotton Mats) on the floor. They brought two big wooden cots and put them near the wall and spread a big white Chadder (White Sheet) on it, there job done, they went off to come back at five in the evening to collect their stuff.

The Halwai (A Cook) came out at six in the morning, brought out big Patilaas (Big Round vessel Made Of Brass) and one big Kadai (A Round Iron Caldron for frying) on a Theli (Hand cart), put his wares on the floor and asked for Bhaagmal, when Bhaagmal appeared the Halwai said Ram Ram and told him to pay a Tekka (Thirty second Part Of A Rupee) to the Theliwala, Bhaagmal paid the money to the Theliwala and he left too Halwai Kaudamal, said he be given the Aaloos, flour and all massalas (condiments) and fire wood. So that he could get the food ready by the appointed time, and said he will feel obliged if two glasses of tea could be given to him Bhaagmal said he will be first served his tea and some Daliya and all his other requirement will be given to him. He called for Kaka, when he was came he told to go and bring his Chacha around here, kaka went off and appeared back with Brij Bhan, Bhaagmal told him to take over this job, so that he could look after other Sundry jobs. They both went inside and brought out the requirements of the Halwai, the assistant of the Halwai was told to collect fire wood from a corner, where it was well stacked up.

The guests started appearing around ten, the Paath was to start at twelve and was to end at two, then the lunch will be served, Lekh Raj took the responsibility of looking after the guests and Kaka and Didu were told to help him around in bringing water etc for the guests.

Nikko and Chotti were asked to help the Halwai in rolling out the purries (Un Cooked Pan Cakes Before Frying).

A man in crisp white clothes came and knocked at the door to get some attention, Brij Bhan got up and went to the door and asked the man standing there was Bhaagmal went to the bank and got up bank draft in his name payable at Rohtak for rupee ten thousand only, which he in turn take with him to Rohtak.

The man at door was asked as to what did he want he said he has been sent by Babe Mool Raj Ji to inform Shri Purshottam Lal that he will be there at twelve with five of his disciple and his food should be kept ready. The man at the door was asked to come in and have some water but he politely excused himself and went away. Brij Bhan told the Halwai that the food and Halwa (Pudding) should be ready before twelve by all means and went it to the room of his father and gave him the message of Baba Mool Raj and told him that he will ensure that the food is ready before Baba Jee comes and came out of the room to supervise the Halwai.

Then six people, four man and two women came in, Brij Bhan recognised his maternal uncles and their wives, went near them and touched their feet, was introduced to the son in laws of his maternal uncle, he went to his father room with four man and asked them to sit down came out saw Didu and told him that take five glasses of water to his Dada's room, then he along with his maternal aunts went to the mother's room she saw the sister in law, she got up and hugged both of them and made them sit and told Kunti to bring water for them and told Amrit to cook some tea, she put the tea in eight glasses and called Kaka who came running, she handed him over a tray with six glasses of tea and a plate full of Namak Paras. Then she put three glasses in a thaali and a plate of Namak Paras and brought it before the lady guests, she touched the feet of both the ladies and sat aside, Ram Pyari urged them to take tea.

Bhaagmal was coming from the bazzar after buying Parshaad and aachhar, when he met his both uncle s and his three cousins. They all soon reached the home and were directed to Purshottam Lal's room, Bhaagmal went to the kitchen put the aachaar and the Parsad there, then he took out a thaal (A Big Platter) and told Sulakshmi that he has brought the aachaar, but was told to take the aachaar to the place where the lunch will be served, Kaka came and took out six glasses of water and told his mother that she should prepare some sharbat for the guest and some for him and Didu, may be about ten people will take the sharbat. He was told to take water come back with all the empty glasses in his Dada's room and the veranda, he came back in five minutes with about fifteen glasses Kunti cleaned and washed all the glasses. When sharbat was ready ten glasses of sharbat were put in tray and Kaka was asked to take them out and give it to the guests and he should come back and take his and Didu's sharbat and send Nikko and Chotti for sharbat.

Soon more guests came and were welcomed offered water and asked to sit down, all the men sitting in Purshottam Lal's room came out exchanged pleasantries and talked in general, tea and sharbat was offered but declined.

Ten minutes before twelve the Halwai Kodamal annoweed that the food was ready and Purshottam Lal asked Lekh Raj and one his brother to taste the food, everybody in unison said it was delicious. Exactly at twelve o'clock Baba Mool Raj Ji came with his five disciples, everyone got up touched the feet of Baba and requested him to be seated, a message was sent to the guest room that the Baba Ji has came and all the ladies came lead by Ram Pyari, touched the feet of the Baba Ji and went away.

Purshottam Lal brought water washed the feet of the Baba Ji and songht his blessing and the permission for bringing out the food was allowed to bring his food, a thaali was brought which had Purries (fried pan cake) Aaloo Subzi (vegetable made up of potato) and Halwa (Pudding), Baba Ji took out some part of Halwa put on a Purri and put some Subzi on the Purri, which Purshottam Lal took in his hand and went to add blessed food to the main food. He prepared one more thaali of the food and took it to the Baba, which Baba put it before the photo of Hanuman Jee (Hanuman is most reverened Monkey God in Hindu Python). Baba ji took his food slowly and left some food uneaten in the thaali, which was given to Kaka to eat, five more thaalis were prepared and served to the five disciples of the Baba.

Baba Mool Chand ji, said he was ready to start, so ask everyone to come and sit, the message was sent to the guest room and veranda, everyone come touched the feet of the Baba and sat on the floor before the Baba. Baba closed his eyes and sat in silence for few second and then lighted the lamp and said a small prayer, opened the book of Sunder Kaand (Sunder Kaand is the story of Hanuman the monkey God, his act of daring of crossing the Sea, burning the kingdom of Ravana finding of Seeta Mata, the wife of Lord Rama) it is said that rendering and reading of the Sunder Kaand removes the obstacles faced in one's life.

The voice of Baba was booming with variations according to the unfolding story and audience was hearing the rendering with rapt attention.

At one thirty the rendering came to an end and the Baba said in very loud voice Seea Pati Ram Bhagwaan ki Jai, Bajrang Bali Hanuman ki Jai(Sita's Husband be hailed powerful Hnuman be hailed). Then a disciple of the Baba said, people may make a Ardaas (it is a paid offering) to seek favours and blessings of the God and the god man). The Aardass were offered and announced and at the end of every Aardass a request was made to the God to accept and grant the prayer at last Purshottam Lal and Ram Pyari made their Aardass, gave clothes to Baba ji and all his desciples, Baba ji gave them parshaad and his blessing them Baba Mool Chand Ji got up and lift along with disciples.

Purshottam Lal stood up with folded hands and requested the guest to have their food and at three o'clock they will sit in a meeting for one hours and then tea will be served to them and then everyone can do as he pleased.

Everyone took his lunch which was mostly served by Lekh Raj and Kaka. The water was brought by Brij Bhan and Kharbooja and mangoes were served by Bhaagmal.

Food for ladies was taken by Ram Pyari with the help of Nikko and Chotti.

Then Lekh Raj and Brij Bhan and Kaka and Didu sat and Bhaagmal served them the food, Bhaagmal took the food for Ram Pyari and Nikko and Chotti and then put his food in the thaali and sat to take it, after taking his food he went out to the Halwai and asked him to prepare some more purries and told him to take his food and also give food to his assistant. He was eagerly awaiting for Bhootia Baba to come, as he knew that the Baba will appear only when the Paath was over and Baba Mool Raj left.

Bhootia Baba said loudly Alakh Niranjan Bhaagmal touched his feet and took him to his father's room and urged him to be seated. He sat down on the spare cot in a crossed leg position, Bhaagmal went out informed his parents that Bhootia Baba has come and took Parshaad to the Baba and requested him to grace the parshaad then he went out and brought food for the Baba, which the Baba ate without a word and asked Purhottam Lal to start the meeting, when the meeting started Baba listened to everyone and at the end said that this partition is going to be very horrifying and many lives will be lost and property destroyed and human values gone and greed and caprice will go up, everyone will suffer and will lose his moral character, all good values will be lost and suffering will be rampant and will go a long time death and disease will be common and poverty rampant, but we should always keep our faith in the God and pray to him for mercy, God is merciful and will not give more suffering to anyone than he really deserved. You will have to leave your home and hearth and lot of belonging and trudge a long distance of safety, and the safety will be at a very high cost, both financially and physically and morally. Please move in a caravan, don't carry heavy loads, keep the ladies and children especially protected, don't mind to spend any money to protect the honour of ladies and the safety of the children, arm yourself and be ready to kill and be killed to save the women and child. Be brave, Be God fearing and Be helpful to each other, God is with you, and he may protect you from the worst and if you deem it fit to take me with you. I shall be available to go with you as one of you, Now go back to your places and start preparing for the biggest shock and adverse event of your life. May God bless you.

The Baba asked everyone to come and take parsad, let ladies come first and Purshottam Lal at last. Everyone went and touched the feet of Baba and took parsad, at last Purshottam Lal touched the feet of Baba and took parsad. Bhaagmal walked with Baba to say fare well.

After some time tea was brought in and served to everyone who took it. The guest started saying good byes and soon all the guests had gone. Then the tentwala came and collected the tent and floor spreads.

When everyone was gone, Bhaagmal, Lekh Raj and Brij Bhan came out of the house and Lekh Raj and Brij Bhan lighted their cigarettes and started puffing out in hurry. They went to the market as Bhaagmal wanted to buy some toys for Mool Chand and Phool Chand and Bangles for Todamai and special Beeris for Bhaana Ram, he bought whatever he had planned to buy and they all stared back then he saw some DOKAAS (Raw Dates) in a hand cart, he bought a seer of it for the house Brij Bhan and Lekh Raj lighted another cigarette and puffed on it slowly they were at the house, Bhaagmal went to his room and put the things he had brought on his bed accept for one seer of Dakkas, which he gave to his wife who was standing at the door of kitchen. He went to the room of his father where his mother and two brother were sitting, Purshottam Lal told Bhaagmal to go to the kitchen and ask Kunti, Amrit and Sulakshmi to come to his room at the earliest, the three ladies their faces and head covered with their dupattas, came to their father in laws room, touched his feet and stood there they were told to sit down, they sat on the floor.

Purshottam Lal spoke in a gentle but clear voice, that they have heard Bhootia Baba, but they need not be afraid, as the God is merciful and will take good care of them their husbands, their kids and their parents, and they should plan to go to their parents house to meet them, as they may not get another chance to meet them any soon. As thing are turning out to be and they should take their husbands and children along, so is the case for Ram Payari but she has already met his brothers and their wives, but he will be happy to accompany him if she decided to go to his parents house, but Sulakashmi can go to his parents either tomorrow with her children without his husband, because he has to catch the evening train and I shall go and drop at her parents' house and when Bhaagmal returns he will bring her back, now they should sit with their husbands and plan and let him know of their plan, all their plan have his approval with his note he ended his address, got up and went to his room. Ram Payari came and sat besides her husband, she told her husband that he should go on Monday morning with Sulakshmi and the kids and drop her at her parents' house and she will also accompany him to Sulakshmi's parents house and meet the mother of Sulakshmi who is her first cousin Purshottam Lal said he will decide only after Sulakshmi tells him her plan, but he approved of her purposal.

All the women went to the kitchen to prepare for dinner, while in kitchen Kunti said she will ask her husband to take her to her parents house tomorrow itself, stay there for a day than she will go with him to her house and sort out the things keepings in view the partition and the biggest problem is her jewellery though she does not have much but she can not afford to loose it, her husband is suggesting that she sell her jewellery and deposit the money in the bank and once they were settled after the partition, she can buy new jewellery by taking out money from the bank, but she does not want to part away with her jewellery.

Amrit said new jewellery is already in the and she will keep it there only as the bank has confirmed that it will be safe there and it may be transferred to another place if it is kept in separate box and her husband will go to the bank on Monday and keep it in separate sealed box with a lock, one key of the lock will be given to him, they will charge rupees twenty for the transfer.

Sulakshmi said that she will give all jewellery to her husband and he will take it to Rohtak to be kept in safe vault in the bank if he could get one and if he does not get a safe vault in the bank then he will keep it with Bhanna Ram for safe custdy, and as far as she knows her mother in law will also give her jewellery to her husband for safe keeping at Rohtak. Then Kunti asked her, if that Bhanna Ram is reliable enough to be handed over the pericious jewellery for safe keeping and God only knows when can an honest man may becomes dishonest and so she is not taking any chance with her jewellery at all. Ram Payari come in and asked in general if they are preparing dinner and she said she has to cook tea as his husband is asking for it, Kunti said she will cook it and send it soon. Kaka came and said at least four glasses of tea are required and when ready he will take it to Dada's room, as he is expecting some prize money as he worked very hard this day and he will share his prize with his sister and brother. Kaka took the tea in a tray o his Dada's room and was given a Duvanee (one eighth part of rupee) by his Dada as reward for his good work of the day, his uncles paid him a Chavani (one fourth part of rupee) and his father gave him a Athani (half of rupee). He had one rupee and two annas, and he went to his mother and he asked of his mother should he bring kulfi for everyone as he has two Annas with him which he must spend his mother said you can bring kulfi for everyone but you will have one anna more and I shall give it to you, Kaka went out and brought Twelve kulfis and gave one to everyone. Everyone said thanks to him and very much apperciated his wise act Dinner was put in the veranda and everyone asked to take dinner, Purshottam Lal was the first to come, followed by Lekh Raj and Brij Bhan, Bhagmal was the last as he had gone to take bath and change his clothes. He took the dinner and asked the kids if they had eaten. Both Lekh Raj and Brij Bhan asked Bhaagmal Lal to accompany them, they went out Lekh Raj and Brij Bhan lighted their cigarettes and Lekh Raj said the Bhottia Baba has unnecessarily created a sort of fear in everyone's mind and nobody will appreciate his observation, Brij Bhan said in a sence the Baba is very right in his observation but he should have used caution and he very much agreed with the observation of the Baba and instead of fearing from his observation, he should act according to the advise of the Baba to be on the safe side of the events.

Lekh Ram told Bhaagmal to study the geography and topography of the town Rohtak and should also study the economics and business potential and also the main trade and business of the Muslim population and also the social relationship between Hindus and Muslim population and the degree of animosity between the two communities and also find out about he most prominent Hindus shrine and its religious leads and also find out if there are many Sikhs living in the town and their main avocation. He should also find out about the number of the schools and colleges if any and the avenues for the girls students. Brij Bhan wanted him to find out if the town has a hospital and how far is it from Delhi and which are the big towns nearby having good Muslim population, they reached the house, Bhaagmal went in brought out the beddings and spread them. Then he went to his room and called Sulakshmi, she came and sat near him and asked him what was the matter, asked her of her plan to visit his parents house to which he replied that she will go to her parents with kids and her father in law and when he is back from Rohtak, he should bring her back and not take any eatable from a stranger, rather he should take some biscuits and live by it, while travelling and he should try and return at the earliest possible, he assured her that he will be careful and will try to return as soon as possible and he will bring some gift for her, he came out of the room and went to the veranda to say his night prayer and then sleep, he sat on his bed in crossed leg position, folded his eyes and closed his eye, he was praying.

Oh, my very dear God, oh my very dear God.
You are my friend my dear God.
You are my Saviour my dear God.
You are my benefactor my dear God.
You are my mentor my dear God.
You are my lord my dear God.
Oh my dear God, oh my dear God.
I await your light.
I await your Guidance.

I await your mercy.
I await your pity.
I await your benevolence.
I await your compassion.
I await your love.
I await your blessings.
Oh my dear God, oh my dear God.
I look forward to your light.
I look forward to your pity.
I look forward to your teaching.
I look forward to your munifunce.
I look forward to your preaching.
Oh my dear God, oh my dear God.
You have always loved me my God.
You have always blessed me, my God.
You have always helped me, my God.
You have always guided me my God.
You have always rewarded me my God.
Oh my dear God, oh my dear God.
God I am at your mercy only.
God I am at your wish only.
God I am at your feet only.
Oh my dear God, oh my dear God.

On Sunday morning when everyone had his bnreakfast, Brij Bhan and Lekh Raj went to their father's room, where their mother was also sitting and told them that they will go with their wives, to their in law's house and on Monday they will attend their offers and on Wednesday, which is a holiday this time, go to their in law's house and bring back their wives. Ram Payari got up and went to Sulakshmi's room and told her that she should be ready to go to his parent's house with the kids on Monday morning. She and her father in law will come with her but will return back on Tuesday and for today's lunch she should cook kadhi (Kadhi is made from curd milk and gram flour and is allowed to thicken) and rice.

When Lekh Raj and Brij Bhan had left with their wives Bhaagmal went out to meet Ashfaq Ullah, the man who had offered to buy his all stocks at discount on payment Ashfaq met him outside his house and they went to a tea shop and Bhaagmal reminded him off his offer to buy the stocks Ashfaq said his offer still stand and he is ready he can just now finalise the deal, on hearing this Bhaagmal said he will go to his father and discuss the issue and they can meet at his shop at three in the afternoon, Ashfaq readily agreed and said that the payment will be made with in three days Bhaagmal came back to his house and told his father about the whole issue and deal is genuine, if the price offered by Ashfaq is genuine he should accept it and hand over the stocks when the payments is made to him.

Bhaagmal went to his room and told Sulakshmi about the deal and told her that he should be given his lunch by two as he has to meet Ashfaq at his shop at three in the afternoon. Ashfaq and Bhaagmal met at three, Bhaagmal opened the shop, Ashfaq took out a note book and a pencil and started making an inventory of the stock and the total value come to rupees fourteen thousands and he agreed to pay rupees twelve thousand, Bhaagmal said he will Settle for rupees twelve thousand and five hundreds, Ashfaq thought for some time and agreed to pay the amount in about four days but he put a condition that if any of the counted stock is sold in between that sales amount should be paid to him, to this Bhaagmal readily agreed upon, they both came out of the shop went to the tea shop and had tea, when departing

Ashfaq paid rupee one hundred to Bhaagmal as an advance for the deal and left.

Bhaagmal brought seven kulahars (Earthen glasses) of Rabbari and went to his house. He informed his father that the deal has been done and he has received an advance of one hundred. He went to his room and handed over Rabbari to Sulakshmi and told her that he is in luck and the deal has been done and the final payment will be done in four days and hopefully he will be back by that time, he told Sulakshmi to cook some food for his journey as he will be leaving by seven in the evening.

At seven Bhaagmal left for the Railway station to catch Punjab Mail, which left at eight in the night, he boarded the train and found the seat near the window. When the train started moving he ate his food, had some water, went to the toilet and relaxed himself, came back and sat on the window seat, soon he dozed off, by the time the train reached Rohtak it was late by three hours, he got down at Rohtak, Bhaana Ram spotted him on the plateform and shouted for him, they embraced each other asked about the welfare of each others family, then they went to a tea stall had a tea and came out of the platform, Bhaana Ram had brought the bicycle of his friend. Bhaagmal told him that since he has some work in Rohtak he will come to the village at evening, Bhaana Ram said no they both will go the village, he can have his bath and some rest and after taking breakfast he can return to the town and he can use the cycle for next two days. Bhaagmal agreed and they both paddled to the village, before seven they were at the village home, Mool Chand and Phool Chand came running, touched his feet and embraced him, Todamai come out touched the feet and went in. He brought out the toys and gave it to the boys, they jumped in happiness, he handed over the packet of beeris to Bhaana

Ram and asked for Todamai and when she came he gave her the bangles and said that these have been sent by his mother and wife.

After a bath and breakfast he left the village at nine by bicycle, he stopped at the very first big tea shop and asked for tea, and asked the shopkeeper if the town has any hospital and was told that the town has hospital and was told that the town has three hospitals, one is general hospital with thirty bed and other is female hospital with ten beds and then there is a veterinary hospital, as the dairy farming is the biggest business of the town, and the town supplies milk even to Delhi and it also supplies beef to Delhi and Neena Kasai is the richest Kasai (Butcher) of the town and there are more than 100 Dairies in the town which export catteles to different places and supply milk to whole town and all the dairies are owned by the local Muslims with their the servants, the town has the biggest Cow Dung industry and Cow Dung is used as manure and as a fuel in in most of the houses and it provided good employment to many poor women Bhaagmal paid the tea man, and started for the bank, by ten he was outside the bank when he entered the bank it was almost deserted, the Agent was sitting in the main hall, where the Head Clerk Mouddin had sat on his last visit, Bhaagmal saluted the Agent who recognised him and asked him how is everything, he said things are good as for him. The Agent said you are lucky as you find the things good, but for him things are no good as all his Muslim staff has left and he is all alone to manage the whole branch here and he is getting mad and asked him anyway how can he help him, Bhaagmal gave him the draft of rupees ten thousands to be deposited in his account and asked him can he hire a safe deposit vault. The Agent told he can allot him one but the rent will be rupee ten per year, Bhaagmal said ok. Let us complete formalities, papers were filled up and singed a vault allotted to him, a key handed over to him, then he told the Agent he will like to operate the vault first now, he was taken to the strongroom and asked to open the vault and then the Agent went out, Bhaagmal put the jewellery and other important papers in the vault and locked it, checked the lock twice and came out. He gave his passbook for the entry. The Agent made the entry in his passbook and asked him, would be mind to go out and bring two cup of tea. Bhaagmal went out looked for the tea shop and brought two cup of tea and kept the cups on the table before the Agent, the Agent took one and asked him to take the other after having his tea Bhaagmal got up to go, the Agent asked him to sit down, when he sat down the Agent asked him as to what was his educational qualifications, he replied that he had passed B.A. 1st year, the Agent asked him if he can read and write English, Bhaagmal replied yes without difficulty, then he asked how good he is in arithmatre that is in adding, subtracting, division and multiplication Bhaagmal told told him that he has been running a book and stationery shop for four years. The Agent asked him does he know how to calculate simple and compared interest Bhaagmal said that he can calculate the interest without difficulty. Then the Agent asked him if he will be willing the work in bank as clerk at monthly salary of rupee sixty. Bhaagmal was taken aback, but he said he needs some time to decide on hearing this the Agent said if he decides to work for the bank then he should come back at two in the afternoon and he will be given a test to write and if he passed the test he may be offered a job in the bank.

All this talk about a bank job made him giddy and muddled headed and he could not find an answer to meet the new situation created by the offer of the job, this was what his father has always wanted out of him, but he could not get a job with the bank as he had no backers who would deposit large sums of money on his request, now he went to the tea shop and asked for a cup of tea and some wafer (salted chips), he suddenly remembered what the Sadhu had said that he will get a big opportunity which he must avail and even the Bhootia Baba had hinted something like this only. Now his mind was clear and he had made up his mind to take the test and wait for its result and if he is offered the job he will accept it, the time was now around twelve, he had two hours for taking the test, he asked the tea wala, was there any school or college nearby. The tea wala said the town has three colleges and four schools but there are not many students available and no girls student there, the college are up to it and inter it is rumoured that after the partition the Government college will be upgraded up to B.A., it is also being said an education college offering teacher education like J.B.T. and B.T. may soon come up in the town as this town is a very important District Head Quarter town in this part of Punjab as it is very volatile District that is why there is total ban in the drinking and selling of liquor, Bhaagmal was happy that he has collected lot of information and he will collect more information after the bank work is over and done. He looked around to have something to eat, he found a rehri (hand court) selling chholey bhuture (cooked craw and oil fired pan cake) he approached the rehri and asked for two Bhuture with Chholey. He was asked to pay anna (sixteenth part of a rupee) he paid the money took the Chholey bhuture, ate it and had some water from small tank nearby. He went to a nearby paan shop and asked him as to what films are running the cinemas, he was told are two cinema Halls in the town, one is Subhash and the other is Partaap, but he does not know what films are running he said may be you can know it from the nearby the Nai (Barber).

Exactly at two he went into the bank and sat before the Agent he was told to wait for some times. After about fifteen minutes, he was given a question paper which was typed and was asked to write down the answer against the question in a given space and he was told that he has to write the paper in the forty five minutes Bhaagmal read the paper from end to end, he re-read the paper, was not very sure as to how much answer he will be able to write, he closed his eyes folded his hands in a prayer, remembered the God, mentally bowed before the Bhootia Baba and Saadhu and hoped that he should be writing the right answer to the most of the question. He started writing the answer and soon was asked to stop writing as the time was up, he had hardly realised that forty five minutes have elapsed, he stopped writing and handed over the paper to the Agent and was told to come after half an hour. Bhaagmal came out of the bank, relaxed himself in the corner and then went to the tea shop, sat there on shop bench, how far is the Anaaj Mandi (Grain Market) he was told it was about two miles away and his informer asked him as to what he intended to buy, he said he has nothing to buy or sell, he just wanted to have some information about the mandi and its business potential the man told him it is a very big mandi as there was no other mandi in the town and these about sixty traders dealing all kinds of grains. The main grain which is traded in the mandi is millet, gram, wheat and other small grains, the mandi has shops cum residence and there are at least five very big trades one of the trader has its branches as far as Madras, few dealers have petrol and kersone dealership and run petrol pump in the town the entire business is in the hands of the Hindus traders, Muslims mostly worked as labours in the mandi and provided local transport by mule cart and buffaloes cart and the town also have a Kaath Mandi (Timber Market) where Timber fuel wood and stone and cement is sold. It also has iron traders especially the steel girders, here also the whole trade is prosperous and the entire business is owned by Hindus and there was no Muslim population in his particular area, he started walking and asked for the direction for the Partap Takies is controlled by the Hindus and customers from as far as Jhajjar, Sonipat, Bhiwani and Dadri come here to buy their requirements. Bhaagmal thought it was time to go back to the bank, so he said Ram Ram to the man and left for the bank.

In the bank the Agent was busy and told him to sit down, after sometimes the Agent said to him that he has passed the test and he can seek employment with the bank, he will have to come tomorrow to collect his letter of appointment letter and he can join the bank at the earliest but not later than 1st July 1947.

Bhaagmal said he will join the bank by that date if nothing untoward happens in view if the uncertainties of the partition he said that he will come the next day to collect his appointment letter and was told to bring his certificates for verification. Bhaagmal thanked the Agent for his kindness and came out of the bank and took his bicycle and asked is controlled by the Hindus and customers from as far as Jhajjar, Sonipat, Bhiwani and Dadri come here to buy their requirements. Bhaagmal thought it was time to go back to the bank, so he said Ram Ram to the man and left for the bank.

In the bank the Agent was busy and told him to sit down, after sometimes the Agent said to him that he has passed the test and he can seek employment with the bank, he will have to come tomorrow to collect his letter of appointment letter and he can join the bank at the earliest but not later than 1st July 1947.

Bhaagmal said he will join the bank by that date if nothing untoward happens in view if the uncertainties of the partition he said that he will come the next day to collect his appointment letter and was told to bring his certificates for verification. Bhaagmal thanked the Agent for his kindness and came out of the bank and took his bicycle and asked he went around the Partap Takies and came to know that the nearby locality was Muslim occupied, but most of the houses were of small size and were inside narrow gated lanes though the town had electric connections. He roamed around and reached near Lal Masjid it was big red Masjid and the entire area had large Muslim population many houses were quite big and in the side lanes houses were of poor people and the area beyond it was the dairy farms the area was totally dominated by the Muslims, even the Bhiwani Stand, which was basically a bus stand the entire transport services were controlled by rich Muslims, except of Jhajjar bus service which was owned by the local Hindus Jamindaar (Land Lord).

As he was on a road which led to his village Dobh, he paddled to Dobh and observed the entire street was barren and unirrigated except for a rain water drain called Badron, it was at least eight feet deep and twelve feet wide, but it had little water at the given time, soon he reached the house of Bhanna Ram, the door was open and he went in Mool Chand and Phool Chand came and touched his feet, Todomai came with a glass of water and asked him if she should give him some tea or will he wait for Bhanna Ram to come as he is expected Soon, Bhaagmal said he will wait for him soon Bhanna Ram came and Tosdomai brought two glasses of tea —and some snacks while having tea Bhaagmal told Bhanna Ram about the job from the Imperial Bank, Bhanna Ram congratulated him and said it was real good news and it was a God sent opportunity for him in the present difficult times caused due to the purposed partition which will cause umpteen problems for million of people who will have to shift their base and may be the new environment and re-settlement may not work well for them. Bhaagmal asked him if he can have the bicycle for the next day as he has to go to bank again and will like to catch the train back home and he has to gather some information about the town, Bhanna Ram he can have the cycle tomorrow, Bhaagmal thanked and told him that he has some impotant papers and a key which he will like to hand him over for safe keeping and he should arrange for a house for him either in the town or in the village, to this Bhanna Ram the house in the village is not a problem as he has another house in the village but it was somewhat small, but he will keep looking for a house in the town Bhaagmal paid rupees two hundred to Bhanna Ram and thanked him, Bhanna Ram said he could still keep the money if he needs to but no thanks as they are not required and he can get some information about the town if he likes as he know few people in the town who could provide the required information Bhaagmal asked him can he come with him to the town and once his work at the bank over they will go together and gather the required information to this Bhanna Ram said that he has no problems in going to the town with him next day.

Purshottam Lal, Ram Pyari and the four kids and their mother Sulakshmi went to the house of parents of Sulakshmi who lived in a nearby small village, Sulakshmi's parents welcomed their daughter, her kids and parent in law all were accorded a rousing welcome, were served sharbat and some sweets. At lunch the father of Sulakshmi who was a Government Primary School Teacher, asked Purshottam Lal about the information he had about the partition, he was given all the information which Purshottam Lal had Shivan Ditta the father of Sulakshmi said that he will migrate to a village which has a Government School so that he could get himself transferred there and as he had lost all his major possessions in a family division, so he is not very much worried about the transfer of possession and he always pray to the God for his good health safe migration of self and family and continuity of his job, but the safety of three daughter and two sons does cause him some worry, but he is very much hopefull that God will take good care of them and their family Purshottam Lal told him that he and his entire family plans to migrate to Rohtak as his both son have already applied for their transfer to Rohtak or a nearby village and ask his other members of the family to try and migrate to Rohtak and then he narrated the advice of Bhootia Baba.

Lekh Raj and Brij Bhan and their wives had reached their father's house and has relayed the advice of Bhootia Baba and their intention to migrate to Rohtak.

Bhaagmal and Bhanna Ram reached Rohtak near the bank at about ten in the morning. Bhaagmal went into the bank and saluted to the Agent, who told him to be seated and wait for him for some time, he sat on the chair, brought out his certificates before him, after some time the Agent called for him, he placed his certificates before him he had a look at it and told him to go to the Aarzi Navees at Tehsil Office (Petition Writer At The Land Revenue) and obtain two attested copies of his certificates.

He came out and told Bhanna Ram that he will have to go the Tehsil Office and see the Aarzi Navees, Bhanna

Ram told him he knew the Aarzi Navees and he will take him to him both walked to Tehsil which was very near by the Aarzi Navees welcomed Bhanna Ram and asked him what brought him to him, he was told that a certified copy of few certificates was required, he said give me the certificates I shall copy them and get them certified he was told by Bhaagmal that two copies of each certificates were required and asked him to what it will cost, Aarzi Navees told him that it will cost rupees twenty instead of thirty as he is guest of Bhanna Ram and he should come after half hour to collect them.

Bhaagmal told Bhanna Ram that he would like to move about the town to know more about it, so they cycled towards Lal Masjid (Red Mosque) beyond it was Chameli Market, it was mainly known for its prostitutes had a Shishe Wali Masjid (Glass Mosque) the whole area was Muslim populated beyond it was Kewal Ganj and Babra Mohalla and Mata Darwaja populated by Baniya Hindus (Traders Hindus) on the other side were Muslim localities of Salara Mohalla, Pahara Mohalla, Pardhana Mohalla, Dobhi Gate having mixed population but mostly middle class locality.

The major land owning people were Sainis (A Farming Cattle Rearing And Government Employee Community).

Bhaagmal and Bhanna Ram went back to the Aarzi Navees money was paid to him and he handed over the certificates copies Bhaagmal went to the bank, handed over the papers to the Agent, he had a look at it, brought out his appointment letter and was made to sign the copy of the letter Bhaagmal thanked the Agent for his kindness and came out of the bank, Bhanna Ram said he felt hungry and would like to eat some thing and said that he had seen a halwai (Cook) near the court and they will go there and eat some samosa or aloo puri whatever was available they both went back to the halwai Shop, first they had one samosa (A Snacks) each and had four Purris and Aloo Subzi (Cooked Meshed Potatoes) they came out and went to near by tea shop, both had a cup of tea, Bhanna Ram lighted Cigarette and puffed it.

By now it was almost three in the afternoon, and Bhaagmal had completed his bank work and had by now all the required necessary information he asked Bhanna Ram if he was ready to go back home, he said that he has nothing to do in the town so he will be happy to go back to the village. They both cycled back to the village, soon they were home.

Todomai opened the door, brought water for them and asked if she should cook lunch for them, she was told that some Sharbat and snacks will do for now, but keep the dinner ready by seven. sarbat and snacks were given to them. Bhanna Ram told Bhaagmal to take some rest as he may not be able to sleep in the train, and went out of the house, Bhaagmal went to allotted room collected his things and lay down on the cot, soon he was snoring, he was woken by Bhanna Ram at six and was told that the dinner will be served at seven, after having his dinner, he collected his bag and thanked Todomai for her hospitality and blessed Mool Chand and Phool Chand. At eight they both had reached Rohtak Railway Station, the Station was pitch dark, he went to the ticket window and brought a ticket for Jhang, the train was about two hours away, they both sat on a bench there were hardly any passenger at the platform, he asked Bhanna Ram as what was the talk about in the village and the nearby villages he said that his village do not have a even single Muslim family, but the next village Lalhi where there are about four hundred Muslim families it is tense though there is no under current or rampant animosity between the Hindus and Muslim farther away in Kalanaur, Aanwal,

Nigana and Chimney most of the land is owned by Muslim but no family has more than 10 killas with them and many of the Ranghar Muslim are in the Indian Army, these village are getting panicky and are arming themselves at the same time Non- Muslim population is afraid of the unknown and during his visit he last went to Gohana a pre dominantly Muslim population town, two Muslim were killed for their Anti- India tirades and the situation become tense and a dawn to dusk cerfew was clamped and the situation has normalised, Bhanna Ram said that there are about 20 big or small village with a sizeable Muslim population mostly land owning though the business is controlled by Hindus Bhiwani and Bahadurgarh are the biggest Muslim populated town, then there is Jhajjar, Dadri and Rewari having good Muslim population and almost every a single Muslim family is planning to migrate to be created Pakistan. Since it will not have any infidel Hindus in neighbourhood Bhanna Ram said that he is meeting with many people in many villages and most of the people are not happy about this partition and say that this partition is not good for the country and its people, as a major part of the country will be given away especially the most of prosperous and fertile land of Punjab will go to the Pakistan and even the name of Punjab will lose its meaning because Punjab means the land of five rivers, two of the rivers Ravi and Jehlam will go to Punjab and most of the mighty river Sindh will also be divided all developed cities like Lahore, Multan, Rawal Pindi, Peshwar and Karachi will also go to the Pakistan, the agriculturally weak portion of Punjab will come to India, most of reverend Hindus Temples of Hinglaz and Katesar will go the Pakistan and these Shrines will decay soon for lack of proper care and maintance, even the Gurdwara Nankana Sahib will go to the Pakistan which will cause lot of pain to Sikh devotees.

The only one to benefit from the partition will be Congress and Muslim League and its leaders like Gandhi, Nehru and Jinnah, the people of divided countries will suffer for the sake of political partitions by the selected few. The division of Bengal and Sind will kill the cultural heritage of people of both states, the sacrifies of Bangalis in 1902 will go to sheer waste, but common people are born only to suffer for the scheming ruling class and for about thousand year India had suffered for invasions and adventurer invaders and traders who have only looted the country and killed its people and reared greed, dishonesty and debauchery the women have suffered the most for least of progress has been said to be made in India is meant only to keep the British Empire flourishing and the British have taxed everything heavily and has even imposed tax on salt and water. Death and destruction is common and so is the corruption at Government level.

The train was announced and they both had a tea and waited for the train to arrive, when the train arrived and halted, Bhaagmal said farewell to Bhanna Ram and boarded the train, it was almost empty, so he sat on seat meant for four people and when the train got out of the platform, he kept his beg breath his head and lay down on the seat, but he did not sleep as the sleep was evading his eyes. He was awake throughout the journey and had tea at Firozpur, he got down from the train at his destination and walked fast to his house, soon he reached his house, his parents were awake and sitting in the veranda, he went and touched their feet and told them about his job with the bank, his parents were happy and thanked the God, his mother got up and went to bring tea for him, he had his tea and passed on the whatever information he had gathered to his father, he told his parents that he will go to his in laws house today itself and bring his wife and kids, his plan was approved and he went to the toilet and then he had his bath, said his prayer and was given breakfast by his mother he soon left for the village of his wife on the way he bought some mangoes and Jamuns(Black Berries) for the kids. He reached at his in laws house at the lunch time, he touched the feet of parents in law, Nikku and Chhoti came and embraced him, he gave the kids the fruits, his mother in law brought some sharbat for him, which he drank, he told about his job with the bank to Sulakshmi, who was over joyed and said that she will go and first light a lamp before the God his in laws were also very happy to know about his job with the bank. soon his mother in law brought lunch for him and for his husband, both had their lunch in silence after the food his father in law told him that he has submitted his application for transfer to Rohtak or nearby as was advised by his father and the informed if he is given information about their plan of migration. He will join them when he saw Sulakshmi, he told her that he will glike to leave by the five to be at their place by six and he will go out and fix a tonga to take them, she said she had no objection than Bhaaagmal told his father in law about his plan, who said it would have been very good if he had stayed for the night to which he said that he has to finalise the deal of selling his shop stocks the next day so he will have to leave soon. At four Sulakshmi brought him the tea, he took his tea and soon the tonga arrived he touched the feet of his in laws and boarded the tanga along with his wife and kids, kids were sitting in the front, he he and his wife were sitting in the rear, the back curtain fully drawn, he pressed the hand of his wife to reassure her and in about half an hour they reached at their house, all got down of the tonga took out their bags, he paid the money to tonga wala and all went into the house, there parents welcomed them,

Sulakshmi touched the feet of his in laws and was blessed and was asked to prepare some halwa to be offered to the God, since Bhaagmal has got a good job with the bank. The kids started playing in the court yard Sulakshmi asked him to fetch some vegetables but he said Daal will do and he will buy the vegetables the next day and rather he will lie down for sometime as he did not sleep during the last night while in the train and he went to his room put on a tehmat and Bundi and selpt on the bed, he was woken up at nine, he got up lazily and had a bath and sat for his dinner, his parents and kids had had their food by that time and had gone to sleep.

Bhaagmal and Sulakshmi had their food from the same thali, he told her about his visit and the gift he had brought for her, she took the gift and thanked him for the favour, Bhaagmal went out relieved himself and came back and lied down on the bed, Sulkashmi got up and went out relieved herself, came out with a glass of milk and water, first she gave the glass of water to him and then gave him a glass of milk, he drank half the milk and gave her the glass and asked her to take the milk which she did at once and then she got up and bolted the door and went to tlie beside him on the bed, he put his hand around her waist and snuggled to her, she put his arm away and got up lighted a lamp and then undressed herself, came near the bed loosened his tehmat, took his number in her hand and brought one of his hand to her breast her nipples were taut and he could not resist any more and made her lie flat on the bed and mounted her without any warning, both ejaculated very soon and both dozed off in a deep slumber, it all happened without a word being spoken.

Sulakshmi got up at her usual time and found herself without cloth and recalled as to what has transpired the last night. She gave a shy smile and started dressing up went to the toilet and had a bath. Lighted a lamp and profusely thanked the God for his mercy and said her daily prayer, went to the kitchen cooked tea, she took her tea, but did not wake up her husband.

She started preparing Daliya and looked for some vegetable did not find any except potatoes, she cooked potatoes and Waddi (waddi is home made from water soaked lintel grounded into thick paste, spices added to it and is allowed to ferment for a day and then small lumps are spread on thaalis and is allowed to sundry).

Bhaagmal got up only at nine, went to the toilet had a bath, put on fresh clothes lighted a lamp and said his daily prayer, after that he went to kitchen and asked for his breakfast, Sulakshmi gave him his breakfast and was told that he would like to have some tea, she brought tea for him sat there, he took the tea and what vegetables are required, she said since she does not have any, so he should buy two three vegetables, some potatoes and onions. He took a thaila (hand bag) and went out bought vegetables and went to his shop, swept it clean and scrubbed the shop floor with mop. Ashfaaq came at eleven, Bhaagmal went out and asked for tea both had tea, they both helped each other in packing the stocks, when all the stocks were packed, he paid the money and Bhaagmal counted the money and found the it as per the agreement, Ashfaaq said before he took away the stocks, he want to know if Bhaagmal is ready to sell the shop also as he sure he will be migrating to the New India as he is a true Hindu, Bhaagmal thought for a moment and said he is redy to sell his shop but as per his knowledge the sale and Baianas (Advance for sale) have been put on hold till the partition is announced. So he will not be able to finalise the deal, after hearing Bhaagmal, he said he had made arrangements for the sale deed for the shop in back date, but it will cost the money which may be up to rupees three hundred and he is willing to bear half of this cost Bhaagmal said he will have to talk about the deal with his father and only than he can give him a firm reply, Ashfaaq said he can come to his house at five in the evening and bring money if he agrees to sell his shop of course he will deduct the amount of expenses on this count, Bhaagmal said he will be waiting for him but as yet can not commit anything in this regards. Ashfaaq harked a hand cart put the stocks on it and went away.

Soon Bhaagmal walked back to his house, kept the vegetables in the kitchen and went to his father's room, where his mother was sitting he told them that he had sold all the stock to Ashfaaq on discount and collected the money and Ashfaaq has offered to buy the shop, and has told him that he will be able to manage the sales deed in back date at a cost of rupees three hundred, of which he is ready to bear half of the cost, his father said he has no problem with this deal and he should finalise the deal, collect the money and deposit it in the bank along the money from stocks.

At five Ashfaaq came to the house of Bhaagmal he was welcomed, Kaka brought some water for him, Bhaagmal took him to his father room, where they exchanged greetings and Ashfaaq was ready to buy the shop for nine thousand and will arrange for the sales deed on Monday after noon, and he will pay the due money and take the key of the shop, Purshottam Lal said he trusted him and Bhaagmal will sign the sales deed and collect the money, Kaka brought the Sharbat in three glass and gave one glass of Sharbat to everyone there after taking sharbat, Ashfaaq said fare well and left. Ram Payari came and asked if the deal was finalised and was told it has been finalised but will be complete only on Monday evening when the deal is signed and money received, Ram Payari God wasmore merciful than she had expected as the both the shop and its stocks have been sold and money for the shop will be realised tomorrow and Bhaagmal having got a very good job in the Bank, things could not have been more good. God is great Bhaagmal having nothing better to do, went to his room spread a mat on the floor of his room, lighted a lamp and sat in a prayer, he was numbing very softly.

Thanks O Lord Thanks for your Mercy O, Lord You Know every wish of everyone.

O, Lord You are kind and you full fill wishes of everyone.

But Alas not every time, O Lord

You must have good reason to not full fill every wish of everyone.

But you only know What is good for everyone.

O, Lord you have full filled all my wishes and I bow before you in gratitude and reverence.

O Lord be happy with me always I cannot afford your displeasure

O Lord be my benefactor always as no one else can benefit me any unless you wish benefit.

O Lord you are always kind how so ever unkind I may be to your Glory, may your Glory live forever and let me bask in your Glory.

O Lord let there be peace, pity and purity in every home every man, every nation.

O Lord you are Great and your Greatness is your purity.

When he had said his prayer, Sulakshmi came and asked him if she should bring some tea for him, he said he will be obliged to have some tea, the tea was brought to him soon, he drank the tea in silence.

At about eight in the evening Lekh Raj and Kunti arrived, Lekh Raj and Kunti touched the feet of Purshottam Lal and Ram Payari. Kunti went to guest room with the bag of clothes and went to the kitchen and said Ram Ram to Sulakshmi, Sulakshmi acknowledged her can she help in preparing the dinner, Sulakshmi told her that Daal had been cooked and she is making Roties on the Tandoor (an earthen over) and she is ready, call for Kaka and he will serve the dinner along with Nikko, soon the dinner was served in veranda and food was given to kids, soon used utensils were brought to the kitchen and Sulakshmi cleaned and washed them, then both of them had their dinner Kunti went to the guest room and prepared bed for two, there was a loud knock on the door, Bhaagmal went and opened the door and there stood Brij Bhan and Amrit they were taken to the room of their parents where they touched the feet of their parents and were asked to sit down a massage was sent to the kitchen to prepare meal for two people, Lekh Raj on knowing about the arrival of Brij Bhan came to his father's room and sat there, Amrit went away to kitchen, where she met both of his sister-in-law. She said that her parents are very much perturbed because of the partition they are very much worried about their property, jewellery and possessions as how they are going to take all their possession with them, apart from their other possession what about their cows and two dogs and five donkeys can they take them along on hearing Amrit. Kunti said her parents were very much worried about their safety, as the daily news of rape, abduction, looting are causing them lot of worries and they are very apprehensive as to what will happen to their house and what kind of new house they will get once they migrate to New India and how will they travel, whether by rail or mule cart or will have a trudge to their destination where ever it is, will they have good neighbours and will they continue to get good milk and desi wheat (organic wheat) and makki ka atta (Corn flour) and Sarsoan ka saag (mustard green) Sulakshmi said that due to partition she has to shift to Rohtak very soon, as her husband has got a job with Imperial Bank at Rohtak and he has to join on 1st July. So she will to go, so the kids could be admitted to school at Rohtak and she is not worried because she will try and face the situations whatever these are and there is always a God there to help. Food was cooked Kaka was called for and when he came a thaali with the food was given to him to be given to his uncle, Didu came and took a glass of water, Amrit was given the food which were brought to the kitchen by Didu.

While in the veranda where Purshottam Lal was sitting with his three sons and telling Lekh Raj and Brij Bhan about the sales of all stock in the shop at a discount and money having been received and the possibility of the sales of the shop itself, a sales deed made out in a back date for about rupees three hundred, on hearing this Brij Bhan yes a sales deed in a back date is possibility with the help of registry clerck and Tehsildaar (Revenue Officer) and of course it does cost money and a registry clerk a favoured man of the higher ups in the revenue department and he said if his father allows him he can find out if a their land could also be sold and a back date sales deed made out for a price, but for that we must find a prospective buyer for the land. Let the sales of shop be completed successfully, then only we will find a prospective buyer of the land. Lekh Raj who has sat only listing intervened that he had met a man at Jhang who is a RSS man (Rashlriya Sawam Sewak Sangh) and he told him that we must carry arms with us as there is great apprehension that the Muslim goons may attack with an intent to loot abduct and molest the woman and he has given me an address of a Hindu man, who can supply us the arm for a price, of course the arm are illegal and contraband he also said that we should move only in a large caravan and the faces of all women fully covered and women should have a big sharp knife or a Suaa (A Sharp Pointed Thin Steel Rod With A Handle) for self defence, they may all so have some poison pills which they could Swallow to save them for their rescue and every member of caravan should know where they are headed to he further said that caravan should carry lot of food like parched grain and rice bread, matter and lot of water and match boxes also said that RSS volunteers will try and contact them on the way to help if possible.

Now it was Bhaagmal who was speaking, he said that Bhanna Ram has met Vetram of INA Subhash Bose, who told Bhanna Ram, Muslims have always despised Hindus because they had a notion that they are born ruling class and they are only pure people around the world and even the Christian people have the same ancestry where as the Hindus may be rich to an extent but have been only a minion when Muslim Empire was ruling India, the Christian represented by the British are just a greedy trader, who tries and hood winks each of his customers whether Hindu or Muslim the INA man also said that the English linked Muslim more because they ate Beef like them and Hindus always protested against their beef eating which caused them a lot of problems to handle such protests. He further said that since the British Empire has suffered a heavy loss of men, money, material and manliness during the Second World War, so they find themselves in capable oto sustain the British Empire in united India, so they are again using their famous strategy of divide and rule and that is why the India is being divided into Hindu India and Muslim

India to be named Pakistan because their experience tells them with Nehru, Gandhi and Jinnah around these newly created nations will always be at loggerheads. Pakistan will remain feudal and militant and New India will be epitome of foolish democracy, the Congress Government always trying to appease the Muslims at any cost of the Hindus and Congress always in power, because the powerful Brahmin lobby behind Nehru, the rich Baniya (Traders) community being Vaish will follow their Vaish the Gandhi, the Brahmin are respected in the society and Baniyas feared in the villages and the farming community has to follow the money leading Baniyas in the village and the town market Nehru, Jinnah and Gandhi to seem good and influential will create a mess in the divided areas in the name of patriotism, peace and prosperity, the poor will suffer everywhere a new kind of hunger, greed avarice, treachery, Sycophancy will develop, debauchery and Sodomy will rise women will lose their importance and will be used as a tool for prosperity and seeking favours, daughters will be killed in infancy and telling big lies will become the major characteristics of the society in general and leaders in particular democracy will become a sham and the God and its good name will be facade and mascot for every lie and deceit Kaka who was sitting there and listening to whatever was being said with rapid attention got up and said I have made up mind after hearing all this, that I will try any and become a good leader of people and pray to the God to make me the greatest Liar, Cheater and people's leader, so that I could amass lot of Wealth, power and if not King of the Government but at least the King of the all cheats in India and preferablely the world over, Please do bless me respected Dada Jee (Grand Father), Dadi Jee (Grand Mother), Tau Jee (Father's elder brother), Pita Jee (Father) once I am blessed, I will seek the blessings of my mother and the God, but I assure you that for you all I will only be your Kaka and will always sub serve you. Please do bless me.

Before any one could say anything he was out of the room, Purshottam Lal heaved a deep sigh and said Oh God have mercy and keep Kaka to make him shake this idea out but only this will of the God will prevail, I can only pray which I will.

Lekh Raj and Brij Bhan got out and started going out, Bhaagmal followed them when they were going out of the house and on the road, both the elder brother lighted cigarette and puffed on it, as if they were in a deep thought, nobody talked and kept on walking, when they were near the main road they saw many Police men, Brij Bhan asked one of the Police man, whatever has happened and was told that a Magistrate a Christian has been murder and it is suspected that it is a political murder, they all turned back and walked back swiftly towards the house, once they were at house, they felt somewhat relieved when Brij Bhan narrated his Conversation with the Policemen to his father Purshottam Lal was spurred deeply, regained his composure and said that the Christian deserved it badly because most of the time they adopted an antagonistic attitude towards the Indians.

Bhaagmal spread the beds in the veranda, Lekh Raj and Brij Bhan, immediately went to the bed and slept Bhaagmal went to his room put an a tehmat and Bundi, relieved himself had a glass of water and came to sit on his bed on the ground, he was sitting in a crossed leg position and folded hands and tried to say his prayer as usual, he was saying in very low voice

O' My Dear God In Heaven
You Created Hell for men
And men with whatever little knowledge
You had bestowed upon them
Started ravelling in the Hell
Man enjoys the Hall
And never tried to get out of it
As he thought Heaven could not have been
Any good, because of his greed has many desires
Wishes and sensual pleasures
And men in their own wisdom has only
Strived to make Hell its abode
O' My Dear God In Heaven
I will contend with the Hell.
As long as you have heaven.

Bhaagmal tried to sleep, but he could not because an apprehension and premonition was haunting him that he may not be able to face the atrocities of partition and will have to suffer a major loss which may be irreparable his wife had already been defiled by a Muslim although he had revenge with the help of Bhootia Baba, but Bhootia Baba may not be around the next time when the calamity befalls him, he decided he will procure some arms and should make arrangement for his safe and early migration even if lot of money had to be spent to buy required level of safety and he was sure that money could buy the required level of safety for his family and it will be a good idea of he could find a buyer for the land, may be he will settle for a low price, but his money will be safe in the bank, and you never know as to what will happen to their land once they migrate he did not think the new government in the new country will pay any money to anyone whose land or property is left in the new country, so he must find a buyer for their land at the earliest, before things take turn for the worst, when there could be chaos everywhere and for everyone, maybe he should seek the help of Bhootia Baba in this regard, he will go and seek Bhootia Baba's help tomorrow having made this decision, he slept peacefully.

When he got up in the morning, the sun was up over his head, he got up went to the toilet had a bath, put on fresh clothes, went to the kitchen and asked for tea, he was told he have his breakfast and then he can have the tea and the vegetables have been brought by Lekh Raj and Brij Bhan has gone out and will be back at lunch time. He to went out and sat in the veranda, Kaka brought him his breakfast, he ate his breakfast, when he heard a knock at the door, he went and opened the door, he found well built man with a big forehead and wide eyes in the robes of Saadhu (Wandering monk) he touched the feet of the saadhu and invited him to come and sit inside, the saadhu came and sat on the cot lying in the veranda and asked it is the house of Purshottam Lal was told indeed it is the house of Purshottam Lal, then he asked please call Ram Payari, Bhaagmal was puzzled by whatever the saadhu was saying however he did as the saadhu bid, he went in and asked his mother to come out and meet the saadhu. She came out with her head covered with Duppata and touched the feet of saadhu and asked the saadhu if she should give him some milk or anything to eat, the saadhu said Ram Payari you do not recognise me, but well it is almost forty year before we last met, it was the day of your marriage, when I came to your housewith my Guru Maharaj (Holly Teacher) who happened to be your mama(Maternal Uncle) he had come especially to bless you, and once again being commanded by the Guru Maharaj, I came here to bless you, so that you do not suffer much in the coming days due to the partition, my blessing for you and your family, now please do give me some water to drink, before I leave as I can't stay any long, Ram Payari got up went out to brought water and gud (jiggery) gave it to the saadhu, he took a small piece of gud and gave the remaining gur to her and asked her to distribute it as parshaad (Blessed Offering) had water and walked out in an instant by this time Purshottam Lal also had come out and asked Ram Payari about the saadhu, she said she did remember or recognise this saadhu, but she do recalls that one her of mama (maternal uncle) was a great saadhu of his time and many people bowed to him for his blessings.

Purshottam Lal said the sudden coming of a saadhu, is part of warning system of the God, which may bring good news or bad news but almost it is a bad news, but most of the time you cannot fathom the import of the warning and its consequences unless they really take a place and by the time it is too late to be of any use or help and by the God the saadhu had come to warn about an impending misfortune.

Bhaagmal recalled the saying of the saadhu who had come to his shop and had made a reading of his hand and had a made some predictions and of course one of those pridictions had come true and he has got a job in the bank without even asking for it but he was now afraid of the other predictions so he asked the God to be kind and merciful and give him the strength of bearing any adverse situation and predicament. On Monday he met Ashfaaq at the office of Tehsildaar, he had brought the old deed of the shop, which was given over to the Aarzi Navees for making a certified copy and rupees ten as asked by him were paid. Ashfaaq went away to come up with stamped up duty papers of rupees fifty for the purpose of sales deed and gave it to Ashfaaq, the Aarzi Navees was paid rupees ten, and then

Ashfaaq went to the registry clerk who came out with him and went into a little far away corner, where Ashfaaq paid him rupee three hundred, Bhaagmal was called in and asked to put his thumb impression to the sales deed and also put his signature, a Numberdar (Petty Revenue Official) witnessed it for rupees ten and Ashfaaq also signed it and put his thumb impression, they were told to come after one hour, they went and sat at a tea shop, had a tea, while having tea Bhaagmal told Ashfaaq that his father has six killas (Acre's) of irrigated fertile land at the out skirts of the town which he would like to sell at the earliest Asfaq asked for trhe price of the land and was told it would be rupees six thousands for him only. Ashfaaq told him that he can get back to him only the day after tomorrow, but on that if he could bring money the sales deed will have to be signed and hopefully the fore dated sales deed will cost the same as it cost this day and he will have to bear the full cost of predated sales deed on which Bhaagmal said no it should be as it is today, both agreed and sat there before going to go to the registry clerk, when they went back to the registry clerk gave them to sales deed and Bhaagmal counted the money and handed over the key to the shop to Ashfaaq, they said farewell and parted and went about their ways.

Bhaagmal went straight to the bank and deposited the money received except rupees two hundred, which he kept in his pocket to meet, other expenses his bank job done, he started walking to his house on the way he bought half seer jalebi, when he reached home he offered the jalebies to the God said a small prayer, kept two jalebies there and took the rest of the jalebies to his father's room, where his mother was also sitting and told them that the shop has been finally sold, the sales deed made, money collected and deposited in the bank, that is why he has brought jalebies, Kaka was called and asked to make an even distribution of jalebies to all but he must keep the share of his two uncle Bhaagmal told his father that may be day after Ashfaaq gives him some good news about the possibility of their land being sold for rupees six thousand less the expenses and the expenses for a back deed may run upto rupees four hundred while Bhaagmal was sitting with his parents his both brothers came and sat there, Kaka gave them a jalebi each and was asked what was reason at this point Bhaagmal told them that he has sold the shop and sales deed has been made in the back date, the money has been collected and deposited into the bank and there seems to be some possibility of their land also being sold in about two three days and money being received for it was far below the expected price, but at least it was a certainity as other opition are a gross uncertainity.

Brij Bhan and Lekh Raj both said that they will leave tomorrow morning to return in the evening of 30th and their wives will be here only till further moves are finalised and Brij Bhan said he is trying to hire a truck so that can all go in one go with most of their possession and hopefully Bhanna Ram will accomadates for a couple of days.

On Wednesday Bhaagmal received a message from Ashfaaq to come to the tehsil with Purshottam Lal and Bhaagmal reched Tehsil at ten in the morning. Ashfaaq met them look the land deed gave it to the Aarzi Navees, who copied and certified it and wrote the sales deed on the stamp paper which Ashfaaq had given to him, the stamp deed was taken to the registry clerk who came out went to a corner took his fee and told Ashfaaq to come after sometime, Ashfaag. Purshottam Lal and Bhaagmal and the witness number daar appeared before the clerk, Purshottam Lal signed and put his thumb impression, Ashfaaq followed, Namberdaar signed as witness took his fee and went away, they were asked to sit down, the clerk went to the Tehsildaar got his signature and seal on the deed and came out, handed over the sales deed to Ashfaaaq. They all came out Ashfaaq gave the money to Bhaagmal who counted it and they parted, Purshottam Lal and Bhaagmal went to the bank and deposited the money there, Purshottam Lal took rupee hundreds for himself and told Bhaagmal to hire a tonga for Sham Shaan Bhoomi as he will like to go and meet Bhootia Baba and don't forget Jalebi's and Pakoraas for the Baba and half a seer of Burfi for the house and to give him eleven rupees, which he will offer to the Baba.

Bhaagmal hailed a tonga and told him to take them to Sham Shaan Bhoomi, on the way he bought Jalebi's, Pakoraas, Burfi one paav each and another half seer of Burfi for the house. When they reached outside the Sham Shaan Bhaagmal got down first and told the tonga wala to wait for half an hour, he took out the sweets for the Baba, when Purshottam Lal got down they walked into the Sham Shaan Bhoomi, the Bhootia Baba was sitting in a meditative position at his usual place, Bhaagmal went near the Baba, touched his feet and sat down on the ground before the Baba, Purshottam also sat on the corner stone, soon the Baba came out of his trance and saw Bhaagmal and Purshottam Lal he immediately got up and went and bowed down to Purshottam Lal and said why father, why did you came, you should have called me to you and I would have came at once, Purshottam Lal said Baba it is very kind of you and with your grace. I have sold my land today and have come here to ask you to keep your grace on me and my family for ever as usual, here is some Jalebi's, Pakooraas and some Burfi and rupees eleven please accept them, the Baba took all he took out Pakoore one Jalebi and piece of Burfi and rupee ten and gave one rupee to Bhaagmal and said keep it safe you may need it and take the Jalebi and Burfi to home and distribute and give me the Burfi you have bought for the house. I shall bless it, Bhaagmal went out and brought the Burfi to the Baba to bless it, he touched the feet of the Baba and came out of the Sham Shaan with Purshottam Lal and boarded home and gave him the address, when they reached home, they both got down, he paid the one rupee to the tonga wala plus two Jalebi and two pieces of Burfi. The tonga wala made a big Salaam (Salute) blessed him and left.

Ram Payari was the first to come and was given two pieces of Burfi and eleven rupees and was told that the land has been sold and money received and deposited in the bank, then all the other three ladies, Amrit, Kunti, Sulakshmi were called each came and touched the feet of Purshottam Lal were given two pieces of Burfi and eleven rupees each, then Nikku and Chotti came got two pieces of Burfi and five rupees each than it was the turn of Kaka and Didu who came touched the feet of their grandfather and their father and were given two pieces of Burfi and five rupees each, Bhaagmal was given two pieces of Burfi to each and Ram Payari was told to keep some Burfi for his other two sons.

Lunch was served and eaten and Purshottam Lal and Ram Payari went to rest in their room, the kids played in the veranda, Bhaagmal went to his room and lay on his bed, Sulakshmi kept herself to the guest room with the other ladies. At four tea was cooked and served, the kids were given some snacks, at six in the evening the Agent of Imperial Bank Of India, knocked at the door and asked for Purshottam Lal, he was asked to come in and taken to Purshottam Lal who remembered Allwyn Decosla, got up and Shook hand with the Agent and asked him to please sit down, the Agent sat on the single chair lying there, Kaka was called in, when he appeared he was told fetch some sharbat and snacks, the Agent told him that they must leave their two trunks for safe custody but if they intend to migrate they must leave their forwarding address with the bank, so that they could be sent their safe holdings at their forwarding address, as and when conditions prevail for their safe transfer, if they are not sure about their forwarding address then they must remember their key number and keep their papers safe to claim their holding from banks after the partition and it may take up no less than a year for the safe transfer of their goods to the local or nearest branch of the bank, from where they will have to personally collect it after paying the due forwarding charges and safe keeping charges and if he agrees to these term he can bring his trunks before 30th May in any case for safe keeping and this gesture is being made to him to be cause he is very good customer of the bank and it has been learnt that one of his son has been employed by the bank and if his son is at home, the agent will be pleased to meet him, Bhaagmal was called for, when he came he saw Mr. Decosta he shook his hand and welcomed him and when Decosta came to know that Bhaagmal who was a regular customer and visitor to the bank, he said it is good to know about your job with the bank and he has explained the safe keeping of trunks with the banks and he will be happy to help in all manners and got up, Bhaagmal offered him some tea which he declined, he was offered dinner, he said he must go home as his wife will be waiting for him and he left Purshottam Lal told Ram Payari to sort out the precious things like all silver wares her jewellery and costly clothing etc. And also tell all her bahu's (daughter in law) to do the same and Bhaagmal should check two trunks in good conditions which can be sealed and locked, so that could be handed over to the Bank for safe keeping.

Suddenly a man came running and barged into the house and shouted for Bhaagmal and when Bhaagmal appeared before him, the man said he has a very sad news that hisshop has been burnt by a fire and no one knows how this could have happened but he must go to his shop and salvage whatever he can, Bhaagmal was stunned like a stone he gave the disturbing news to his father and told him that he was going to the shop and look around, when he reached the shop many on lookers were gathered and two police man were asking the on lookers to keep moving, he went near the shop and saw that the shop was completely gutted he did not need go to into the shop. Since the wooden door was completely charred and so was the total furniture, when he got down, he saw a folded paper, which he took up and opened it written in Urdu was "Hindus Ke Saath Aisa Hi Hoga" (This Will Happen to all Hindus) and in the corner was written Sachha Musalmaan (True Muslim), he left the paper there and told the police man to check the paper as he cannot read Urdu. The police man got up lazily and went, where the paper was lying, picked it up, probably he was a Muslim or a Coward Hindus who did not want to get into any trouble at this most troubled times. Bhaagmal was very sad not only for his shop which was no more his, but Ashfaaq also who had shown lot of honestly in keeping his promise like a true Muslim, but he did not dare to call on Ashfaaq because of a lurking fear to the unknown, but he did pray to the God to be kind to Ashfaaq and shower his mercy upon Ashfaaq. He walked back to his house with a very heavy heart, he went straight to his father and narrated the horrible news and his strong reservation about the likely events of destruction once the partition is announced, his father did not say a word. He was walking to his room when his mother met him in the veranda and asked about the fire, he told that the shop has been put on fire to teach a lesson and strike a fear in the minds of all Hindus on hearing this his mother told, first the Muslim invaders through their brutality and then the British by their oppression and cunningness to made the Hindus a cowards and now it is Congress and Muslim League aided and abetted by the British Government through English educated Indians are making the Hindus the cowards, but she was sure that the God will help the Hindus and take good care of them.

Bhaagmal felt very uneasy and went to his room, put in the tehmat and bundi and lied on the bed in his room, Sulakashmi soon came enquire if he was fine, he told her about the burning of his shop by a fanfare Muslim, who did not benefit in the anyway by burning the shop, but his action was not for any profit but to create a sense of fear amongst the Hindus, who will soon have to vacate their long lived houses, well playing jobs or business and will have to move out to place they have never heard about and hoor they are going to reach there and which ever will they will do at the unknown end unfriendly places with nothing to help and they all have to start from a scratch in an atmosphere of despair uncertainty hunger and rivalry coupled with the Great and caprice. Sulakshmi said that her father was told by Muslim colleague of him that in many mosque aerie the land Namaazis (those who pray) are being told not to show any mercy to the feeling Hindus and not to left them carry their precious wares ever if they have to be looted or killed, but the new nation of pure is laws (Pakistan) should retain its wealth and Hindus should not be allowed to carry it away he further said but there is large body of honest and human musalmaan who are volunteering to ensure that these who migrate should be safe and be provided all help, so they carry a good will for the people of Pakistan, but unfortunately mostly the Satan and evil prevails. She went away and in few minutes returned with a glass of hot tea and a glass of water, she handed over the glass of water first and then gave him the tea, which he sipped absent unkindly Sulakshmi kept sitting there, until he had dozed off and was snoring. She got up and went to the kitchen where she narrated the episode to Kunti and Amrit who also because very sad Kunti said that she can't understand why this partition has been agreed upon by the leaders, without knowing the opinions and feelings of the people, she had a very good friends in the school especially Aaliya the most beautiful and intelligent Muslim girls and even her parents were noble and love able people, Aaliya's mother always made her to eat something or the other whenever she went to Aaliya's house and her brother Jubair was very handsome and if he were not a Muslim, I would have to sure married him, Amrit said most of the people whether Hindus or Muslim are good and behave socially very well and take pains for each other without considering the religion, they share their food and festivals of course marriages between common Hindus and Muslims are unheard, both the religion teach compassion charity and humanity and faith in the God and urge it followers to be honest and morally strong and help those who are in distress and she is unable to comparehend the necessity of partition, so that the people should have a new set of rulers, who do not understand people whom they want rule, so that their greed for power is stated and they could claim for posterity that the, got the people got freedom from the British Rule, even at lie great cost of partition. It has been truly said that all leaders whether Religious political, social or financial always treat people as puppets whome they make dance to their personal tune by the late evening both Lekh Raj and Brij Bhan had come and all the men of the house were sitting in the veranda. Purshottam was seated on the wooden cot, Ram Payari was sitting near him on the cot itself Lekh Raj, Bhaagmal and Brij Bhan was seated on the ground, Lekh Raj was saying that he has heard a rumour that in a village near Pasrur mostly populated by Muslim weavers, have been burnt, with about hundred people including children have been burnt alive and the rest of people have fled the village for safety, a heavy police force mostly comprising of Hindus have been deputed to surround the burnt village and two Hindus have been arrested to protest the burning of the village and in action of police, everyone in Pasrur whether he is Muslim, Sikh or Hindus shaken and is very apprehensive of strong retaliation and oppression, daily supplies of milk, bread have vanished from the market, partition is causing a mortal fear in the mind of everyone even the officers of the Government are perplexed and have lost the propose of Government and are looking for their and their family's safety as the most of them know that the divided government will not be able to provide safety or protection to the million of people on the moov, Brij Bhan said today the SDM (Sub Division Magistrate) Mr. Kennedy Bruttan Anglo Indian Chrirstian called the meeting of all the Hindus staff in which Mr. Waqaruddin Tehsildaar was invited, Mr. Brutt said that any Hindu who is migrating once the partition is announced can ask for his immediate, release and transfer, one condition is that he must handover all the papers and property under his charges, he must also return and deposit all Government money with him and he should provide a forward address a joining periods of only five days will be allowed and no transfer allowance or travelling expenses can be claimed and paid, they are free to put in their transfer request today itself and they will be relieved as soon as they handed over the charge and have been relieved and I have to join at Rohtak by next few days, but before 9th June 1947 and I have been given the option to migrate or stay and everyone has opted to migrate to "to be created Pakistan" I have been informed by an ex-serviceman, whose son is an army officers posted at Peshawar that Army is likely to be deployed to ensure safe transist of people in sensive areas, but there is difference of opinion among the top Generals and the Government the Generals insit on the modalities of the division of forces before the partition is formally announced, so that the forces personnel know their alligence and their masters whosoever they are The British Vioceroy in Council has assured the Generals that they will be communicated the division of forces within forty eight hours. Further all the Government records especially the land revenue records are being kept in steel trunks to be stored at a very high safe place, so there can not be put on the fire or destroyed and the Government is sized of the reality of large scale arson and looting and rioting, but as yet has no firm plans to meet the situation likely to be caused by the announcement of partition and its after math.

Suddenly there was very loud and hard knock at the outer door, Lekh Raj got up and went to open the door closely flowed by Brij Bhan, when Lekh Raj opened the door, he saw two well built up and strong men standing at the door who both had a latthi (Bamboo Stalk) in their hand, they both said Ram Ram in unison and asked is Lala Purshottam Lal was at home as they want to have a urgent talk with the Lala Jee, Brij Bhan asked him their names and where from they had come and what kind of business they have with Lal Purshottam, who is his father.

The men outside said they are Taakan Dass and Lokan Lal and they are the distant relatives of Purshottam lal and they are from Sukh pura village, Brij Bhan told them to wait there and told Lekh Raj to go and tell the father these gentleman, Lekh Raj said Yes he will go and tell his father and he shall get back with whatever his father said.

Soon Purshottam Lal came to the door and asked the callers to come in they were taken to the veranda and made to sit, Bhaagmal was asked to bring water for them and Purshottam Lal asked if they will have something to eat, or will they have dinner the callers said they had their dinner and they shall be happy to have some tea if it were not very inconvenient, Bhaagmal brought water and was asked to arrange for tea, at this time Lekh Raj and Brij Bhan said they all will have tea.

Lokan Lal said Lala Jee I have come to inform you the conditions before the partition are becoming very disturbing and six women of which two are young girls have been abducted and three houses of very poor Hindus have been burnt, people of the villages are very very afraid of further looting abduction and destruction they have met the police Inspector who is in charge of the village he is Hindus gentlemen, but he has expressed his inability to help in the matter as he is very much certain that his help at this time will further aggravate the situation so we have come to Lala Jee, so he leads the villagers when we meet the police kaptaan (police superintendent) so that the police provides us some protection from the rioters and the looters till we migrate to New India. Topan Dass said Lala Jee the people of Sukhpura have a lot of good will and respect for you and they pray and hope that you will lead them. We can return to own village only if we get your consent to lead the people, hearing them Purshottam Lal he will lead the people of village of Kaaptaan as they have reposed a great faith in him. But please ask all the people not to come here and they shall assemble peacefully before the offers of Kaptaan, but no one should carry arms not even the laathi or stones. We meet at nine in the morning now if you want to stay for the night, the arrangement will be made, both the callers said no they must leave now since Lala Jee has been kind in accepting their request, they will go and inform the people in the village, who will be waiting for their return back very eagerly and then they left.

In the given times and circumstances of lingering fear and total uncertainty rumours provided substance to survival and survival was the most important thing to be yearned for, everyone wanted be survive, whether Hindus, Sikh or Muslim and Chrisitian every one was working and planning for survival only and was willing to pay for

Its, if it was money, one was ready with the money to buy the guarantee for survival even within new risks or doubts if it was property that can ensure survival people were ready to forgo the property, if the survival seemed a possibility, did not seem important to buy survival people were not bothered if survival was obtained through dishonest characters, but the most sought after was the honour of woman against which the gooms were ready to promise and assure survival and safe passage across the borders to be established, but such painful and degrading decision were not very rare or uncommon.

Next morning when Brij Bhan and Lekh Raj went to the market to buy vegetables, grocery and fruits, the market was closed on ascertaining it was found that Ghasita Halwai and his family had been murdered and in protest all the shopkeepers whether Muslims or Hindus closed their shutters, though the shopkeepers were not allowed to sit in protestr before the office of Deputy Commissioner or the SSP all the theli walas (stand cart owners) were asked to move away from the market. Both the brother went to the Subzi Mandi, some distance away where rumours were rife that in the areas which were to become the part of New India many Muslim have been butchered, looted and forced to migrate to, to be created Pakistan and the army has been called in those area to stop loot and arson the other rumour which was a very rife that the Deputy Commissioner of Multan, a Christian has been shot at and being in serious condition has been shifted to Lahore and at Lahore a Muslim Tehsildaar has been killed in his office and in Rawalpindi a Hospital has been burnt partially and that due to fire about ten people died. Both the brothers brought whatever vegetables and fruit and some groceries and walked back to their home, vegetables, fruit and grocery were sent to the kitchen and both of them went to the room of their father and told him about all the rumours they had heard and the killing of Ghasita Halwai and closure of the market Purshottam Lal asked Brij Bhan if he has brought his news posting order, to which Brij Bhan said, he has the order with him then his father told him to proceed to Rohtak at the earliest, but before that he must send a telegram to Bhanna Ram about his visit to Rohtak and he should stay with him at his village Dobh, as it has no Muslim population, join his duties at Rohtak and try and get a deserted house allotted to him, even of he has to pay some gratification once the arrangement for their transportation and safe journey are finalised as he is working seriously with some reliable people and have committed to pay upto rupees three hundred for safety and security and another three hundred rupee for the proper transportation and in every likely hood they will settle at Lahali village some five miles away from the Rohtak it is likely that about three hundred Muslims have shifted or in the process of migration to be created Pakistan by this 31st May 1947 let us hope everything goes as planned.

On hearing his father Bhaagmal said yes I have been to Lahali once it is a good village but most of the houses or not puuca and many of its men are in the Indian army or Punjab police, the land is fertile and irrigated and it also have a Canal Rest House and the village is situated on the main Rohtak-Bhiwani Road and it will be convenient to all of us if we can have a bi cycles, even the boys can go to the school at village Lalahi and we can build a new house at Lalahi after sometime of we find it convenient and suitable.

The lunch was served in the veranda everyone was eating and brooding, suddenly there was a big noise outside the house, Lekh Raj got up and opened the door a slogan shouting procession of mainly made up Sikhs was shouting against the police Kaplaan and the DC on enquiry is was found that the main Granthi (head Priest) of Gurudawara has been murdered in the premises of Gurudawara and the police has not been able to arrest murderer who were doubted to be a Muslim and in the nearby village a Molvi of the Masjid(Priest of Mosque) has been severely beaten, soon many Hindus and Muslim joined the slogan shouting procession which was headed towards the house of the DC Horse mounted police was keeping a tight vigil over the procession lest it goes berserk. Lekh Raj narrates everything he had heard or had been told by one the other man. He further found that the situation is getting bad with every passing day and safety and see unity of the people is under great challenge and what good or bad turn the situation and it will take no body knows and it seems that even the Government does not understand the exact import of the situation and it does not seems to have a definite plan to meet the situation squarely so as to ensure the safety of the life and property of the people it Governor and the political leaders of all hues are ensuring that they gets the maximum benefits from the situation and every policeman seems to mislead the public at large to believe in a make believe story and even the Viceroy General has lost interest and control of the Provencial Government and the police is finding itself as helpless and and have resigned themselve to the unpredictable situation and lack the will and direction to act effectively the worst is people who are being guided by greed and self serve and their total surrender before the situation.

On 30th MAY 1947, an official notification is

The Gazette Extraordinary of India duly signed and approved by the British Viceroy in Council on behalf of the Crown of the British Empire that the sub continent of India will become Independent Nation, through it will be bifurcated into two nations of India and Pakistan. The division has been approved by the Crown Congress and Muslim league, the existing territories of the state of Bengal Sind and Punjab will be divided on the basis of majority on religious basis the Muslim are as being remaining in India territories have the option of choosing their nation of choice as agreed upon by the Congress led by Mahatma Gandhi and Muslim League led by Mohammed Jirrah. But Hindus will have to vacate territories which are predominately Muslim Independence for Pakistan will be effective from 14th August 1947 and for India it will be 15th August 1947. The Government will try to ensure safe transit and passage to every recoiling man, women or child and even the pet animals. The division of assets will be worked out to the satisfaction of both the parties and the British Government commonly known as the Government of India will remain in control and command till such times as and when the both countries have their own effective Government people need not panic or break any law or take law in their hands, arson rioting and looting will be severely dealt with and punished. The notification started a rumour mill and fear distress and mental turmoil ruled people had no exact information or knowledge about the circumstances and the course of action they had to follow.

On 31st May there was large scale arson rioting, looting in Gujran wala Town and Okara, in which it was reported that about 500 people had been massacred mostly women and children, the Government called in the Army to quell the rioters, but as this contingent of the Army was commanded by a Muslim officer, it was not very effective and rioting it continued for next three days, when people started fleeing without any possessions and directions.

They were trying to run for safety like manic, but the new Indian Borders were miles away and there was no merciful or helpful villages on the way at least ten percent of the fleeing people could not survive and reach at any point or place of safely, for there probably God was on a long vacations.

Parshuttam Lal told Brij Bhan to go and send telegram to Bhanna Ram, about his arrival at Rohtak on 3rd June 1947 by Punjab Mail, and told him to make preparation to move and seek direction to Dobh village from Bhaagmal, of course he can always find his way to the Revenue office at Rohtak, join his service and arrange for allotment of some Evacuee property preferably a house in the centre of the town, as there should be plenty available Brij Bhan went to the telegraph office and sent a telegraph to Bhanna Ram informing about his arrival at Rohtak by Punjab mail, while he decided to go to the railway station to know about the position of rail service. He found that Punjab mail was running late every day on an average of three hrs, on the railway station he saw a big and strong contingents of Army soldiers on enquiry it was found that they were headed for Ambala and Kernal. A police man came and asked him if has a rail ticket, and if he was not travelling then he should leave the railway station and go home because soon a curfew will be imposed in the area around the railway station on hearing the police man, he hurried back towards his home. on his way he bought some vegetables and fruits and some salt and sugar as he felt if curfew is clamped, nothing will be available, he went to the house placed his purchases in the veranda and asked Kaka to go and fetch a jug from the kitchen, he went back to market to a halwai to give him three seer of milk unsweet, and aadha (half) seer jalebis, paid for his purchases and rushed back to home, once inside the home, he heaved a sigh of relief and told Kaka to go and bring some water for him to drink and ask someone in the kitchen to get him some tea and he went into the room of his father where his mother and two sons were also sitting he asked of them if they need some tea, except for Ram payari every one said that he will take some tea, he sat down and told them everything that he has found on the road and asked everybody not to venture to the road without confirming and making sure about a curfew being clamped his father asked him that how will he catch the train if the curfew is imposed, to this he replied that he will manage to sneak some way but he will not be able to carry any luggage even his clothes bag as he may have to run at place and times but he will keep a strict vigil on the situation and see as to what best can be accomplished. Since they had nothing to do, so they kept setting there and chatted wish to kill the time, Ram payari got up and went to the kitchen and told his bahu's (daughter in law) to cook only one vegetable as vegetables are not freely available anymore and also to ensure that they do not run-out of anything in the kitchen and they should keep her informed if they need anything, but keep the wish as small as possible in the evening Naib.

Subedar Madan Lal a friend of Lekh Raj came, he was asked to sit down and was offered tea or sharabat which he refused and said that he has only come to meet his friend whom he has not met for a long while, as he has been asked to join his duties at Firozpur immediately and he will board Punjab Mail, as the day trains have been suspended or cancelled to meet the shortage of coal and railway staff. Since he had some spare time he thought he will go and find about his friend.

Lekh Raj told him that he is on leave these days, so as to be with the family on hearing this Madan Lal heaved a deep sigh, that is the biggest advantages of civil service, but if you are in the Army, you hardly have any choice and you may be away from your family for a very long period and you can be of no use to your family in case of their need or difficulty, this is what has actually happened, he had hardly met his family for only five days after two years and has been asked to report back for duty, if you do not obey the orders you may be discharged without pension. When he was told the proposed visit of Lekh Raj to Rohtak by Punjab Mail, and possible curfew. He said you need not to worry as he will ask his Haveldaar (corporal) Joga Ram to come and escort him to the railway station, Joga Ram will come in complete Military Uniform and accompany Brij Bhan to the Railway station, thus he will not be stopped or checked, Kaka brought tea for Madan Lal with some snacks, which he took and thanked and left.

Dinner was served, everyone had his food, since Lekh Raj and Brij Bhan did not wish to go on the main road, they both come out of their home, and lighted cigarettes and puffed on it, the road was deep silent and there was no movement on the road. They came back in to the house, their beds were already spread in veranda, they wait on lay on their bed. Bhaagmal, went to his room, had a bath, put on his tehmaht and bundi, came back to the verandas and sat on his bed, crossed leg, his hands folded in prayer, he closed his eye and started praying, he was mumbling slowly.

God, I am your serf in your prayer.
God, I am your slave, happy to be slave.
God, I am your servant and you pay me well.
God, I always look up to your for benevolence.
God, Have mercy on me be merciful.
God, you are always merciful, have mercy.
God, you always take pity on your slave.
God, I am a slave please take pity   on your slave, God
I am your slave.
God, I am poor and impure.
But you are wealthfull and pure
God, please make me wealthy and pure.
God, you are very great
God, I am very ungreatfull
God please help and make me greatful
God, you are here, there and everywhere
God, make me your devotee forever
God, you are complete
God, I am incomplete, make me near complete
God, your decide, design and dispense
God let me live happily with your dispensation only
God you are my Father, my mother

God let me be your son your good son
God I am your serf in your prayer

For the next two days no un towered occurrence
happened at the house, and as no one ventured out of the
house, and nobody from the outside came hence there was
no good or bad news, there was nothing to talk about excerpt
to laze away, and the ladies were mostly busy packing the
things which should be and could be taken along when
travelling to new land which did not seems to perceived as
friendly or comfortable and they had no idea non what so
ever, as to how the thing and life there will be every man
and women was subdued by a lurking fear of the unknown
and hypothecating and visualising the unfathomable.

On second June 1947 at seven in the evening havildar
Joga Ram knocked on the door of the house and was allowed
in and asked to sit down and offered food, tea or sherbet,
whatever he wished to have, he declined every offer and
said let Brij Bhan accompany him to railway station, but he
should not carry and heavy luggage or more than two small
packages, Brij Bhan went to the guest room where his wife
Amrit was there, he embraced her briefly and consoled her
that the God will take good care of him, and. She should
remain calm and happy and pray, to the God for his and
her welfare and came out, went to his father's room, where
his mother and two brothers were also sitting touched the
feet of his parents and hugged his brothers and came to the
veranda, to meet both his sister in law who had came and
the kids were, there he blessed the kids and said Namaskaar
(an Indian form of salutation) took two bags and put them
on his shoulder signalled havildar Joga Ram to move, Joga
Ram took one bag from him and they both came out of
the house and both walked towards the railway station,

nobody on the way checked or stopped them. When they reached the railway station, Brij Bhan went and bought a ticket for Rohtak and came to know that train was running late by one hour, they went to the platform, Brij Bhan took one cigarette and offered one to Joga Ram, who took one, they lighted their cigarette, Joga Ram asked him to move to the far end of the platform where a military coach will come, Brij Bhan said let us have a tea before I get into the train, both went to tea stall, asked for tea, were given tea, sipped their tea and both lighted another cigarette, and then moved to the far end of the platform, after a very long wait the train chugged in, when it halted Joga Ram went to the last but one coach which was indeed a military coach on the door of the coach a Naik (A senior solider) was starting at gaunt Joga Ram for his attention and asked him to take Brij Bhan in, Brij Bhan went into the all packed compartment, wave to Joga Ram and soon train started moving out then it accelerated its speed and Joga Ram could not be seen anymore, when the train had left Joga Ram walked back to the house of Brij Bhan to inform the parents of traveller that he has boarded the train safely was offered tea, but he declined and said fare well and left. Ram Payari loudly thanked the God and prayed for the safety of everyone.

When the train reached Firozpur, the name of Brij Bhan was shouted, he peeped out of the window as to who was calling his name at an unknown place there he saw Naib Subedar Madan Lal was shouting there at the platform, Madan Lal asked a soldier who was looking out the window to take care of him and shoved a packet of samosas in the hand of Brij Bhan the train started moving and was soon out of railway platform, there were four samosas in the packet, Brij Bhan gave one samosa to the soldier who identified himself as Kallu Ram and was headed to his new place of posting at Bhatinda, a burily man who identified himself as Subedar Bhai Ram was also going to Bhatinda his new place of posting, a samosa was given to him, he asked Brij Bhan how come he was in a military coach, in reply he said it was Naib Subedar Madan Lal who arranged it and was asked but he had been posted at Firozpur only and was told it was Madan Lal who had brought these samosas for him at Firozpur only. The fourth samosa was given to Havildahr Bhoje Ram, Brij Bhan was offered a seat, he sat there and told them he was headed to Rohtak and is clerk with the Revenue department and he has been transfered there and he is to join there, but his family was still in Jhang facing the challenges and turbulences of the partition and the fear of the unknown. Subedar Bhai Ram said the Government is ruining India and politicians out of greed are feeding the Government with its ill-thought plan of partition and in spite of the Army, millions of people are `going to die not because the God want them to die, but it is politicians who have ordained, planned and organised their untimely and most painful death, I being in the Army may live and if I lose my family will I live to bear their lose people always presume being an Army man I should have a high degree of endurances but that endurance is only against the enemy alone and not against the loss of near and dear ones, but no one want to accept this truth sitting nearby the Havildar Alme Ram, the British were for sure are very cunning but they always cared for sentiments of the Indian Army men, but now these Kale Angrez whether in new India or to be created Pakistan do not care a forth for any one especially not for any Army man as they think that Army men should be above human sentiments and feeling and they should be only trigger happy even if they have to fire at their Kins Clans, friends or family, and he has heard a rumours that the Muslim contigeut of Army Soldiers based at Karachi have refused to fire at the looting goons who happened to be Muslims and were looting Hindus, soldiers have killed many women in a fleeing caravan made up solely of Muslim under the present Government which is under the influence of Congress and the League no Muslim or Hindu is safe in his house, his village, his town, his country. God save us from these greedy politicians, but I can only say that humanity just cannot die, but for a temporary change and foolish ideas. Let us pray to the God to be kind and make people see reason and religion of humanity. He said he overhead a message between the DC of Multan and the DC of Mianwali on his wireless set that there was large scale arson and looting and Hindus were being massacred and women being raped before their husbands, brothers, father and sons and the local police has not acted impartially and the Army is being called in to restore confidence, law and order but not to crush the looters and the goon the train reached Bhatinda for coal had a very long stop at Bhatinda for onward journey to Delhi. When it reached Julana it was almost morning it meant that the train was running late by at least three hours, he started peeping out of the train, the compartment was almost empty as most of the Army men had de boarded at Mukelsar, when he was near Narwana, he could see in distance a large fire raging, as if the whole village has been put or fire and this entwined around Jind and Julana and beyond it. The train reached Rohtak five hours late he got down on the platform, it was filled with people waiting for train which would take them up to Firozpur, they all were Muslim who were headed to be created Pakistan the land of the Pak, The pure with all their impurities of body and mind, he felt agonized, depressed and distressed, but he did not care as he was in the same tired mess hoping against hope for a good news from home and lot of peace though he will miss his friends mainly the Muslims who were good people and good friend, but he has no role in this pre dictament and horrible atmosphere which was born out of greed and malice of powerful politicians weather Hindu or Muslim people like him never counted in the scheme of things, which were devised, designed and dispensed by those people who were privileged and always enjoyed privileges at the cost of poor who willingly paid the price for the power they enjoyed and possessed, he was so much engrossed in the thought that he jumped when Bhanna Ram tapped on his shoulder, he recognised Bhanna Ram with some effort and then hugged him, pleasantries over, Bhanna Ram took one of his bag and took him to a tea stall, where they both had tea and smoked, after they came out of the Railway Station, Bhanna Ram took him to his mule cart and told him that they will go to village, he will have his bath and change, have his breakfast, after that he will be given a bi-cycle and lunch pack and he can be in his office by eleven o'clock, Brij Bhan did not object and went with the plan, when they reached home in the village Bhanna Ram shouted for Moola and Phoola they came running and touched the feet of Brij Bhan, they look his bag and entered the house, where Todomai was standing with folded hands, he was taken to a room and shown the bathroom, where he can take bath, he brush and had his bath, changed into fresh clothes soon Mool Chand brought his breakfast, the usual daliya, which he ate without a word and was told that Bhaagmal will back soon with the bi-cycle and his lunch will also be ready before he left, is Bhanna Ramhad brought the bi-cycle and he explained the route to his office and telegraph office from where he should send the telegraph to his father Brij Bhan took the lunch pack and the bicycle and started for the town, the road was not metteled but had few pot holes, but was narrow, he kept on cycling till he reached the start of the town, there he stopped and asked for directions for the Telegraph office, he soon was at the Telegraph office, took a form and filled it and handed it over to be Telegraphed, paid the price for the wire and sought direction to the revenue office, when he reached the Tehsil (revenue office) he took the bicycle inside the building, put it in a corner and locked it he looked for the room of head clerk, located it and went in said Namaste to a burly man seated on a chair across a big table on which many files were stacked and paper were lying, the burly man asked him his purpose of visit, Brij Bhan told him that he had come from Jhang on transfer and kept his order before the burly man, who looked up and said, good please sit down and I shall see if he has received the copy of his transfer order, he shuffled a bunch of papers, but did not see the copy of his transfer order, so he shall have to wait, while he will talk to the Tehsildaar if he is in his office and if he allows, he will be allowed to join otherwise he will have to wait till such times his transfer order copy is received here, the man got up from his seat and went towards the office of Tehsildaar, after five minutes, he came out and asked Brij Bhan to accompany him to the Tehsildaar Sahib, both went to the office of Tehsildaar Brij Bhan folded his hand and politely said Namaste, which was duly acknowledge and though copy of his transfer order has not been received in this office, but since he realised the ground realities of these troubled time he is allowing him to join, but his pay will be released only after his transfer orders are received and the head clerk was asked to complete the necessary paper work and let the man join and assign him work, they both came back t o the office of head clerk, a tea was asked for and papers were signed and work was assigned to Brij Bhan and he was asked to go and sit in the adjacent room and start going through the files and papers lying stacked on the table and he should report to the Head Clerk Shoor Sain Saini at four in the evening. In the evening when Brij Bhan reported to Mr. Saini, he was asked to sit down and was asked as to where he is staying and what are the arrangements he has made for his meals, he said that he is stalking with an acquaintances at Dobh and has no problems with his meals, Mr. Saini told him to be careful and cautions as he is new to the place and danger is lurking in the air, and he should not carry lot of money with him as the goons are stalking people to rob them off all valuable and he should leave at the earliest to reach the village before it is dark and if he could come early in the morning may be by eight, he shall allow him to leave by four in the evening, and now he can leave, he went to his office room, cleared the table, brought out his bicycle and came out of Tehsil gate, two man clad in white Khaadi (handmade cotton cloth) kurta, pazama, accosted him and introduced them as leaders of the Congress party, and asked him if he needed their help in any manner, as soon many people like him from the West Punjab will be storming this town and with all kind of help from local people like them and sure they have a direct link with Mr. Alferd Bornto the Deputy commissioner Rohtak and in all likely hood the DC, will be acting as Custodian of Evacuee property left by the migrating Muslims, whom there party is helping them of course for a token fee, but there is and no large scale looting may be there is some pilfering with few wealthy families and since he is new to the town and does not have a house may be he was to bring his family here because of worst law and in order situation in the major parts of Punjab which will for sure go to Pakistan, they can have a house allotted to him by the Custodian of Evacuee property and for this he will have to put in an application and they will get it granted and if he cooperates with them in small ways they can be an asset for him in these perturbed time, but of course the country will be governed by the Congress and its members Brij Bhan thanked them and assured them that he will put in his application for the allotment of a house, once he selects the house and he started to walk with Bicycle in one hand towards the Bhiwani road, the road was deserted he could not see any activity and only one or two people on the road. Then he came to crossing and asked as to what was this area, he was told that on his left hand was Killa mostly occupied by Muslim, but now deserted and straight was Bhiwani stand and Lal Masjid again having been deserted by the Muslim population, he took a left turn and entered the Killa through a big and heavy iron gate one part of which was lying on the ground, he went straight and saw a lane which was upward gradient, he went in to the lane, he did not see a man only a buffalo tied with chain squatting on the ground, he saw a pig on his right hand side but it was licking a fierce looking dog which sat on the door, he went ahead and on his left side, he saw a gate of the house open and unlocked, he went into the open door and into the house, no one was there, but he could see broken cots, glass bottles and other useless things, it was double storey pucca house having two rooms veranda, kitchen, toilet and a court yard, he locked the house again, on the door of the house he saw a name plate which read Waquar Mohd. 333 Killa he came out of house, he had made up his mind, he rode the bicycle and paddled fast in less than twenty minutes. He was in the village Dobh and into the house of Bhanna Ram, Moola and Phoola came, saluted him, Moola went away to come back with a glass of water. Soon Todomai came with a glass of tea and some snacks, which he took and sipped the tea and murmured the thanks, after that he went to his allotted room, changed clothes and came to sit in the veranda, after about an hour Bhanna Ram came and sat there and asked him, how did the things in the office were, he told him whatever had transpired about the house he had seen in the town and his desire to get the house allotted to him, on hearing him Bhanna Ram said that he will come with him tomorrow to the town and then decide after seeing the locality and the house soon dinner was served, both ate in silence, and came out of the house. He lighted a cigarette and Bhanna Ram lighted his beeri, walked for some distance and walked back to house, Brij Bhan went to his allotted room and slept like a log, he woke up at four in the morning, Bhanna Ramand Todamai were also up, tea was brought for him, he sipped, went to a toilet, had a bath and was ready, breakfast was served by seven. Both were ready to leave, a packet of lunch was given, and they paddled the cycle by turns and reached the town Bhanna Ram was shown the house and locality, Bhanna Ram approved of the locality and liked the house and told him that he will go to the Mandi (whole sale market) to attend to some work and then go back to the village, and he can keep the bicycle and return to the village after his office hours, they parted and went their ways

Ram Pyari was sitting beside her husband and asking him to give her a date by which they shall have to move so that she can plan the use of vegetable, daals (pulses) etc. And to find out if more grocery and rice can be purchased if required, Purshottam Lal said as yet he has not made a firm plan of movement, may be by tomorrow, he will have a plan ready as by this evening, he will receive the supply of arms and ammunition and suaas (ice-picks) and the confirmation of some reliable transport which can take them safely to Rohtak and Dobh. Lekh Raj said that he can take them on 7th June Night, he has said that he is also arranging an escort in military uniform of course it will cost little more money, but it will be worth and I had a talk with the Bhootia Baba and he has said he will be there at two hours notice, Bhaagmal said that he has deposited the four trunks in the safe vault room of the Imperial Bank with a forwarding address Care of Bhanna Ramat Dobh- Rohtak, but nobody is sure of safety on any road, as many areas of Bannu, Kohaat, Mianwali, Peshawar, Abbotabad, Karachi, Mzzaffer garh and Multan and especially Lahore and Rawalpindi are seeing lot of migration to the part of New India and cattle Trains are being used to ferry people to the new territory, but most of the trains are being stopped and looted, women are being kidnapped, abducted and raped and some of women have been raped before their fathers, brothers and sons. Most of whom have been maimed and tortured many kids have been snatched from their mothers, and many pregnanent women had been forced to abort, the similar news is coming from Ambala, Kernal, Jakhal, Panipat, Merrut and Delhi. But all these news are based on unfounded rumours and the Government is keeping a studied silence, most of the news are being broadcasted on B.B.C.

RSS is finding itself handicapped as almost every one of its worker is busy in ensuring the safety of himself and his family and is no way a match for organised mob of Muslim goons, who in hoards are looting and killing the people and defiling women and abducting young girls, there is total chaos all over India and the Government has lost all control and command and the will to act it seems that the admistration has surrendered before the goons and is allowing them a complete field day, who dies or suffer do not seems to be of the concern of the Government any more.

After reaching the office Brij Bhan wrote an application for the allotment of House Number 333 Killa, and submitted it in the office of the Custodian Evacuee property, the dealing assistance told him that it will take some time, some gratification and some recommendations for the allotment to take shape and on enquiry the dealing assistant said recommendation, it can be done by the Congress leaders who met him yesterday and he will be happy to help for a token gift of rupees twenty in cash, Brij Bhan paid him the required asked for gift and told him to get the recommendation done, as he does not know how to contact those Congress leaders. when he was back to office he sat at his place and completed the work assigned to him and went to the records room, he brought out the locality wise property details register and looked for Killa, when he found House Number 333, he noted the details, the house was owned by Mohammad Yunus photographer by occupation, 48 year old, born at Rohtak only. The property was registered in the joint name of Hasina Bibi and Mohammad yunus, the house measuring one hundred fifty yards, a double storey pucca house built in the year 1944 and at the time of registration was valued at rupees ten thousand. After finding the record he had his lunch at his table only got up fetched some water and gulped it and realised the taste was different and it was not saltier, which he used to take at home and the village, he went out and got two glasses of tea and went to the room of the office of the head clerk, where Shoor Sain sat, he folded his hand in Namaste, Shoor Sain responded with a warm salute and hailed him to sit down, he sat down on the opposite chair and placed the glass of tea before Shoor Sain who immediately took it and started sipping the tea and asked him, has his application been granted, he said he has done whatever was asked of him and he is awaiting for the word to come, Shoor Sain told him not to worry and he will ensure it is granted in next two days for sure, but in the evening he should go to the house and put his lock to it, but he should take Tikan Ram peon with him, he said Tikan Ram will agree to come along with then he will take him with him for sure, as he gives one a sense of security and protection, Shoor Sain called for Tikan Ram and instructed Tikan Ram, to go with Brij Bhan to Killa in the evening and he will be offered some jalebi for his effort but he will have to tell Brij Bhan as to where he can buy the jalebi. In the evening Brij Bhan and Tikan Ram went to Killa and Brij Bhan having purchased the lock at a small shop locked the house and Tikan Ram took him to Babra to buy Jalebi, after taking jalebi's Tikan Ram took him to Bhiwani Road, so that Brij Bhan could go straight to Dobh. After dinner when Bhanna Ram and he came out of the house he told him about locking up of the house and his application for the allotment. Both smoked and walked back to the house. Next day, a peon from the office of Custodian came to him in his office, and asked for Baksheesh (tip) he gave him and asked him his name and was told that his name was Jagbir and he is Dhanak(who beat rice) Brij Bhan went out of his office and went to tea shop, he bought two samosas and two peras (a sweet meal) and went to the room of Shoor Sain, touched his feet and offered him a pera and was told to take a seat, he sat and kept samosas in the table, soon the tea came, they both had tea Shoor Singh said he was happy because he could help a refuge, but soon there are going to be thousands of refugees in this town. whom he will not be able to help in any way and the next kala Angrez Deputy commissioner may take his effort to help refuges otherwise soon a peon from the office of the Deputy commissioner came and asked for Brij Bhan clerk, revenue clerk, when he was directed to a room where he could find the clerk, he went there and said Namaste to the man sitting across the table and said he was Dhola Ram from DC office and the Sahib (DC) had called Brij Bhan the revenue clerk to call on him, immediately, Brij Bhan said he will seek the permission of the head Clerk and accompany him, when he was ushered in to the office of the DC he stood there with folded hands Mr. Alfered Bronto. looked at him and asked him was he Brij Bhan, when he said yes he was asked to sit down and tell the DC about Jhang as a town and the social conditions there.

Brij Bhan said Jhang is distract town and has five Tehsils, an inter collage, two schools, a hospital, railway station on Peshawar-Delhi line, the social conditions were good, sometimes but since the announcement of the partition, the situation have taken an ugly turn, the brotherhood and social relationship between Hindus and Muslim has ceased and there is mismatch in everybody's mind, and arson in which about Sixty Hindus died, a Granthi of a Sikh Gurudawara was killed in the Gurudawara, partial curfew was announced in the town, when he left on 2nd June and since then he has no information, the information which was relayed to this DC on his wireless, the Jhang is on fire, people are trying to get out, three cattle trains have been arranged to evacuate the people to safety and Rohtak town has been assigned to people of Jhang town, the cattle train leave on 5th June1947 and he has been transferred to Jhang as a Deputy commissioner and he will not be in any position to help his family, but if gives him his Jhang address he will try to receive his family left over, and he would be glad to know that he has been allotted the house he had asked for, the meeting over, Brij Bhan came out of the room and saw a booklet lying on the floor, he picked it up and read it on the front page it said for Christian Deputy Commissioners only- Confidential made Brij Bhan was very curious about the contents of the booklet, he kept the booklet in his inner pocket and went back to his office, cleared the table and went to the head Clerk room and said to Shoor Sain that he is leaving, he took up his bicycle and came out instead of riding the bicycle he simply walked, when he reached near Lal Masjid he saw a large gathering there, an old man was who was said to be Hazi Azahurddin Moulvi, Masjid Khaas Gohana, was speaking hoarsely I am a Musalmaan a Deen of the allah and pray to Allah to give wisdom to the people whether they are Hindus or Muslims, because they do not realise that all Muslims in India, had Hindu ancestors. The Turk, Moughal, Persian, Muslims who came as mercenary soldiers, abducted and married Hindu women here and produced children, those children grew up married, but the women whom they married were from the same kind of Hindu women, it was about hundred year back but now every Muslim man and women are of Hindu origin and ancestry and even if the Pakistan is created it will not be Pak. Or pure and it is being built on the blood of innocent Hindus and Muslims and this seed of hatred sowed by the politicians will yield only the harvest of greater hatred and more women will be killed, raped and shamed both by the Hindus and Muslims, who so ever gets an opportunity in the name of dignity and religion and a foolish nationalision, let Allah have mercy, Amen, Amen and he stopped speaking and want into the masjid. People gathered there dispersed and went about their ways. Brij Bhan rode his bicycle and paddled to the village Dobh.

On the night, of 4th June 1947, at about two in night, there was a big thud, which woke up Purshottam Lal, he came out and found that his houses main door has been pulled apart and down, and about seven to ten men, with covered face fully armed had raided the house, a tall well built man with a strong built up pointed his pistol at him and shouted let every man of house out and tell us where is your gold stocked and of the women are wearing any jewellery it should be brought out at once, and the other man advanced in a threatening posture Purshottam Lal was full of fear, he shouted for Lekh Raj and Bhaagmal, both came out of their room followed by their wives, the noise also woke up the kids, who came out to see as to what was happening at this hour of night, the women were asked to hand over the jewellery they were wearing. The leader saw Nikko hurried to her and picked up her and ran on to his mule and ran away, the other men followed the leader jumped on their mules, by now Lekh Raj was ready with his pistol, he shot without a particular target or aim, a man fell from the fire of his pistol. The raiders had left two mules, Purshottam Lal asked Bhaagmal to ride a mule, and also rode a mule and spanked the mule to run as fast as it could, they went about two miles but could not trace the raiders, then Purshottam lal took the ride to the house Deputy Commissioner Bhaagmal followed him, when they reached the house of deputy commissioner, the door was closed and sentry on duty told them they should come only at Ten in the morning, Purshottam Lal told him that it is very serious and urgent that they meet the DC. The man on duty simply refused to budge Bhaagmal aimed his pistol at him and told him to lead them to the room where the DC is sleeping. They were taken there and the sentry knocked at the door, the door opened and DC could see the pistol trotting Bhaagmal and Purshottam Lal with pistol in readiness the DC, could make it out, why did the sentry had to knock at the door. He said in loud noise put down your pistol if you don't intend to shoot me and I shall listen to you for the metter which brought you here in the dead of the night, Purshottam lal narrated the incident, the DC listened in a deep silence, then he spoke, well gentleman you are pained at your loss, not the jewellery which you can buy again, but the loss of the girl. But unfortunately, I cannot help you any, not that I do not want to help you but because my wife and daughter has also been stolen two days back and I could not help and I was unable to trace them, at this given time Muslims have become fan awes and are of the view that this is Pakistan. So Hindus have no business to be here, and any wealth, any property and all young women and girls are here only to satisfy their carnal Lust and the Government has no business to intervene on the behalf of Non-Muslim and the official orders are to show utmost restraint towards the Muslim and direct all energies towards the migratation, so a train is leaving on the night of 5th June and my most sincere advice is to board the train and save whatever you have and head for the safety of New India at all costs, and I am really very sorry that I cannot help you in any way and my name is Pete, but I want to share your agony and anger and convey you my deep sympathy. Bhaagmal paid rupee two to the sentry and said sorry to him and he along with his father turned back, Left the mules there and walked back to their house when they reached home women were weeping and Ram Pyari swooning, it was Sulakshmi the mother of Nikko, who was trying to console everyone, but she started sobbing when he saw the very sad face of Bhaagmal. Parshottam Lal called for Kunti and Amrit and told them to cook food for at least three days, which they will carry tonight only, and every woman should put at least three pairs of clothes and so should the children and men. Sulakshmi brought tea at six in the morning; nobody was sleeping, but was behaving like a mechanical toy. The Bhootia Baba came at seven in the morning. He was informed about the entire happening of the night and he said he knew it and had predicted it, but he was unable to prevent it. He told Purshottam Lal to reach the railway station by seven in the evening, go and occupy the rake near to the railway Engine, as there will be five Army men on the railway engine and he should also send message to as many people as he can and they should also go by this train, Baba promised to meet them at the railway station at the appointed time before the train departed and left.

Purshottam lal and family along with another sixteen families boarded the cattle train at seven, Bhootia Baba reached there before the train chugged off at eight in the night, it was just crawling, all the sixteen rakes packed beyond capacity, there were minor scuffle in every rake more space, more comfort, more safety, none of which seemed to be possible, the horse mounted police men were following the train, but as many mule gangs of looters, hounded the train, took away whatever they could lay their hands on and ran off, police did not fire a single shot, except for the pale moon light there was complete darkness everywhere, darkness in everything feeling of the heart.

Bhaagmal was engrossed in his thought that he has become a refugee in hi own nation, because the politicians have refused to understand that every man is rooted in his land, home and his immediate neighbourhood and to uproot him to go and fend for his new home, new land and new neighbourhood as a refused native to become as a REFUGEE, and live with this label and sigma till he dies,

Purshottam Lal, when he boarded the cattle train looked up to the sky and said to the God, as if the God was present and listening, he said oh God, once upon a time you rescued me and sent me to the well from heaven and you have again refused me from the comfort and consolation to become a REFUGEE in an Alien well into no home and wealth and unknown neighbourhood, oh God, be a God only and now do not act as politician.

Brij Bhan was busy in his work at his table on the morning of 5th June1947, when one Tikaya Ram called on him and told him that he has come from Delhi and has been appointed as an office assistant in the office of the custodian of Evacuee property which will be under the control of a Newly Created Department of Rehabilitation for the refugees, and he has been directed to obtain the records of the properties vacated by people who have migrated to the newly created Pakistan, which is yet to take truth officially and legally, but he has to act only as he been directed. Brij Bhan told him that unless he has official instruction in writing he will not be able to give him the records and he took Tikaya Ram to the office of Head Clerk, and introduced him to the Head Clerk and told him as to what he wanted, or hearing Brij Bhan, Shoor Sain said he will talk to the sahib and whatever he decides, it will be done, but the Sahib will came after lunch, on hearing this Tikaya Ram asked the Head Clerk to allow Brij Bhan one hour leave, so that they could get acquainted well, as in the future they will be required to work almost together, Brij Bhan was given off time and he came out of the office and walked towards a Tea Shop at some distance of the Tehsil Office, when they reached the Tea Shop, he asked for two glass of tea, by the time tea came. Tikaya Ram told him that he is from Multan and lives in Delhi with his parents and his two elder brothers and sister are still living in Multan and will soon migrate to Delhi, but he is very apprehensive as he had heard very bad news in many parts of West Punjab, at the office of Viceroy. where Pandit Nehru was a very regular visitor and it was a very common knowledge that Pandit Nehru valued only those who could speak perfect English, support a Neat Suit and support a tie and had his schooling at good school like Eton, Modren, Mary and Jesus Lawrence or Sanawar and had higher education in England to be in power of position all those who studied in Indian Tradition were fit only for Subordinate position. Brij Bhan told him that his family is in Jhang and shall migrate only after the partition is officially announced, Brij Bhan told him that he can share his lunch, which he has brought, Tikaya Ram said he will be thankful to him, as he has not seen a Dhaba (eating place) anywhere, and by the night he will be back to Delhi and once he is permanently transferred to Rohtak, he will be commuting between Rohtak-Delhi, though he will have to spend more than six hours everyday for this and he will start bringing his lunch with him, they both came back to Tehsil, had their food an went to the office of Shoor Sain, on seeing Tikaya Ram the head Clerk said he can get the records only if an official requisition is made by a competent officer, who will have to give a personal guarantee for the safe keeping of the record, and the request should be counter signed by the Deputy Commissioner, Tikaya Ram said thanks to the Head Clerk, Shook hands with Brij Bhan and thanked him for the lunch and left. Brij Bhan want to his seat and started going through the booklet he had found outside the Deputy Commissioner, he read, then all Deputy Commissioner in East Punjab Area, should ensure that the migrating Muslim population is provided the maximum safety and local Hindus should not be allowed to indulge in loot and arson even if the DC has to resort to mass arrests of Hindus suspects especially of people sympathetic to Hindu Mahasabha, RSS and Sanatan Dharam Sabha and Arya Samaj, no mosque should be left to volunteers of Congress, Army should not be deployed unless situation so demands and if some Muslim comes for any kind of help he should be extended swift help without any reservation, a special survey of land is to be carried out in all Muslim population villages, a very strict compliance of these instructions is directed and any dereliction will be viewed seriously. P.S. Churehes, Christian and Anglo Indian should be provided special care and attention the cattle train was moving very slow, there was no air, lot of humidity, which caused lot of personal flare-ups, there were no toilets and you cannot de board the train and you dare not venture out in the dark out of fear of the unknown goons, who were trailing everywhere to kill man and, loot and rape if it was a woman, the train took more than eight hours to reach Firozpur a distance of about sixteen miles, the last rake of the Cattle train was detached and about four hundred Refugees were dumped in a place, about which they may not even have heard to lead new life to start from a scratch and perish or survive the ordeal if they were enough strong, physically and mentally. Firozpur was supposed to be First or last Indian town on partition. After about one hour the train moved out of Firozpur and stopped at many places including Aboher, Kotkapura and many people had to de board the train as decided by the police, when the train reached at Bhatinda, two rakes were detached, nobody was being asked to express his opinion in the matter, the tea was being sold at Bhatinda for one Anna, four times more than the usual price, Bhaaggmal wanted to buy some tea but he could not buy any as his pocket has been picked on the rake itself, though he had more money in the inner pocket of his bundi, but he dare not bring it out, nobody had a wink of sleep for the last sixteen hours as there was hardly any space to lie down, after about three hours train started again to stop at Jakhal, where another rake was detached it was dark there and no tea being sold, soon the train moved about two hours later again stopped, it was Tohana, no lights, no tea, a rake was detached, half an hour at Narwana, it was almost morning some volunteers gave water, there was a scramble for water. But only few could have any, a rake was again detached here, when the train left, it had only eight rakes now, it reached Jind in about two hours it was broad day light, every passenger was exhausted, few had swooned and the children were crying, a force of volunteers mainly villagers approached every rake and gave a packet of food to almost everyone. But no water was given, four rake were detached two of them to be attached to a train for Kaithal after about five hours stay, the train again moved, it had only four rake now, soon it stopped in a jungle, after about two hours it again moved and stopped at Kharenti. Where a rake was again detached by now it was five in the evening the train chugged out and reached at Rohtak at eight in the night it had taken about three hours to cover a distance of seven miles every one was asked to de boarded the train. there was a mad rush to de boarded and everyone was pushing his neighbour, whether his family member or a relative, it look Purshottam Lal, Ram Pyari and the other member of the family more than half an hour to get out of the rake. There was no place to squat on the platform no water in the tap, no tea stall open and everyone was relieving himself or herself at where they were, the place had become a living hell and it was amply clear that a Refugee is nothing but a Refuse, who can survive on any kind of refuse. The whole family came out of the platform since Bhaagmal had been to the Rohtak Railway Station on two three occasions he took the family towards the Maal Godam Road and asked them to sit in a lane near the Railway Quarter, and he will go and find out if some food or tea or something to eat. He told his father and brother Lekh Raj to be vigilant as the other refugees may not try and rob them off anything they could lay their hands on. Bhaagmal knew of a Dhaba and a Dharamshalla (an inn) near the Dhaba, when he reached the Dhaba it was closing itself he talked to man who he thought was the owner of Dhaba and asked to have food for about ten people, the man walked away and looked into Caldron and said Daal (linted) will be good only for five people of course they may have Rotti (Pan cake) and some chawal (Rice). Bhaagmal said it will be very kind of him and asked him the price of 40 Rotti's Daal and two plates of Rice, he told it will be rupee fifteen in all and he will also provide him with some achhar and onions. But he will have to bring some utensils for Daal and Rice or he should bring his family here only he will serve the food. Bhaagmal paid the money and said he will be back soon. He entered into near Dharmshala a man was lying on the cot, he woke him and told he and his family of ten people wanted to spend the night in the Dharmshala. The man said he can allow him, but there are no cot and Durries (Bed spread) and he will charge rupee ten for the night because a Refugees like him has enough money with him and he should be spending it for a night sleep after a gruelling cattle train journey and he must be knowing the town to have located this Dharmshalla. Bhaagmal told him that he will go and bring his family and paid him ten rupees. He hurried back to where his family was asked to stay. When he reached there except for his father, everyone was fast asleep on the ground he sobbed silently. This is why they are called refugees and the irony of it is that all these people are Refugees in their own nation, their own country, their own birth land, he restrained his emotions and asked everyone to get up and walk with him, Didu had to be carried on shoulder, soon they were in the Dharmshalla everyone washed his or her face from the small water Tub and sat on the ground, Lekh Raj and Bhaagmal went out to the nearby Dhaba and brought food. Didu also woke up was given food, everybody was hungry, so food was eaten quickly. The used utensils were returned to the Dhaba. The balance of eight roties was saved in a cloth and put in a bag everyone soon went to sleep, Bhaagmal just could not sleep though his eyes were drooping low due to sleep, he crossed his legs and folded his hands and started praying.

Thank you, God, for the kindness.
Thank you, God, for the safety.
Thank you, God, for the food.
Thank you, God, for the ground to sleep.
Thank you, God, for making us good Refugees.
Thank you, God, give us the refugees the succour. We need and deserve.
Thank you, God, for your mercies on all poor refugees.
Thank you, God for the food we would earn.
Thank you, God for keeping us alive.

On the 7th June 1947, Brij Bhan was sitting in his office, reading the second part of the secret book, he was reading.

India has more than 686 princely states, some as small as a ten acre farm, some as big as ten distracts of the Punjab. West Punjab had only few princely states which are predominantly Muslim and ruled by Muslim ruler. But there other in India which are ruled by Muslim rulers who are the friends of the British Empire notably the Nizam of the Hyderabad and Junagadh, who will like to go with to be created Pakistan, though these states cannot accede to Pakistan because of their geography noteably Hyderabad a very big and very rich Muslim state, Junagadh, has some border with the Sind in Pakistan and the most important friend of the British and likely to be friends and collaborator of Congress and the League are Rai Bahadurs, Khan Bahadurs, Rai Sahibs, Nawab Sahibs, Jile Daars, kiledaars and various Knighted Sir, and these important allies of the empire will ensure that people in the India do not harbour ill will for the Empire of course the disgruntled people are always there, so we place the burden of lowering the dissent brought the officers of covouted Indian Civil Services and well educated and mentally English people like collage teachers, lawyers, Government servants in the middle rung who had the fortune of having worked with an English man. Brij Bhan was interrupted in his reading by Tikan Ram and was told that he should present himself before the Tehsildar, he at once got up went to the office of Tehsildaar Mohan Singh asked him was from Jhang now in Pakistan, Brij Bhan said Yes Sir and he was asked to sit down, when he had sat, Mohan Singh told him that a cattle train has brought two rakes of people approximating about seven hundred people, does he has any idea or information about his family having arrived by that cattle train, he replied that he has no information or knowledge as his house in Jhang never had a telephone and even his total locality had no telephone, he was told that he can leave just now to check at the Railway Station and if his father and his family knew where he was staying, he should go there and find out he left the and sought directions to the Railway Station. When he reached the Railway Station he saw a swarm of the people squatting on every rich of available space, he went to the platform it was full and there was no passage to walk, he took two rounds of the platform, but could not locate his family. He came out and took another two round of the Swarm of the people, but did not see his family then he saw a man who he thought was from the same locality. as his family, he went and approached the man and said Ram Ram, the man also said Ram Ram, asked the man was he from Garhi. The man said that no he was not from Garhi and then asked him as to whom he was looking for, he told him that he was looking for his family of Lala Purshottam Lal of Garhi, the man said he did not recognise Lala jee, but he saw a man of Garhi who runs a stationery shop in the main bazaar with about ten people and they were riding a mule cart, for Brij Bhan it was a very heartening news, and he thanked the God profusely in a loud voice and started walking very fast towards Dobh in about forty five minutes he had reached Dobh and he swiftly barged into the house of the Bhaana Ram, he saw all members of his family sitting in the veranda on a Durry (a floor spread), he went and touched the feet of his father and mother, his wife Amrit came and touched his feet and threw a tear on it, then Sulakshami touched his feet, Lekh Raj and Bhaagmal hugged him, Kaka and Didu came and touched his feet, Chotti came and did a Namaste he did not see any sign of Nikko, he went near Sulakshmi and enquired about Nikko, Sulakshmi, was at brink and started weeping very loudly, Kunti went near her and consoled her Todamai brought water, Pyare Lal called Brij Bhan to come and sit with his father, he was told as to what had happened to Nikko and how they were refused any help by the DC and his advise to catch the cattle train on 5th June and now they are here as a bunch of Refuse to be referred as Refugees forever and the irony of fate, but not now the irony of the fate, but irony of greed and cunningness of politician of the Congress and the League who have created a mount of Refuse of fifty, sixty lac people who will be called and known as refugees in their own land and in their own nation

Brij Bhan told his father that he had arranged house in one of the central and better locality of the town, which has been vacated by a Muslims family which has migrated to the land of. So called Pure the Pak, when in the present times and atmosphere no one has remained pure, because the will to Survive to live, lead to greed, caprice and dishonestly to get more and moreof what one does not possess and hopefully the house will be allotted to him soon by the office of Custodian Evacuee property, however he has already put his lock on this house Purshottam Lal said this is a very good news and how soon he can be sure of the allotment,

On the 8th June 1947 the three brothers left for Rohtak at seven in the morning. and they walked to have a look at the likely to be allotted house, when they reached the main road they hailed a mule cart, the coachman said he will charge a anna for the three of them, they were told to get down at the Bhiwani stand as the cart will not go any further, they got down and walked towards the Killa, where the to be allotted house was situated. Brijj Bhan lead them to the house brought out the key to the lock and opened it, they all entered to the house went into every room, the stairs and first roof and the top roof, from the top roof, they could see a big part of the town as the house was about seventy feet high from the main road they had a look at other houses in the neighbourhood the house seemed to be more reasonably good and it seemed to be bigger from their house at Jhung which was only a single storey house, this house was double storey and a big roof and large court yard they did not see any water storage tank or a well they come out of the house locked it and took a round of the lane on which the house was located. But did not find any water well or tank. This was matter of concern as they had no idea as to where from they will get water and how far the source of water was and how they could carry water from a long distance. Brij Bhan was asked to enquire, if there were Bhishtis who could supply water and what was the likely price of water for a month. They started walking towards the tehsil and it was almost nine, Lekh Raj sought directions for the Irrigation office and went on to his office, since the Bank opened only after ten, Bhaagmal went to the office of Brij Bhan, where he was introduced to Shoor Sain who offered tea to both of them, soon Tikaya Ram came and said he also deserves a tea, because he has a very good news for Brij Bhan, saying this he delved deep into his pocket and brought out a folded paper and gave it to Brij Bhan. Brij Bhan opened it eagerly and there it was his formal letter of provisional allotment of house 333 Kila as a requisitioned property at a monthly rent of rupees eight per month. The allotment letter seemed to be an absurd effort by the Government to placate a refuge who had lost his house and has been allowed to live in this foresaken house, whose rightful owners having fled as refugee to find a new home in an unknown and god forsaken land.

Lekh Raj reached his office and presented himself before the office Super intendent. Mr. Dayal Chand Sangwan a study Jat, well built, who told him to sit down and called for peon Ummed Singh a small limping man and asked him to bring two glass of tea, after both had tea, Dayal Chand said you are the new clerk, transferred here from Jhang, but how did you reach here as I gather the whole area of Jhang is facing looting and arson and what not and especially the travelling for Hindus is said to be very unsafe and Punjab mail running upto twelve hours late, when Lekh Raj narrated his travelling experience by a cattle train, the abduction and kidnapping of her thirteen year old niece by Muslim goons, the Refusal of the DC to help and his advice to leave the town at once by a cattle train on fifth night, he told him that one of his elder brother was a clerk in the Revenue Department and had joined his duty here from third of June only and how his family are staying at village Dobh with an acquaintance who is a land lord of the village and is very kind, considerate and helpful person and they have yet to arrange for an accommodation in the town. After hearing Lekh very patiently Dayal Chand said he knew that Government created new thing through planning, developing new vistas, new public welfare, new railways, dams, canals, schools, hospitals and many other. But I never knew or thought the Government also created millions of refugees and refugees in their own nation, own country, own land, but he has heard or has came to knew it only during the past few days he had developed a very strong doubt about the competence of the Government and he is very apprehensive that this Government of the day will be able to really rehabilitate these millions of refugees who have lost their home, hearth, land, friends, families and their God heads and now they have a very collective identification as refused Punjabi, refugee Sindhis and have lost their identity as Indian first, they are refugee first, Punjabi, Sindhi at last.

Dayal Chand said he felt sorry and ashamed, he helped a lot of Muslims to migrate safely to be created Pakistan, he helped them as a man, a human and never thought them Muslims or Pakistani, will look, rape and murders in their to be created country and forget that God has created only man and not Hindus and Muslims and Sikh or Christian, because the religion is the choice of man though you are a refugee I dare not refuse you, your right to be an Indian of greedy politics has been made by the Government of India, which did not realise that the regime, territory and treasury of the Government of India will have to be shared with the Govt. Of Pakistan soon and rich land which will go to Pakistan it will also loose major cantonments, airports and sea ports and what not but greed does not see reasons and repercussions of the greedy decision to self serve the politicians. So Lekh Raj you are welcome here and always let me know if I can be of use to you in manner not only in the official affairs, but also affair outside the office. Lekh Raj wrote down his joining report and handed over to the office Superintendent, who wrote accepted to told him and write an application addressed to the Custodian of Evacuee property for allotment of some requisitioned property and he will get it forwarded by the Executive Engineer. Lekh Raj wrote the application specifying Killa as the preferred locality as it was near to his office and he does not own a bicycle and gave his application to Dayal Chand who said it will be for sure granted, may be at some cost.

Brij Bhan was sitting before the Head Clerk Shoor Sain, when a peon from the office of Deputy Commissioner came and handed over an official letter to the Head Clerk, who read it shortly and asked Brij Bhan to bring some tea, Brij Bhan went out and was soon back with two glasses of tea. He sat on the chair Shoor Sain handed over the letter to him it was regarding his additional duties in the Ration Office which was to register the Refugees for issuance of Ration Cards. Soon he was called into office of Tehsildaar, when he went in he was told to sit, the Tehsildaar Mohan Singh asked him if he could find a refugee who could read and write English and Urdu, such a person should also be able to read Hindi and Gurumukhi, to be able to read application as there is a temporary vacancy for such a person for about four months and he will be paid rupees three per day of work apart from rupees ten per month extra. But this type of man must join his duties very soon and should be ready to take a reading and writing test in English and Urdu.

Bhaagmal went to the bank and learnt that a new agent Mr. Peterson had joined while in the bank he observed that there were no clerk or peon around, he presented his cheque of rupees thirty to Mr. Peterson, he was asked to wait after few minutes his name was called by the Agent, he went and presented himself, Mr. Peterson, counted the money and gave it to him, he counted the money and put it in his pocket and thanked the Agent on an impulse he asked Mr. Peterson can he get some tea for him, Mr. Peterson hesitated somewhat and said he can bring him tea, but he will pay the price of tea Bhaagmal went out and soon returned with two glasses and two big Biscuits, kept the tea and Biscuits on the table pulled a chair and sat opposite the Agent both had their tea without a word Mr. Peterson took out a Chavanni (a four anna coin, quarter of a rupee) and offered it to Bhaagmal, Bhaagmal said tea was his pleasure only and told that he has an offer as clerk with the bank and he is supposed to join on the 1ˢᵗ July 1947, on hearing Brij Bhan Mr. Peterson got up and went into his cabin he brought a file and searched for the copy of an appointment letter, he asked Bhaagmal his name, and when he was told that his name was Bhaagmal of Jhang. Mr. Peterson said, see Mr. Bhaagmal, if it is convenient for you to join immediately he will be very happy as he has no official at present and with prevailing situation in the country and the horrible partition, which is a pain in his neck, he had no hope of any kind of hope until this most foolish adventure of the Government comes to an end, which do not seems to be any distinct possibility in the near future unless Army is called in to quell the arson rioting, wanton killing of women and child, and you Mr. Bhaagmal look to me as a God sent Messiah to me who can elevate some pain, apart from my forced separation from my wife and children about which I am not sure as and when will be united again any soon, so please join your duties tomorrow it and be assured that I will train you very well and you can depend on me for any kind of help, on hearing Mr. Peterson, Bhaagmal said he is a refugee of course in his own nation of birth, but the Government of his own nation has treated him as refugee and thrown him in another corner but please be assured I will report for duty tomorrow as desired by you Bhaagmal came out of Bank and went to Teshil and searched for Brij Bhan, when they both met he told Brij Bhan that he had withdrawn the money, and he will join his duties the next day and now he is going to the Anaaj Mandi and then he will go to Dobh on the way he will buy some vegetables and grocery, when he reached Anaaj Mandi, the first thing he did was to buy two big cotton hand bags to that he could carry his purchases, he bought some pulses and condiments, sugar and tea. Then he bought whatever vegetables and fruits he could buy and walked towards Bhiwani Stand on reaching there he looked for a mule cart headed towards Lalhi or Dobh. He found one and boarded it, he got down at Dobh and paid for it, carried the hand bags and went to Todomai who in turn told him that Bhanna Ramhad already brought the requirements. Todomai told Bhaagmal to wait for some time and she will bring some lunch for him or send Sulakshmi to give some food, Kaka and Didu came and embraced him, he put his hand on their head and patted them, then he went to the room where his father would be and tell him that he will join the bank the next day, Chhoti came told him that mother had brought food for him in the veranda and he sat down and told. Sulakshmi that he will join the bank next day, he started eating his food, while he was eating his food, Bhanna Ram came and sat there Bhaagmmal told Bhanna Ram that he will be joining the bank the next day.

Lekh Raj and Brij Bhan came back at five in the evening, all the male members of the house were sitting together when Kaka brought tea and snacks for everyone, Brij Bhan told his father about allotment of additional work to him in the Rehabilitation Department and the requirement by his office for a man who could read and write Urdu and English and read Hindi and Gurumukhi. It is daily wage job paying rupees three per day and the job is for four months only and it is open only for a refugee, if he thinks he is interested in taking up the job then he should accompany him in the morning to his office, Purshottam Lal said he will think over the matter and let him know his decision in the morning.

Lekh Raj told his father and brothers whatever had happened the office and the information he has got that a full catle train of refugees will arrive tomorrow, but the district administration is not ready to accommodate the new batch of refugees it is rumoured that at least thirty thousand refugees will arrive in this town in next few day refugees from Multan, Muzzaffergarh and Jhang will from the bulk of arrival. The whole rail road is being patrolled by the police and the Army, but arson rioting looting, kidnapping and raping of women is still rampant almost on the entire street of area likely to go to Pakistan the district administration is expecting about ninety- ninety five thousand refugee in the district, but total number of refugee likely to migrate is about four to five lakh people including old, young and adolescents and even infarnts.

The Government is finding itself unequal to the task for instance in Rohtak apart farm space the biggest challenge is arranging for water and toilets unfortunately there are no voluntary organisations that may help the Government in the enamours task of elevating the suffering and hardships of the arriving caravans of refugees, without food and shelter. All schools and colleges are being instructed to let the refugees occupy their premises till such times, the Government can arrange for some viable alternative, sales and registration of land has been suspended till further order.

Next day the three brother left the village by a mule cart, Bhaagmal reported to the bank and joined his duties and was advised by the Agent to apply for a requisitioned property for his acommendation, he wrote the application which was recommended by the Agent and was asked to go and submit it to the office of DC, he did as advised. He was to receive training for at least fifteen days in banking operations, before he could act independently. Purshottam Lal, was given a test in English and Urdu writing, and was found proficient and was given the job, which he accepted and joined instantly. Late in the evening the four men reached the village house and were given water and tea Purshottam told Brij Bhan to scout the Killa locality to find if some cart is available, so that they can shift to the town at the earliest after about a week both Lekh Raj and Bhaagmal were allotted accommodation. Lekh Raj in Salara Mohalla and Bhaagmal in Partaap Mohalla, both the houses were occupied by their allotters, soon the neighbourhood houses were occupied, Brij Bhan was last to occupy the house at Killa with his parents.

One day Sulakshmi told Bhaagmal that she will complete her education, of class eight examination and matriculation exam, Bhaagmal promised to find out the options.

In July Kaka, Didu and Chhoti started going to school, Kaka was to appear for matriculation Examination next session. Didu was to appear for class eight exam and Chotti was to study for ninth class on a Sunday the whole family met at Brij Bhan's house and came to know of the pregnancy of Kunti and Amrit Ram Pyari asked Bhaagmal to try and find about Bhootia Baba, so that she could have grandsons with the blessing of Bhootia Baba.

By now about thirty thousand refugee had landed at Rohtak and some of these shifted to nearby village like Kahni Bansi, Kalanaur, Aanwal, Kahanour, Petwapur, Nigana, where ever they should find a house or land to occoupy and to wait for some announcement by could the Government, the entire refugee population was dependent on distribution of free ration but very irregular and insufficient supply of ration mostly rotten. The prices of all goods of daily use had rocketed up and the Government did not seemed to be concerned, brawls for water and ration were routine and were not being even noticed. Hunger was rife shortage of clothes was very acute and many of the women had only one cloth mostly a Tehmat to cover their selves most of the people defecated where ever they were and sanitation was not of any importance or concern. All refugees lived and behaved as refuse only, with no shames or regret, survival was the only thing that mattered at all.

Bhootia Baba appeared at the office of Brij Bhan because he had a definite knowledge about him and he was not sure as to where the family was staying. Brij Bhan on seeing Baba got up from the seat went near the Baba and touched his feet brought water from the pitcher and offered it to

Baba, Baba had lost one leg and Brij Bhan was surprised, so he asked Baba was told that he was attacked by some Muslims with swords and in an ensued brawl, his leg was wounded it got infected and had to be amputated, he asked Brij Bhan to get him some tea and biscuits and take him to his parents as soon as he could, Brij Bhan went out brought tea and biscuits for Baba and himself. after they had tea, Brij Bhan went to the office of Shoor Sain and asked him for the permission to leave as he has some personal work at home, the Head Clerk accorded him the permission, after that he asked the Baba to wait for some time and he will go and ask Lekh Raj if he too could accompany him and ask his father to come and meet the Baba, Purshottam Lal came and bowed to the Baba after about half an hour both Lekh Raj and Bhaagmal came and touched the feet of the Baba, Lekh Raj said he will go and fixed a mule cart to take them to the house, Bhaagmal said he will be home by six in the evening.

Bhootia Baba, Purshottam Lal, Lekh Raj and Brij Bhan soon reached home, Rampyari came and touched the feet of the Baba and wept very loudly, Baba consoled her and asked her to stop crying and go and cook some Daliya for him and send the three daughters in law only. Kunti was first to come, she touched the feet of Baba, the Baba told her she should not worry and the child will arrive and live safely, then came

Sulakshmi came and touched the feet of Baba and wept at his feet Baba told her that he is trying to find about Nikko and as and when he has some definite news, he will do whatever could be done, so don't you worry and take up to your studies seriously and Kaka will do well in his matriculation exam. At last Amrit appeared touched the feet of Baba, was blessed by the Baba and was told that she will give birth to two baby boys at the appointed time and she should not try for any more child.

When Rampyari came back with Daliya. She had cooked for the Baba, she placed the Daliya before the Baba, took a hand fan and started airing the Baba, Baba ate his Daliya and asked for some more of it, Chotti was asked to go and bring it, she came back with some more Daliya, which Baba ate and asked her to go and ask her mother to cook some tea for Baba and the other for Ram Pyari. Kaka brought tea for Baba and his grandfather and uncles. After taking tea Baba addressed to Ram Pyari and said you be brave and take care of your husband as his health is failing, because he has not been able to live in peace with his status as refugee and he finds it difficult to behave as a refugee. The Baba back oned Lekh Raj to take him to the Shamshaan Bhoomi behind the railway station, Lekh Raj asked baba to wait for some time, so he could find a cart, Baba said don't bother it buy a bicycle with a carrier at the earliest and try and learn the local dialect and customs as fast as you can, so that you do not feel an outsiders here, take good care of your wife during her pregnancy and afterward, they soon reached the Shamshaan Bhoomi, and Baba asked him to go back, he touched Baba's feet and walked back, he went to Brij Bhan and inside house and sat with his parents, Purshottam Lal said he was happy that the Baba has re appeared but it was very sad that Baba had lost his leg to the goons, but he is sure that the God will punish the guilty who attacked Baba, Ram Pyari said you all have your dinner here only and went into the kitchen and told Kunti to cook food for all Amrit and Sulakshmi extended their help in the cooking of food.

Mohkan Singh and Shoor Sain were sitting in the office of Deputy Commissioner they were told to carry out the survey and registration of all the refugee in next ten days, so that they could be issued a ration and other Ration card. A police ASI and six constables were assigned to them as to prevent any incident at the venue of registration and an announcement to this effect has to be made through a dhol (a loud sound making drum) in all localities where ever the refugees are squatting, each family is to be registered as one unit and the name of the head of family and other members of the family to be recorded with age, a team of twenty person is to be assigned to this job so as to meet the dead line, this work is also to be carried out on Sundays and holidays. The General Assistant to the Deputy Commissioner will oversee and direct the entire operation.

In next five days more than ten thousand more refugee mostly starving and sack landed at Rohtak, three were many flares and scenes of rioting and the police had to act tough to stem the Rot. there was acute shortage of water food, vegetables, Atta, Rice and even salt was difficult to get there was no space to stretch even milk for infants was not available, there were not any voluntary or charitable langers doing free distribution of any food items had to be discontinued as soon as it resumed because of rioting by then starving refugees women old man, children and the infants were the major casualty of the total mismanagement by the administration and refugee put together.

As per rumours which were rife the Muhajirs were (Refugees) to Sindh had become aggressive and the local Sindhi population was afraid of refugees, where as the Muhajirs to west Punjab faced the similar problems as the Hindu refugees to the New India. Muslim dominated districts of Bengal, the East Bengal Hindu refugees were looted and lynched an masse, the many refugees from West Punjab which was to be part of the to be created Pakistan, went to places like Bareilly, Pilibhit, Moradabad, Luckhnow,

Merrut, Ghaziabad, where ever their cattle trains took them some even went in to Madhaya Bharat and Rajpulana. By 6th July, India had more than four million refugees at least fifty percents of them had lost at least one of member of their family, about 50000 widows whose husbands had been killed by muslim goons. There were about 50000 infants without mothers and 60000 or phan children and no of widows was nearly one lakh about 20 tonne of gold and silver has been lost, lootted or left away Indian economy was at its worst, agriculture in total disarray had come to a standstill the banks were not functioning normally. Everyone was living in dispair, there was hardly any enthusiasm for the most touted independence, rather independence had become a curse, cruel joke played by the British, Congress and the League. There was a very strong sentiment against the surrender by Mahatma Gandhi And Jawahar Lal Nehru, before Mohammad Ali Jinnah Muslim who as a result of division and scheming by the Congress and the British and the Pakistan were not feeling at home and were rather, were scared of their future prospect in Hindus dominated areas the League was goading and demanding their right with Zeal and force and were assured Pakistan will always support them in their assertion Hindu religious leaders were absent from the acne as the Hindus in South, west and East India did not find them close to Hindus of North India. The Arya Samaj, Sanatam Dharam Sabha, Hindu Maghasabha And the RSS could not make any impact at all in alleviating the sufferings of refugee it was mostly the Congress men who were be looting the refugees with great hopes in any independent India under Nehru.

The process of brifurcation of assets was a road full of pot holes and Mahatma Gandhi looked to be more benevolent and patronising to the cause of Pakistan, India being a big brother had a Moral responsibility to appease the younger brother, the principalities whether big or small on the Indian side were trying to flex there mussels and demands before they were ready to sign the instrument of accsetion. The predominantly Muslim principalities of Rampur, Junnagarh, Tonk were torn by communal riots. The division of the Army, Air force, Navy, Railway stations and Post Offices was causing the biggest challenge due to its composition. Indian negotiator were getting wary of the stubboreness of their counterparts but yielded under pressure to keep the Pakistan happy as far as they could, people were in mess so was the Government and the nation in a complete mess without an inkling of any just resolution.

Refugees were getting restless and were loosing their tempers when face to face with subordinate Government official greed and graft were in grand scale at least fifty percent of refugees had forgotten the taste of Milk or Sugar, for them fruit was only part of long forgotten story which they had heard in past, school and colleges were yet to open and teachers were hard to find. Hospitals were in total disarray there, were hardly any doctors or nurses or compounders, private doctors were also hard to find as most of them were scouting for space to start their service and set up their clinics the town was not fully electrified and piped water supply was unheard of.

Punjabi's by nature are loud people and making lot of noise is their habits and all the refugees in this town were Punjabis, so they made lot of noise at every opportunity, the local were getting tired of their noise, so there were daily at altercations between the local and refugees and since refugees had no work to perform, so they always indulged in verbal duels and even those refugees who had started working as street vendors fought among themselves for a customer, which did not buy from them an official statement was made that the New Nation of Pakistan to be carved out of India will come into being on 14th August 1947 and it will be independent of the British Empire and a sum of rupees seventy five million will be given to it by India a sum of rupee twenty million was paid immdiatetly, there was celebrations in area that were to from the part of Pakistan, the land of the pure Muslims and the Hindus infields will not be welcome in geographical territory of the newly created Pakistan, even most of the Indian Muslims who had decided to stay in India amongst the Hindus majority rejoiced and celebrated the creation of Pakistan and all foreign educated Indian Hindus welcomed it as a very wise decision of the British and the Congress under Nehru and Gandhi. The Hindu Mahasabha, the RSS and the Arya Smaj did make some whimpering Noises, but to no avail against the Charisma of the Mahatma.

On the night of the 14th August 1947 when Pakistan was taking brith an Indian refugee died in its own nation as refugees Ram Pyari shouted for Brij Bhan, who came running and saw his fatherbreathless his toung almost out of his mouth. Ram Pyari told him to go and fetch Lekh Raj and Bhaagmal and their families as his father is as good as dead, Brij Bhan went to Bhaagmals house which was near and told him as to what has happened, Bhaagmal, Sulakshmi, Kaka, Chotti and Didu walked in their sleep to the house of Brij Bhan, then went to the house of Lekh Raj and brought him and his wife went with him to his house and to their dying father, Purshottam Lal was put on a string cot and taken to the hospital a sleepy doctor attended to the patient and put the patient on the oxygen, but said very loudly that he has no hope of survival and then asked Brij Bhan if the patient was a refugee, when he was told that yes indeed the patient was a refugee the doctor said Alas, the refugee Never deserve better in their own nation a death which this man has met, and he said I am also a refugee not from Jhang but from Kohat and I am here on transfer and his newly weeded wife of three days marriage was kidnapped even before he could sleep with her even for once oh yes, what Great Nation getting independence with five million of National refugees to support a National Government which will take oath to serve its people on 15th August 1947, then he folded his hand and said he was sorry for his ranking, but it all came from within his heart and left.

The body of Purshottam lal was brought home, every one wept loudly only, neighbours gathered and the first thing in the morning that was done to cremate Purshottam Lal a great refugee who chose to die on the very first of the day of Independence of the New India, which had received independence from the British rule, but now will be ruled by the Greed Gandiose, Graft, Grief and general degradation.

On the August 15th, 1947, the Indian Tri colour flag was hosted at the Ram-parts of the Lal Quilla (RED FORT a muslim fort built by a conquering Muslim Emperor's grandson) by Pandit Jawahar Lal Nehru the first Prime Minster of independence India, everyone who had not suffered the lot of family, property, home and hearts rejoined. But nobody talked of the sufferings and scarifies of five million refugees who had made the independence a reality. The tryst with destiny under Nehru has begin, but the refugees were stuck with hunger, starvation and decay which was their destiny.

Long Live Independence –Let Refugee Die For long.
P.S
The people especially the Hindus from village areas who migrated after 15th August 1947, mostly reached safely

without human loss, kidnapping and looting another Army had been called in to oversee the migration of the people across the newly created borders, adequate relief arrangement in the form of uncooked ration were made ration issued as the earliest allotment of Evacuee property was organised as far possible mainly through religions Gurus clan Chiefs village heads, so that migrate live close to their friends and relative, the Government has ultimately taken over and was performing well in the given situations and circumstance, of course there are stories that many refugees suffered theft, when they had reached at place, where they were to settle and it had become a common knowledge that the floor of many houses were dug cup to find the gold, gold jewellery, coins, silver and it was found at many places, the other common happening was the marriage of widows and widowers so that the small kids do not have to suffer for a long time.

Most of the refugees were sent and settled in areas which had lot of similarities with their original place of leaving, like most of the weavers community was settled at Panipat and those in dairy business to Rohtak, farming community of vast natural areas and the refugees started setteling in their new environment, new situation, but all of them accepted the new conditions as divine act and started living with God's design and their fate, but Alas the tag Refugee stuck and stuck hard. At the end of September 1947, almost every Indian had migrated to New India as refugee, for which refugee ration card was to be issued, of course un cooked ration was being provided and many of the refugees had been allotted Evacuee property, the house and the shops and those who could not be allotted shelter were still in refugee camps between the squalor and brawls, everyone trying to find some work which could at least pay for two square meals a day, many of the women were draping themselves in a single sheet of cloth for want of salwaar kameez men were content with a Kachha (a under wear) and a Bundi (vest with three to four pockets). Most of the refugees were content to have roities (flour pan cake) with salt and red paper, business activity was at low ebb because of acute shortage of cash money, gold and silver were being sold at cheap rates under duress to survive and to have some capital to start a fresh, the good thing was that the rain was poor, so you could sleep in the open, petty theft and begging was becoming very common as the days passed. The Government was working at a very slow speed in tardy manners, adding to despair and despondence and everyone was praising the British Rule. The new Leaders were behaving as overlords and had a lot of scorn for the poor and needy of course the rich and well off people were not at all happy, due to the non availability of many customers and poor payments. People did not mind eating the peel of mango, so they may be able to fill their bellies wood as fuel had become very costly even the pitcher was available at almost the double the usual price.

A ministry of rehabilitation was created and also a ration department was created, a custodians of Evacuee property was appointed at refugee affected district and a settlement officer had been appointed land was earmarked for creating Model Town and other refugee colonies to be established and allotted to the refugee, certain fee concessions and job reservation for the refugee were announced at many places Mahila Asharam (women shelter) were established, but charitable activities had mostly died or shrunk to almost none.

On the 30th January1948, Mahatma Gandhi was shot at and died, nobody took the responsibility, but RSS was accused.

Kaka passed out the matriculation examination with sixty three percent marks, and a job for him was arranged in the Imperial Bank, Sulakshmi passed her class 8th examination.

In June 1948, Kunti gave birth to a son, and Amrit had twins in July 1948.

Brij Bhan had been promoted and appointed as Assistant Settlement officer and Lekh Raj became a SDC.

Bhaagmal bought six acres of land at Lalhi and gave it on lease to Bhanna Ramfor cultivation.

Bhaagmal's parents in laws had come to India and settled at Gohana. Many other members of wider family had settled at various refugees' settlements and were in touch with each other.

In October 1948 Pakistan Kabali's had invaded India, India approached the UNO and ceasefire was announced inturn India had lost a big chunk of its territory to Pakistan, which was referred to Pak-reoccupied Kashmir.

Som Nath Temple in Gujrat which was invaded and looted by Nadir Shah, was restored to its past glory with the effort of Sardar Patel much against the ire of anti Hindu lobby.

Tryst with Destiny was continuing on its slow journey but the people did not feel any enthusiasm or hope.

On 26th January 1950 India gave itself a New constitution declaring India as soverigon Republic and a Secular nation.

Ram Pyari died on 26th January 1950 when India had given itself a New constitution, of course. She died as refugee in its own nation.

All other refugees in their own nation are waiting independence from hunger and the Stigmas of being a refugee.

Lapses

Oh, My God, Very Very Sorry
Oh My God I Did Not Sit
In your presence for last three days
Please do not punish me.
I sincerely offer my apologies.
Oh, My God accept my apology.
And forgive me for my lapses.
Oh, My God, you are my saviours.
　　You are my only hope.
I solely depends on you.
And without your kindness.
I can not be there.
Oh, God have mercy.
Oh, My God Do Your mercy.
All my life my God.

Temptation

Oh, My God today I acted dishonestly.
But Oh God how could I not be dishonest
Whenever well placed people were behaving dishonestly.
And inducing people like me to be dishonest.
My only fault is that I could not resist the temptation.
But I accept my guilt, that I did not try and resist the
temptation.
Though I should have and could have repeted the temptation.
But Oh My God Whatever I do is as you
Gave it to me in my mind and i went
Ahead, as I have no doubt your wisdom.
Please forgive me my temptation
As I am capable of resisting everything
But Temptation
Oh My God, be merciful and heaven let
Temptation come my way
As I will not be able to resist it anyway
Oh My God, Please Stop me from being dishonest
And God Please always forgive my dishonesty
Oh God, be pleased, be merciful
Oh God the merciful, please be merciful.

Omni

Oh Lord of the Universe
You Are said to be omnipotent
Omnipresent and omnireach
But if you are omnipresent, then
How can you let bad thing happen
And if you are omnipotent
Why do people then do it ignoring you
Please God do punish those who ignore you and do wrong
But you must reward who acknowledge
Your might and always try do only the right
Since you do not reward easily and freely people get disgusted
and start doing wrong thing sinful act
Let people do only the Good acts
Let Good acts be rewarded fairly
Let Good acts be recognised
Let Good acts only prevail
Of God you are the only just
Oh God You must stop the unjust
Oh God Let only the just happen
Oh God Let no unjust happen
Oh God, Oh God, Oh God.

Blessings

Oh My God You are great
Oh My God You are most powerful
Oh My God You are most merciful
Oh My God You are the Benefactor of the Poor
Oh My God You are My father
Oh My God You are My mother
Oh My God how can a mother forsake her child
Oh My God how can a father not support his son
Oh My God how can your child be orphaned
Oh My God shower your benevolence
Oh My God shower your mercies
Oh My God forgive your son for his lapses
Oh my god Let Your Child re-deem himself
Oh My God please guide your child
Oh My God show the right path to your child
Oh my God be show your favours on your child
Oh my God Let Your child bask in your glory
Oh My God let your child live by your nearby
Oh my God Let Your child be your true devotee
Oh my God Let Your child devote himself to you
Oh my God Let Your child seeks your blessings
Oh My God please do bless your child
Oh My God you are great-your child is blessed
Oh My God Let Your blessing last forever

Vision

I am a sinner, you are my re-deemer
I act only in great, but why do you forced the greed
I am an evil man, but you made the evil
I act foolishly but why do not you pardon me in your wisdom
I am a foolish and a greedy man
But you can help me to shun my greed and foolishness
I look forwards to your help, your guides and mercy
God only you can rid me of my foolishness and greed
Please God be merciful and make me wise
So I shall not act foolishly in greed
Please God bless me with your vision
Please God give me your attention
Please God cure me of my maître

Heaven

O My Dear God In heaven
    You created Hell for men
And men with whatever little knowledge
You had bestowed upon him
Started ravelling in the hell
And never tried to get out of it
As he thought heaven is only for the God
For the men, Heaven could not have been
Any good because, because of his greed
God has no desires no wishes, no sensual pleasure
And men in their own wisdom has
Only strived to make Hell its abode
O, My dear God in heaven
I will contend with the well
As long as you have Heaven

Serf

God I am your serf in your prayer
God I am your slave, happy to be your slave
Gods I am your servant and you pay me well
God I always look up to you for your benevolence
God Have mercy on me, be merciful
God I am slave, please take pity on me
God I am slave, please take pity on me
God I am poor and impure
But God you are wealthy and pure
God please make me wealthy and pure
God You are very great
God i am very ungrateful
God You are here, there and everywhere
God make me your devote for ever
God you are complete
God I am incomplete, make me near complete
God you decide, design and dispense
God let me live happily, with your dispensation only
God you are my father, my mother
God Let me be your son a good soon
God I am your serf in prayer

Refugee

Thank you god for the kindness
Thank you God for the safety
Thank you God for the food
Thank you God for the ground to sleep
Thank you God for making us good refugees
Thank you God, Give us THE REFUGEES
     The succour we need and deserve
Thank you God for your mercies
     On all refugees
Thank you God for the houses and heart
     You will grant us
Thank you god for the food
     We will earn
Thank you God for keeping
Us alive

NATION

Geographical territory is not a Nation
Nation is the cohesiveness of thought of
Its people for its geographical territory of a Nation
Nation is made of its people their culture their traditions
Nation is the feeling of Nationality for its geographically
territory and its fast ruler
Nation is made up of its culture, languages
Folklore and its soil
A Nation does not die as long as
Its Nationals live for it
A Nation survive its invaders, floods
Earth quake and God's fury
Nation cannot survive in inhuman
On slough on its National
Nations and Nationality always Live Long

Refugee

A refugee is a man or group of people uprooted from its roots to fend for itself in hostile terrain for his hunger, shame and morality moving directionless n despair in a string will to survive the inhuman indigenise brought upon him by the political, social and human organisation to live and die with a striking stigma of being a refugee. A refugee in its own Nation is a new phenomenon which happened only in India during the British Empire aided and abetted by the own nation.

Dedication

Dedrealed to My luck which ultimately
Decided to smile for me
Micky my son who made me write this
My wife Pushpa, my son Amit who
Encouraged me to creat it
My daughter in law Anisha who was elealted at the prospect
My Grand daughter Amishi make me smile often
All readers of this book who beard it

Author's Note

This book a Refugee in his own Nation is a pure fiction, the names and places have been picked at random and do not have any bearing on the storey or its narration.

All the characters are imaginer and their thoughts and narrations have been fabricated.

This book of fiction is only a fabrication and has nothing to do with facts or history.

All bad references are sincerely regretted and due apologies are offered for the same. The book is a definite literary blunder as it does not take grammer or any litrary disciplines into account the objective of this function is to qualify refuse as refugee, and the pain a refugee may suffer on being a refugee in his own Nation.

Thanks a lot for the Publishers

SARDANA SURINDER